The
Road
Unravelled

Earlyworks Press Science Fiction

The Road Unravelled

Earlyworks Press Science Fiction

ISBN 978 09553429 98

Published by Earlyworks Press
Creative Media Centre
45 Robertson St, Hastings
Sussex TN34 1HL

The Earlyworks Press Science Fiction Challenge

"We're looking for stories that are a credible picture of where we might be heading - or where we could end up if.... Stories should conform to the sci-fi 'What if...' genre, that is, they should be predictions backed by credible if not actual science.

But the science must stay in the background. We want stories you can read without having an MSc! And they must have real, in depth characters, not just manikins to drive the space ships.

There are lists of 'over-used sci-fi plots' going around the web. Can you make one of these plots worth visiting again, or do you have a truly original idea?"

That was the challenge, and this book is the authors' answer to it. They have given us theories about god, genetics, mortality and human responsibility. They have asked what can and cannot be done with computers, robots and AI, and what it is that makes us human. The result is some startling predictions about our society and our environment based on the social, political and scientific developments of recent years.

Compared with the SF classics of the 20th century, we feel that the mood is both sobering and challenging. The world is in grave danger. Technology is no longer a game. These gripping stories raise some mind-melting questions so enjoy them, think on them, and sleep if you dare!

Kay Green   August 2007

www.earlyworkspress.co.uk

Contents

Chucking Out Time

by R D Gardner

I can't remember any more which pub I was in when I saw Matt Markham's face again. He'd been a skinny Goth of a biologist, in the days when people left university with a degree and some prospects rather than a lifetime debt, and he'd shared my liking for real pubs with other human beings in over the safe, incestuous little ghetto of the Students' Union. We'd been banned from two halls of residence and seven pubs; brought each other home from any number of places that we couldn't remember getting to, and gone straight to afternoon lectures to sleep it off - and then he got a First and a job, and that was the last I saw of him.

He'd cut his hair since then, and left off the black dye, but I swear that in eleven years the swine hadn't aged six months. Two pubs later, he'd had the edited highlights of my career, culminating in how I came to be stamping payslips in the lower echelons of County Hall; we were trying to remember what went into a Purple Nasty to make it a Red Wizard, and it was his turn.

"You're doing *what?*"

"Well, it's not that unusual, mate - scientists have been trying to undo mortality since before they knew they were scientists. That's what the Philosophers' Stone was really for, to change mortal flesh into something that would transcend death and disease: all that base-metals-into-gold business was a side effect. It just took a few centuries to find the right nuts and bolts, and we've only now got spanners that small... There's never any whisky in this; let's go somewhere else."

By chucking-out time, he'd still not convinced me that he was on a tiger team researching immunity to death, and that they were getting it right: as we stood there in the street, swinging our carry-out and temporarily at a loose end, I was still insisting that he must be designing a new kind of anthrax and wouldn't own up. Eventually, he got that madcap grin I should have known and feared, grabbed the carry-out, and set off towards the University; as I stumbled after the beer, yipping questions, all he would do was giggle and say "I'll *show* you!"

"I'm always telling them to get CCTV fitted," Matt muttered as he fiddled around the third-floor fire door. "Just because we've got nothing radioactive in here, no-one can be bothered... and I know the alarms aren't on: Jenna's always checking her mice in the middle of the night." The fire door clicked quietly open, and the smell came out, a smell that took me straight back to the Science Wing at school – gas and sawdust and things pickled in alcohol for decades; the dry smell of cases full of insects and the musty smell of rats. Matt was grinning like Just William as we crept along the corridor, miming "*Shush!*" to each other every time we bumped into a wall. Rats blinked blank pink eyes as the laboratory lights went on, and Matt rummaged in a cupboard for Pyrex beakers to pour the beer into.

"Up your bum!"

The beer tasted dusty.

"Well, this is it, Jim: the end of death as we know it."

He gestured proprietorially toward rows of cages, shelves full of files, and a board covered with neatly ordered photographs.

"We were still at school when they worked out how to switch off the instructions that cause cells to die," he went on, shaking beer off a pile of notes, 'cause if your cells can't die, then you can't die - not naturally, anyway. But they hadn't thought it through, and it went a bit wrong..."

He passed me a curling Polaroid: a ratty tail protruding from an improbable powder-puff of white fur.

"You see, you can't just stop cells dying: you have to stop them multiplying, too, or stuff just keeps on growing. Hair's one thing, but it affects everything short of brain cells; it's effectively whole-body cancer..."

He passed me another photograph, and I sat down abruptly and concentrated very hard on not being sick.

"They suffocated, eventually - couldn't die naturally, of course - we offered them to the cancer research boys, but they bottled out. Then it was back to the drawing board with the old fruit flies, and we've finally managed to switch off both sets of instructions without affecting the rest of the cellu...'scuse me... cellular functions. Mick Jagger here's eleven next birthday."

He opened a cage in which a nondescript white rat was listlessly nibbling at a dish of reddish-brown mush, and grabbed hold

2

of the rat, which twisted round in his indifferent grip and sank its teeth into his finger as though it hadn't seen food in a fortnight. Matt looked resignedly amused at my appalled yelps, and prised the indignant rodent's jaws apart to show me the tiny yellowish stubs barely poking out of its gums.

"Rodents' teeth grow all their lives," he explained, returning Mick Jagger to his cage, "so once you shut cell division down, they just wear away - most of this lot haven't gnawed anything in years."

I imagined two hundred years of eating soup, my teeth worn down to the jawbone.

"Urrgh, would that happen to *you*?"

"Human teeth aren't *meant* to grow," Matt said patiently. "You'd be all right: just don't chew any bricks. In fact, you'd be better off, because your teeth can't fall out or rot. The roots of your hair won't die, so you'll never go bald, or even grey; your eyesight will never fail; you'll never lose another brain cell. – fill mine up while you're at it – and you just generally won't get old. And the punch line is, you'll never be diseased, either: you'll be immune to cancer, because your cells *can't* multiply, and the moment bacteria or viruses get into affected cells, they can't multiply either, so you'll never catch so much as a cold!"

"Hell of a cure for the common cold," I giggled. "Where can I get some?"

He gave me that grin.

"Oh no, Matt... you're out of your mind!"

"Well, I suppose you could say there are side effects: we haven't worked out yet how to shut down normal cell division without shutting down meiso... meios... the kind that splits up DNA to pass on to your offspring, so the rat budget's gone through the roof 'cause we keep sterilising our stock..."

"So if you immortalised me, I couldn't have any children? Well, that's fair, I wouldn't need any..." and then I just sat there, tasting the size of the word 'immortal'.

"Oh, and we can't do anything for veggies. Can't make red blood cells immortal, see – no nucul... nucleus – so you need to keep up the red meat."

Immortal.

"Otherwise, don't jump off any cliffs. You won't become Conor MacLeod: there's a difference between *immortal* and *invulnerable*, and you'd really hate to spend eternity in traction."

Immortal.

"Matt, what would I have to do?"

"Have another beer, and shut your eyes: this has to go in your spinal cord."

"Er, Matt, how much have you had?"

"Relax, I've never impaled a rat yet."

The needle went into the back of my neck.

I don't remember to this day what we did then, or how I got home: the students next door assured me I came home at sunrise, singing:

Never get bombed with a boffin, you never know where it might end,
Don't get laboratory ratted, and do what you didn't intend...

to the tune of that Monty Python song, and I dare say they're right. I didn't experience Sunday at all.

On Monday, I got up with the hangover of a lifetime, and spent the morning holding on to my desk, retching every time the telephone rang. It didn't occur to me that I had a sore neck till well after lunch-break, and then I couldn't come up with a reason; just vague images of Matt Markham's grin and the glass-ball eyes of a white laboratory rat. I was half-way through shaving that evening before something started to dawn on me. I'd scraped my chin twice a day since I was in the sixth form; I last remembered shaving before going out on Saturday night; but what I was harvesting now was barely a night's growth of beard. "Alcoholic amnesia," I said to my reflection, and in the back of my mind I heard Matt's voice: "You'll never go bald..." I got up as clean-shaven as I'd gone to bed, and finally it came back to me: my body clock had ticked its last.

Life stopped making sense. I'd sit there among the yearly receipts for dustmen's safety boots and shake with giggles, the hysterical, unfunny giggles that you have to repress in the middle of a Two Minutes' Silence, looking at my fingernails that never grew, feeling

4

my chin that would never sprout another bristle, my hair that would never need cutting again, and thinking "I am immortal... dear God, I am immortal... what am I going to *do*?" The pavements I walked along on my way to work seemed insane, unreasonable things as I pictured my footsteps wearing them away, left foot, right foot, year in, year out - how many years would it take me to wear a track in the pavement? How many years could I sit at this desk - any desk - doing the same job, until somebody noticed, or I'd tick-tocked through so many meaningless days that I started to cuckoo? I drank more than ever, getting more and more obnoxious until the inevitable happened: somebody on the Quayside took exception to my face with a pint glass, and opened the back of my left hand up as I blocked it. Sitting there in Casualty, waiting to be stitched, beer-sodden trousers glued to the tasteful pink and grey chair, I stared foggily at the posters of Swiss mountains, crooked and curling up at the edges on the soothing pink and grey walls, and it dawned on me at last.

"What am I going to do... well, whatever I like!"

It didn't *matter* how long I sat at that moulded plastic desk, moving pieces of pink or green paper from one side to the other. It might take me ten years to save up enough money to go round the world - so what? - the mountains wouldn't have changed, and neither would I. I could see every mountain in the world; paddle in every sea on every beach I'd ever heard of; watch the sun rise on deserts that had closed over ancient cities, and come back in a thousand years to listen to the wind blowing the last grains of sand from their unknown streets. If the slog of earning money between adventures didn't appeal, I'd rob a bank: suppose they did catch me? I could toss them a life sentence's worth of my years as casually as I'd drop a coin into a collecting tin - plenty more where that came from! – walk out after twenty years, still young, and dig the money up again. Or I could move to California and start my own religion, wandering naked through the vineyards to demonstrate my divine immunity to the malignant melanoma, and abscond with the takings when I got tired of designer drugs and nubile votaresses... the prospect was so gloriously ridiculous that I never even noticed the stitches going in.

From being a numb wreck on a permanent warning, I changed into Mr Powerhouse. I saw foreign suns rising over the ratcatchers' diesel receipts, and heard the foam of tropical seas whispering into the out-tray with the stacks of stamped payslips; at tea-break I salivated over guide-books and accounts of epic journeys. In fact, they were becoming the only things I *could* salivate over: neither a crisp, steaming bacon butty nor Kylie-Anne from Reception's smooth brown legs in her white stilettos seemed to stir any interest any more. The nurse said I wasn't eating properly, when she picked the stitches out of my hand and the cut simply fell open again. She said it at length, and repeatedly, while sewing the rather used-looking skin back together: sounded off about veganism and anaemia, told me to eat more red meat, and sent me to the chemist for iron supplements. I didn't mention that I was eating pounds of the stuff - red meat was about the only thing I could find an appetite for, and the redder, the better - but the iron did help, for a while. I took to eating my meat raw, and that helped, too, but I never went back to have those stitches out. I left them in until they rotted, and then went somewhere else to have the cut closed again: I'd worked out by then that it was never going to heal. Stitching's hard on the skin, though, and ugly to boot: I'm holding it together with silver wire, these days, and telling people it's the latest in body-piercing. So far, it hasn't caught on.

Winter came on, and I was saving money very nicely, and thinking that the world would be my oyster if my hand would only heal up, or at least stop hurting. One night it was particularly cold, and I couldn't sleep for pain and frustration: I tried watching television, but after fifteen minutes of flipping from one gibbering coiffured head to another, I knew I had to *do* something before I lost it completely and beat the screen in with my redundant frying-pan. I left the flat with a resounding slam, and set off towards the river in the angry, jerky quick-march of a really foul temper, intending to walk around until I calmed down and got tired enough to sleep. It was some time in the small hours, but the city was all life: hurrying taxis and cruising police cars; drunks arguing with kebab-shop owners; glass smashing in full surround stereo; the eggbeating rotors of the police helicopter, and suspicious trickling noises from unlit doorways. The anger that was steaming off me like a trail of thunderheads must have kept everyone at a distance, and I ignored everything around me until I trod on someone, and she wailed and flailed around and bled on my trousers. Laid out and legless in a street full of frost and windscreens: her bare legs were splashed with blood and purple with cold, there was glass embedded in the palms of her hands and her knickers were trailing out of her handbag. I went down on my knees, murmuring "Come on, come on now, it's all right, it's all right..." as though encouraging a frightened puppy, and as I had her in my arms and was lifting her up, I smelled her blood. The smell numbed my nose as though I'd inhaled swimming-pool water, stunned my ears like a chord on the cathedral organ, filled the inside of my head like sunlight through closed eyelids... and then it was in my mouth, strong as roast-beef gravy and pungent as Islay malt, and I shuddered and whimpered and felt life flowing back into me as though I'd come into a firelit room from a long and bitterly cold night... and there was a dead woman in my arms, limp and white and bloody like something discarded from a butcher's slab, her neck slashed open with a fragment of glass. There was blood in my mouth and down my shirt, fresh blood seeping out from between the rotting stitches: I was bursting with life, aroused in a way I hadn't been for months, and about to scream. Should I run home to bed and hope it had all been a bad dream? – or run to a police station – run to a *church* and give myself up? – Then I saw something move between the dustbins further down the alley, went straight off the mark like a dog after a cat, and when I saw the knife-blade glint I didn't slow down. I had his shaven head up against the wall before I recognised him, and that didn't make me think of letting go.

"Matt, you bastard... what have you done to me?"

He was babbling "Phil, we didn't know, I swear we didn't know..." but I wasn't paying attention, because I'd just worked out what he was doing in that alley with that knife in his hand, and I smashed his head against the wall as though I was launching a ship. I was already swinging his weight around to throw him down when I saw the headlights on the corner, and it was far too late to change my mind. The car was coming much too fast, barely under control, and as Matt went staggering over backwards I exchanged blank stares with the passenger, who couldn't have been more than fourteen, before Matt was batted straight back at me. He landed at my feet like a second-rate stuntman, and the driver – the twocker – put on even more speed and was gone.

"You're really going to hate spending eternity in traction, Matt."

He was trying to crawl with no limbs left that would take his weight, scrabbling and twitching like a half-swatted insect while he blubbered at me, begging for something but unable to make himself understood, and the smell of his blood that was all over the street was so horribly wrong, not rich and hot and vital, but the phantom smell of a butcher's stall in a closed-down market, and I snapped. I snatched up the knife from where it had landed among the bin-bags, and struck, struck in fury, in revulsion, in desperate compassion, but he still wouldn't stop crawling and crying, and my mind was ringing on one high note like a wineglass about to shatter as I struck again and again, the blade skidding off ribs, the handle sliding about in my grip, struck till he stopped moving and making noises, and I was kneeling there sobbing obscenities with the knife under the arch of his ribs, finally embedded in his heart. I was waiting for the sirens; for the Flying Pig's searchlight to pin me down, centre stage - surely *someone* must have rung 999? As I was staring into the dull orange clouds, listening for the rotors, there was a noise right in front of me – a dry, whispery noise as though the wind had stirred a drift of dead leaves – and I looked down to see Matt's corpse softly falling apart: skin flaking from flesh, muscle slipping from bone, joints splitting like withered seed capsules, bones loosening from bones and rolling outwards under their own weight in the heap of pale brown dust that was all that remained of the flesh I still couldn't believe I had butchered. Then even the bones lost their shape, blurring and crumbling as though they had been modelled from sand that dried out and sifted away on the wind, and nothing was left of Matt Markham but a set of knife-slashed clothes with fine dust in the weave, and my hands were dry and gritty with the dust of his blood.

Nobody ever did call the cops: when I think of all the times I've heard fighting and screaming outside after dark, or shattering glass and wood giving way, and just pulled the curtains and hoped for the best, I'm surprised I thought anybody might. They found her body the next day, of course, but I'd taken Matt's clothes away with me,

8

so they never came looking for him, and whatever questions they did ask, nobody answered. Matt himself never seems to have been reported missing, not even around the University: if his colleagues knew what he'd become, they must have been glad to see the last of him. Sometimes I wonder if they weren't just glad to see the back of the competition; if that rain-streaked slab-concrete block round the back of the Union Building is prowled by the lab-coated undead, petting their toothless vampire rats; but I've hunted round there several times, picking off drunken students, and never caught anybody else at it. I hope the whole project's been hushed up: I don't like to think that they may be starting with the fruit flies all over again.

As for me, well, you don't see me around so much any more; not in daylight, anyway. I found out why Matt had shaved his head when my own hair started breaking off as I brushed it: its roots might not die, but the part you see was dead to start with, and that only lasts so long. My skin's not doing what it should, either: it's becoming pale and stiff, like fingernails or the flexible plates on a snake's belly. I've thrown all the mirrors out of my flat, and I won't walk past one in the street: even in the dark, I don't want to see what I look like now.

This is the immortality Matt promised me: lurking in a dingy flat where the landlord doesn't have to see my face; cowering from the random violence of the outside world like a haemophiliac princeling, knowing that my immortal flesh will never stop bleeding, and the undividing cells of my bones can never knit together if they break; creeping out at night to sustain this existence with other people's blood. Every time I open the door I think of Matt, crawling smashed and bloody in a filthy alley, no more able to be healed than he was able to die, and all my cloudy dreams of desert sunrises and jungle moons have gone out of the window with the mirrors. Yes, I know there's always a way out – don't think it doesn't cross my mind, around three o'clock in the morning – but I can't fall sick and die, and I can't be poisoned; I could take the high dive off the bridge, but I don't even know if I can drown. There are always knives and guns in town, or trains and high buildings if I want to be really sure, but can I be sure *enough*? – one wrong move and I'm spending eternity as a freak in a wheelchair, with generations of incredulous scientists prodding my unhealing bones. God, I even thought of the lion enclosure at the zoo – being eaten should be final enough, and elegantly ironic to boot – but then I thought of the lions.

It's summer again now, and I think I'm slowly getting used to this life. There are even things I'm starting to appreciate about it: the scary sound of my footsteps in dark alleys; the look on her face as she turns round and realises that Nosferatu's behind her... oh, and that first mouthful of blood, when I'm white and shaking from the lack of it – an ice-cold beer at the end of a long, hot day doesn't begin to compare with it. I don't have to kill, if I haven't waited so long that I can't control myself, and since I can't draw blood with my teeth any better than you can, there's no nonsense about bloodless corpses with puncture wounds on their necks. Anyway, my favourite hunting ground's down by the mental hospital, where you go to have the radio transmitters taken out that the little green men built into your brain – who believes those poor bastards when they say they've been attacked by a bald vampire with a broken bottle? Someone's going to get suspicious eventually, though: maybe one day, some East European migrant who still remembers a few things will hammer a sharpened stick through my heart, and as I blow away in a little pile of dust he'll have the satisfaction of knowing that everything great-grandma told him was true. There's so much dust gathered here already, I doubt that anybody else will even notice.

Report: Experimental Use of the Drug
Axenphenicol Lithium Sulphate in Forensic Criminology

by David Dennis

My name is Peter. Peter Haynes. I love the sea – that boiling white spume and spray, with dark green-blue streaks and glassy surfaces, crashing endlessly upon sand and stones. I was hypnotised by the waves in the English Channel as they beat upon the shores near my home. I was often late for school because of it. My classmates, they called me 'Neptune' and mocked me when I was half an hour late after lunch.

The teacher would make me stand up and tell everyone what I'd been doing. Having lost all sense of time, I'd been watching waves crash up against the sea wall. When I think back now, I was hypnotised by it; the power, the smell, the roar and vibration of it all.

I'm a dreamer. I don't have much of a sense of responsibility. If I find something fascinating – a hill to climb, a wood to explore or a wave to watch, then I tend to drift off-task and go and do it. I'm a pleasure-seeker. Not to be rude or ignorant, but to just do that thing and no other. Then reality intrudes and I feel guilty and wish that I'd attended better to the tasks that duty has sent me. Deep down I feel that 'ennui' has an almost sexual effect on me. I get a kick out of being outside the order of things. At these times, I salivate a little.

One day I let my dream get the better of me. I climbed down onto the beach by one of the groynes and slipped. My hands were on cold wet stones at the edge of the sea wall; slippery and treacherous stones, sliding under my hands. As I fell from the wall I reached out to try and grasp it but a wave caught me and I was taken out to sea.

At first, I bobbed and could see myself floating, like a stick with a head. Then I went under and struggled to breathe. The sea was dark blue down there and the sky above lit with a wan sun. A shoal of silver fish passed by and left in its wake millions of bubbles. The sky seemed to clear a little and through the clouds of bubbles the sunlight infused and sparkled, giving out more rays of light which began to penetrate the darkness beneath me. I could see right down

11

to the bottom of the sea. The sea-bed looked strangely like my bedroom carpet with blue and white squares and lines.

Strands of seaweed stroked my face, like the hair of some mermaid or lost maiden. I tried to catch them in the vain hope that they were anchored to some rock which might help me save myself. There was a roaring in my ears. When I came up for air I saw the shining sea wall and on it was some writing in white foaming letters, tall and broad: 'DID DADDY TOUCH YOU?' it said.

Then someone dived in and rescued me.

But now I was a driven man. The next week I went down to the same beach at high tide and I threw myself into the sea. This was to the horror of all those looking down at me from the sea front. Hundreds of faces looked at me, angry, sad, happy, smiling or shouting. I was happy. I was in the sea alone.

This time, instead of the writing on the wall, there was a man chained there. He was imprisoned with a large rusty chain around his wrists and ankles and the final links were welded to a huge iron ring embedded in the wall. He could not escape. The crowds, they seemed not to see him. They were looking at me, shouting encouragement.

"Swim, swim," they said, "swim for the lighthouse."

As the waves came in they smashed the chained man against the giant stone blocks of the sea wall – that man, that rag-doll victim. His clothes were faded. His hands were white, big. His fingers were big. His legs, white like chicken-flesh. I could smell him. He had blood on his forehead. He called out to me: "Did daddy touch you?"

Once again, suddenly, someone rescued me. It was the same rescuer as before. All this happened when I was eleven. When I was this age, I was a man. 'Be a man.' they said – the many faces on the sea front. 'Take it like a man.' and 'This is what men do.'

Then when I grew up out of the sea onto dry land, I became a geologist and went climbing in the Hindu Kush. The narrow valleys and massive high peaks overawed me. The glaciers were snow-covered at that time of year. They looked to me like waves just breaking. In the distance on the ridges were people driving yaks.

The animals were over-burdened with goods. They had so much to carry that they could hardly stand the weight on their backs. They groaned with the effort and the noise of their animal anguish drifted down to me. I wished that I could help them. I wished that I was strong and could lift the load from their sore and bleeding backs.

Then suddenly, as I was climbing higher and higher, I met the man who had twice rescued me from the sea. He seemed very tall, wider at the feet than at the head, so tall – he must have been at least twenty feet high. He had black hair and black eyes. His mouth was large. He was just there, outside a temple, casting a giant shadow across the stones and scree. He stood his ground; some immovable totem. A monolith.

A prayer-wheel turned and the wind-flags blew, red and yellow, streaming out and up into a blue sky. The monolith man smiled, indicated by raising his fingers to his lips that he was dumb and then scribbled a question on a piece of slate he picked up from the ground. He had a large stone in his hand and scratched it on the slate: 'All right then are you, Peter?'

"You mean alright?" I shouted to him.

'No – all right?' he wrote on the slate.

"What do you mean?"

He seemed to transform himself into a cloud. Everything that was black about him became white. I reached into the cloud. There was nothing.

I called out: "Why did you rescue me from the sea all those years ago?"

There was no reply but it was obvious that things had changed badly. This was a different world. My heart was beating on the wrong side of my chest.

The man who had formed a cloud came back into view – slowly, like a Cheshire Cat in reverse.

"Welcome to the other universe, Peter," he said. "You've made a remarkably good transition. Here all the things that were left in the old world are right in this world. All the things that were right in that world are wrong in this world. So that means that all the things that were wrong in that world are right in this world. So if Daddy did touch you, it is okay to tell."

Together we stumbled up the slopes until we could see a glacier snout. He took great strides but strangely never seemed to get ahead of me. A large blue lake came into view and we noticed pieces of ice floating in it. Some parts of the ice were an intense light blue like the flower-clusters of a Plumbago and some the darkest indigo, like Morning Glory. There was a roar from the giant stream of meltwater that ran under the glacier and disgorged into the lake, tumbling over black shining stones. Although the sky was bright, it began to snow. The snow was warm. It was like woollen blankets.

"Wrap yourself in one," said the man.

Then he said. "Are you comfy, Peter?"

"Who was that poor man whose face was bloody? The one hanging in chains on the sea wall?" I said.

"That was a memory of anger," said the man.

"Who was angry? Was it me?"

"You have been angry in the past, Peter. But now, here, all is peace. Just watch the snow fall. Relax. Be warm. Keep the blanket up to your chin. Be sure you are safe. No harm will come to you."

The flakes of snow fell with such quietude, barely hissing into each other as their crystals bonded and layer upon layer rose up about me. Soon I was under the snow.

"It's nice here under the snow, isn't it?" said the man. "Why don't you come closer? Tell me about your life."

"I'm not used to company. I like to be alone," I said.

"Is being alone so good?"

"Being alone is the best thing in the world. When the door shuts and the footsteps go downstairs, then there is peace of a kind. I can climb inside that peace and then I'm happy."

"Did daddy like you to be alone?" said the man.

"I don't remember daddy. He's dead," I told the man.

"Let's climb higher," he said.

The slope was gentle at first, but then it increased. It became harder to take even a small step. My breathing rate was way up. I struggled for air. I sucked icy snow-filled air into my lungs. To get to the very highest point I had to use my hands. My fingernails were broken and bloody. I had to hold the rock. I had to grip it hard.

When we reached the top of the world he showed me my father. There he was, his face covered in blood. He lay there.

"Did you do this, Peter?" said the man.

"I don't know. Did I?"

"You can tell me."

14

"Does it really matter – because here in this universe killing is good, surely?"

"Yes. You are right. Clever boy, Peter. Here in this universe we like good. Well, you and I both like good so much. So tell me, did you kill your father? Did you kill daddy?"

"Yes, I did kill him. Did I do right?"

"Thank you. That will be all, Peter. You are still safe. You are alone. You can go to sleep now," said the man.

Going Away

by Vanessa Lafaye

James Hamilton woke from a pleasant dream on the last day of his wife's life. This was unusual because he never remembered dreams. Julianne entertained them both with the bizarre despatches from her subconscious, while his nocturnal visions remained inaccessible to his waking self.

She was convinced that he kept his dreams from her, assuming that everyone woke like she did, with the shreds of the night's images still hovering in front of their eyes. He was not hiding his dreams; he had no memory of them, good or bad. Until today.

In his dream, he was lying in the bottom of a boat, looking up at the sky of his childhood – a gentle blue with sparse, insubstantial clouds, all warmed by a benevolent sun. With the peculiar logic of dreams, he accepted that he was his adult self taken back 30 years.

The boat drifted to a stop under some overhanging branches, and the light was filtered green through the leaves. He focused on a perfect leaf, shivering in the breeze above his head, its skeleton shown in clear relief against the bright sky. A stranger's voice said: "All colour is only reflected light."

Slowly waking, he felt peaceful and relaxed for a moment. Then he remembered: this was the last day. In a few hours, Julianne would be dead. He wished, like a child, that he could return to his dreamscape and stay there forever, that the boat under the branches was real life. Although they had both been preparing themselves for years, he realised with a surge of panic that he was not ready at all, would never be ready.

The hard floor beneath his back forced him to full wakefulness. He tried to ease the stiffness in his tired muscles and heard the dull ring of champagne glasses nudging against each other when he shifted his legs. He kept his eyes closed for a moment longer in order to collect himself.

He had thought so many times about today, how he would feel, what would happen. He had thought more about Julianne's death than his own. As usual, he had planned everything with military precision. The champagne had been bought two years before. All of Julianne's things were in order, carefully arranged in different piles, each with a label. The taxi was booked, and he had checked the booking so many times that the firm knew his voice.

It crushed him to realise that all his preparations were as futile as sandbags against a tidal wave.

When he finally could postpone it no longer, he opened his eyes and composed a warm, relaxed expression for her to see. Sitting up, he moved the glasses on to the low table beside him.

Julianne returned his smile, up on the sofa. She had obviously been awake for some time. He lay his head on the cushion next to her, guilty for falling asleep; they had intended to stay up all night, their last night, but he must have dropped off somewhere around 3am. The last thing that he remembered was opening yet another bottle and pledging drunken, undying love.

"Morning," she said, reached out to stroke his head. They had the blinds drawn against the sun, which was strong even at such an early hour, but he could still see her blond hair aglow in the gloom.

They had been pair-matched by computer on compatibility scores 5 years previously; like lots of their friends, they knew people whose pairings were a disaster in practice, while fulfilling all of the success criteria according to the complicated algorithm which underpinned the computer's decisions.

Even with low expectations, their first meeting was not a success: he found her standoffish, she found his nervous banter exhausting. Both resigned themselves to another spin of the wheel, but when they arrived home they realised that they had accidentally swapped identical telephones. When they met to exchange phones, with expectations at rock bottom and nothing to prove, the conversation flowed so easily that when the café owner threw them out at midnight it seemed natural to go to a hotel and make love all night. Julianne liked to say that their happiness was the result of both accident and design.

He reached up to wrap his arms around her familiar shape and then rolled backwards, pulling her down to the floor cushions with him. They lay quietly together amongst the detritus of the night's activities: several champagne bottles, a photo album on the

17

monitor, favourite music files making slithery piles around the computer. Gladys was curled up on the biggest cushion, snoring gently.

"I'm sorry that I fell asleep," he said, stroking Julianne's hair in the way that she liked.

"It doesn't matter. Gladys and I finished off the champagne and then talked about old times."

"She doesn't appreciate fine wine," he pointed out.

"You wouldn't either if you spent most of your time licking your butt," said Julianne, stretching out a hand to scratch the cat under her chin. She said, "I didn't dream last night."

"Not at all?" He wondered if he should tell her about his dream, but rejected the idea. Their morning ritual was her story, not his. She shook her head, hand buried in the cat's soft ruff. He kissed her lightly. Their movement disturbed Gladys, who leapt disgustedly off the cushion.

Julianne's face was set, no sign of the fear and anxiety which he knew she must feel. They had talked about this day so many times that there was little left to say.

Fundamentally Julianne was at peace with her fate, except for the pain of leaving James. Naturally she found it hard to embrace her state-sponsored passing, as depicted on all the anodyne public service announcements, where inspirational music accompanied dignified, stoic people, hands clasped as they walked towards the welcoming faces at the Facility.

But after a rebellious phase in her twenties, she had accepted that it was a fair price to pay. The Life Clock provided an ever-present reminder that time was precious, that choices mattered, that wasted minutes – so trivial early on – would be bitterly regretted at the end. The Life Clock had, by setting limits, actually given life more meaning.

In fact, James had many more doubts, although he hid this from everyone, including, some of the time, himself.

Latterly Julianne's main preoccupation had been the soulless efficiency of the Facility, her final destination today. She had said not long ago, "The thing that really disappoints me is that it's all so…ordinary. You go to this place, which looks like a failing dental

18

practice, and you wait your turn for a needle full of morphine. Even the name is boring. Why can't it be more interesting, like 'Death's Door', or 'The End of the Line' –anything that would make it more special, less bureaucratic. Death is the most important event of your life. There should be a ceremony, a festival – anything to stop it feeling like a visit to an accountant."

He would forever regret that he could not give her the operatic send-off that she deserved. Instead, he had to deliver her to professionally sympathetic functionaries who would deal with her in exactly the same way as they would anybody else. To them, she was not someone special, someone deserving of spectacle and public displays of emotion.

And whatever the claims made on TV, he had little expectation that the essence of Julianne could be captured by the afterlife harvester, even if it was a perfect facsimile based on her electrochemical brain activity. It would still be insipid in comparison to the real thing, like a black-and-white image of a perfect summer day.

He shifted his position, the better to see her face, and he could tell from her eyes that she was already partly Gone Away. 'Leaving', 'Going Away', 'Gone Away'. These were the modern euphemisms for the euthanasia program.

He understood. It was the necessary mental preparation for the inevitable, and he recognised the training. Still it crushed him to see his beautiful, vivacious Julianne starting to shut down. None of this would help her, so he tried to concentrate on being supportive instead.

"I will miss you," she said suddenly, passionately, back with him again for a moment. "Don't forget me."

"Are you insane?" was all he could think of to say. The remark was completely out of character, and it told him that there was not much time left. He held her close to hide his face.

Julianne kept her eyes open, not wanting to see her Life Clock. She finally closed them, opened them again, and when she said, "Time to go," her voice was calm.

They both realised that for the first time they had little to say to each other, and busied themselves with leaving preparations.

Julianne said a long good-bye to Gladys, who accepted the adoration as her due.

"Do you remember what a tiny kitten she was?" James asked.

"She could fit in the palm of my hand," said Julianne.

She made her tour of the housing unit, touching objects which held special significance for them – a smooth black stone from the sunken city, a small drawing of the red fox that she had done after her visit to his office at the Zoological Preservation Park.

She stood in the doorway, recalling the immense pleasure that they had taken in the small touches with which they had personalised their home. It had seemed a minor but important victory over the grinding ordinariness of the unit, to make theirs feel different, their own. The walls were the standard, unadorned white, but this just accentuated the rich colours and textures in the furniture, bedding, and even everyday objects like crockery that she had chosen. Julianne said that bright colours nourished her soul, and did not give a damn about looking unsophisticated or out of step with the current trend for shades of neutral: "Oatmeal and mushroom," she liked to say, "are things to eat, not colours to live with."

Each window held several large crystals suspended to refract the sunlight, which only dimmed when the powerful thunderstorms pounded the tinted glass, and sent Gladys cowering under their bed.

As they neared the door, James popped a solar protection pill into his mouth, felt the familiar fizz as it dissolved on his tongue, and offered her the pack.

She shook her head. "Won't need it. I'll be in the transport and then the Facility. Anyway," she interrupted his objection, "I only have a couple of hours left – the sun can't hurt me now."

"What if something should happen on the way?" he argued, always the one to plan ahead.

"Like what, we get lost?" she said, focused on putting on her shoes.

"Like we get a flat, or run out of fuel?" he suggested.

"We both know that if anything stops me getting to the Facility on time, then sunstroke will be the very least of my problems," she said quietly. And for that he had no answer.

They left the building together, into the hot, moist morning air, and headed quickly for the street. Gladys leaped onto the windowsill to watch them go, confident of their return, her squat silhouette visible through the blind.

James had booked the taxi to ensure that they would arrive at the Facility with a comfortable margin of spare time although 'spare' time, as such, did not exist as a concept any more, could not persist in the face of the Life Clock's inexorable counting progress in the zero direction. But James had always been extremely punctual, which came from all the days when he had had to get himself to school while Trish, his foster mother, lost herself in virtual reality soap operas.

On the drive to the Facility, Julianne and James revisited their favourite moments from the past on the handheld viewer. They were conspiring together, both focused on the happy images of their miniature selves being replayed in the back seat of the taxi.

Gladys as a kitten, sleeping inside the soup bowl which she had inexplicably claimed as her first bed; their first real 'date', at the Plant Museum, after the historic meeting to swap telephones; a diving trip to explore the ruins of Westbury, the camera's light piercing the green and blue surrounding the flooded office buildings, shops, and streets of the biggest coastal town yet to be submerged; Gladys again, asleep again, this time full grown, mouth open and snoring; Julianne's father's 60th birthday, his last before he Went Away.

As they neared their destination, James found it harder to engage Julianne's attention. He tried some of their favourite shared memories and private jokes, but they both heard the desperation in his voice. When they were within a few miles of the Facility, she turned her eyes to the darkened windows, and he gave up trying to distract her with conversation. "How long?" he asked. She closed and opened her eyes to view her Life Clock and said flatly, "20 minutes." He stroked her hand, hoping that his touch would register even if she was almost beyond the reach of his voice.

The driver stopped the car, and said gently, "Here we are, my friends." – James found it irritating to be addressed as 'friend' by a stranger, even though he knew it was part of the ambiance that the Facilities wished to create. – "Madam, please look at me for a moment," he said, and Julianne turned her head obediently for a photograph.

A member of staff opened the taxi door, saying: "Welcome, friends, my name is Todd and I will be your carer today." Todd was not tall, but his compact build was solid underneath his white uniform. Physical force was an extremely rare last resort at the Facilities precisely because the staff looked so formidable.

Todd stood unobtrusively by the door, yet James knew that he would take charge in a second if Julianne looked about to faint or flee. She hesitated for a moment too long, as James held the car door, and he sensed Todd preparing himself for whatever action was required. She climbed out, gripping James's hand tightly, and walked with dignity to the front door of the low, white, windowless building. A silver tower rose from the building's core, which reflected the sunlight from every surface.

They approached the reception desk with Todd, who signed them in and led them into a corridor, at the end of which was a private waiting room. Every aspect of the Facility was designed to promote calm acceptance, from the pale lavender walls and honey-coloured carpet, to the soft, uplifting music in the background. There were huge, motion-sensitive hologram faces on the walls. The first face to be activated as they passed belonged to a handsome woman in late middle age. Her silver hair was swept back from her smooth skin, and she exuded health and vitality. "I'm doing the right thing for my grandchildren," she announced, beaming with contentment. Farther down the hall, their approach brought another face to life, this time of a successful business man at his desk, with rain pounding against the windows behind him. "I'm doing the right thing for our planet," he said, his voice strong and deep, the voice of a leader. More faces spoke to them in turn as they progressed towards the waiting room, each one a potential role-model for someone, and even James felt his spirits lift a little. It was working for Julianne too, who was visibly more relaxed.

Todd retired quietly to finalise arrangements. James realised that they had seen no one else except the receptionist and other staff, which struck him as odd. Where was everyone else? On balance, he was glad of the privacy, and thankful for the Facility's clever layout which prevented people from encountering each other as they waited their turn. The reception desk was the hub of a wheel made up of identical corridors; indeed the whole site was circular, with several entrances around the circumference, enabling arrivals and check-ins to be staggered for optimum discretion. It would not do, he realised, for emotionally stressed people to be exposed to the upsetting scenes of others' grief or, worst of all, those situations which required Todd and his colleagues to implement their physical strength.

"How are you?" he asked, aware of the question's inanity but needing to know.

"Okay," she said to reassure both of them. "Really, Okay. I just want it to be over now. They say that the waiting is the worst part..." She shrugged apologetically at the feebleness of the joke.

Todd returned and they stood together. They followed him into the corridor and into a hydraulic lift which carried them quickly above the level of the roof. James realised that they must be ascending through the silver tower.

They stepped out of the lift into a large round room seemingly made entirely of glass, in the middle of which was positioned a long, white padded couch with two stools, one on either side. Beside one stool was a small table on which there was an oblong case, big enough for a pair of glasses. There were no restraints visible, no obvious means of coercing the last-minute unwilling, although James was sure that there were many cameras hidden in the smooth walls.

Julianne allowed Todd to lead her to the chair, where she lay back looking up at the sky. It was a pale, bleached blue with no clouds. It looked flat, one-dimensional, like a painted backdrop instead of the doorway to infinity. She seemed composed, but gripped James's hand tightly when he took the stool beside her.

"Julianne, my friend, tell me when it's time," Todd said, sat on the other stool, in the sincere, caring voice which James already hated.

Julianne closed her eyes and opened them again. "It's time."

James focused on Julianne's face as Todd removed the syringe from its case. He heard the hiss as Todd injected the morphine through the skin of her arm so expertly that she did not even flinch.

"The sky," she said. "It's so beautiful." And he wondered what picture the morphine was painting for her brain, but she wore a tired smile and he was grateful that she liked the view, however it was generated.

"It is, very beautiful," he said, stroked her hand, her arm, her face. He did not notice that Todd had withdrawn to a discrete distance.

James would not say a final good-bye: "Bye for now, my love," he said, as he had done at the end of every phone conversation with her. "See you soon."

"See you," she murmured. "You have the code?"

He nodded, and kissed her one last time, her lips warm against his. The swipe card for her Afterlife Account was always on his person. He held it up so she could see. "Don't forget..." she trailed off.

Her eyelids drooped and she mumbled. He leaned closer, desperate to recover whatever words were left to hear from her. "What was that? Say it again."

With his ear against her mouth, he felt her last breath brush his skin. "More. Time," she sighed, and was gone.

James closed his eyes and immediately saw his own Life Clock, projected via his optic nerve: 02:14:22:05:10. In a little over two years it would be his turn to report to the Facility. They said that it was like slipping into a sweet dream, until you woke up refreshed and carefree in the afterlife.

He opened his eyes again when he felt the weight of Todd's hand on his shoulder, and realised that he still held Julianne's hand. Her face was blank, empty. There had always been an energy about her, an animation hovering over her features even in deep sleep. That was gone. Todd took a blue cloth from underneath the table and gently draped Julianne, leaving her face bare. One of Todd's colleagues, a sad-eyed stick of a man, emerged from the lift.

Todd said, "James, when you're ready, Richard will take you downstairs. I'll meet you in Reception."

Todd insisted on accompanying James back into the unit, and pressed a pile of pamphlets into his hand. He further insisted on giving James a manly hug, which was nearly enough to make James

24

give in to the powerful urge to hit Todd in the face. But once Todd had left, he was undone by the aloneness. He sat down on the floor and leaned his back against the front door, unable to go any further. Gladys leaped onto his lap, butting his nose with her head.

Tucked inside one of the pamphlets was Todd's business card. James brushed the photo of the handsome face with his finger. The card intoned, in that professionally caring voice, "I'm here when you need me." James realised with cool detachment that he had never hated anyone as much as he hated Todd. He folded the card back on itself, over and over, enjoying the sound of Todd's words being strangled, and finally silenced.

Although there had been many instances when he cursed the shortness of his time allocation, at that particular moment, it felt like each minute would last forever. He thought that Julianne would appreciate the irony of that.

Taking the swipe card for Julianne's Afterlife Account from his pocket, James was paralysed by indecision. He ached to see her, but knew that it was entirely possible that it would make the pain worse. Much worse.

He made a decision. Moving Gladys onto her cushion, he went over to the computer and swiped the card. A prompt demanded the code. James typed the number on the card, his finger poised above the key that would abort the session.

Then he saw her. Julianne. Looking just as she had a few hours before, except better. She sat on a green hillside, dressed in loose trousers and a v-necked tunic in pale biscuity linen, a colour she would have hated. Lounging sideways on one hip, she looked relaxed and happy, all the tension gone from her face. The grass looked soft, and it was sprinkled with small white flowers.

"Hello, my love," she called, with a wave of her hand. She got up and approached the camera, her face filling more of the screen. A light breeze swept a few strands of hair across her forehead, and she pushed them aside. She still wore her wedding ring. He was amazed by the quality of the image, the realism of her voice. He so wanted to believe, that it was all worth it, that something of her remained. But somehow the perfection of the illusion gave it away.

"It's wonderful here," she enthused. "You're going to love it. It's beautiful, and the air is so clean. And the sun doesn't hurt any more." Her expression saddened. "But I miss you, my love. Don't be too long in coming. It will be so much better when we're together again." He opened his mouth to speak, but could not say a word. It was so real, so inviting. And so utterly wrong. He had never felt so alone.

She continued to look at him, her smile slightly uncertain. "James? What's the matter, my love?"

He said nothing.

"James?"

His name hung in the air, unanswered.

The O'Malley Portrait, Oil On Canvas, Late 21st Century

by Michael Heery

Milo went into his studio to continue work on his portrait of President O'Malley. He was enjoying the work and keen to get on with it. Over the past forty years or so it had become an essential ritual of British political life that any new President of the Federal Republic of Great Britain should have his or her portrait painted by a prominent artist and then hung on display in the new House of Commons rotunda. And Milo most certainly was a successful portraitist. This was the third of these commissions he'd won. His others, of Presidents Patel and Millington, sadly both subsequently assassinated, had been greeted with acclaim and continued to enjoy popular support. He fully intended to use this new work to cement his reputation as being among the great British portrait painters.

As a young man Milo had graduated from the Global University of Manchester with a good degree in Media Studies. He had, somewhat reluctantly, been persuaded to follow this course of study by his parents, who wanted their only child to graduate in a respectable subject that would guarantee a good income. And they got their way, as within a year of graduating Milo was working for the BBC as a trainee producer on one of the many daytime religious shows. The trouble for Milo, and indeed for his parents, was that he suffered from an obsession that simply would not leave him alone. This desire, or 'The Itch' as Milo sometimes called it, was a passion for art. He never lost his childlike delight in painting and drawing. At school he had excelled in Art, taking top honours in both life drawing and improvised computer composition, and for some years he juggled his more formal academic studies with membership of local amateur painting groups.

One of these, Oldham Old Masters Society, was dedicated to the appreciation and practice of traditional forms of painting. It was closely linked to other art societies in greater Manchester and participated in a network of competitions, some of which were organised by local universities. In this environment Milo flourished, developing a wide range of techniques and a growing list of local

27

awards. It was obvious to the artists he worked with that he was a significant talent. Eventually, much to the disappointment of his parents, he succumbed to his instincts and the advice of his artistic mentors and dropped Media Studies in favour of work as an artist. He had never regretted his decision, and, as he maintained a comfortable lifestyle through his work, his parents gradually came to accept his choice of career.

That, of course, all happened two decades ago. His parents were now retired and Milo was based in London, where the best commissions were to be found. Milo had discovered that he had another talent, one less obvious than his talent for portraiture. He was skilled at making and keeping contacts. He made friends with other artists, with art historians, with media types, with politicians, with the rich and powerful. It was his ability to play the part of artistic Boswell to a succession of worldly Johnsons that secured much of his progress. In fact the commission to paint O'Malley's portrait came as much from Milo's contacts as from his performance in the open competition.

Milo had met O'Malley several times over the years. The first time was back in 2042 when he was called to give evidence to a government committee on the promotion of public art. He had been recommended for this role by several politicians and media commentators concerned to return public art to that of an earlier, less troublesome era. So much modern art was concerned with attacking the government's record on economic policy, on poverty, on its wars. They believed that the country needed artists who stuck to their commission and didn't trouble themselves with politics. Milo was recognised to be just such an artist. O'Malley had chaired the committee that set up a new programme of investment in public art and Milo had been kept busy ever since.

Of course it was obvious to Milo that O'Malley didn't give a damn about art. The President had only one interest, his pursuit of power. O'Malley had got his hands on the top job five years ago and it had soon become apparent that he wasn't going to let it go. His ruthless pursuit of state security had finally begun to stem the tide of terrorist outrages and he won grudging acceptance of his government of national unity from a public heartily sick of social and political unrest. As O'Malley's power grew so too did his intolerance of those who challenged him. This was apparent in his 'reform' of state offices, whereby journalists, lecturers, even artists could find themselves out of a job if they crossed his path. A couple of Milo's own friends had lost work as a result of going public with their criticisms of O'Malley. So, Milo learned to keep his head down and stick to what he was good at. And as a result his commissions grew and grew.

As part of the commission to paint O'Malley Milo had been invited to Downing Street. The great man had given him an hour of his time for a preliminary sketch. O'Malley, being totally ignorant of art, assumed this was the correct protocol. Not wishing to be in any way awkward Milo duly went along and roughed up an outline portrait while O'Malley took calls, signed papers and generally fidgeted about. Their brief conversation went something like this:

"So, Milo, you've won the honey pot again."

"Yes Sir, I'm very pleased."

"Well you did a good job on poor old Millington. You'll make me look equally gorgeous, right?"

"I will try to show you as you are, President O'Malley."

"Will you indeed. You mean 'warts and all,' I suppose?"

"Sir, a comparison with Cromwell would not be unflattering."

"Hah, Milo! No one could teach you much about flattery. Now please get on with it."

When the hour was up Milo showed his subject his likeness, to which he nodded his approval and Milo was dismissed.

As a professional painter Milo worked to a routine that varied little from day to day. After a light breakfast and two cups of strong coffee he walked his Afghan hound, George, round the adjacent park for about thirty minutes. This was long enough for George to get some exercise and attend to his bodily functions, and also to allow Milo to reflect upon his artistic progress. Painting was more productive if he had determined in advance the detailed stages needed over the next couple of days. That way he worked efficiently and was able to keep everything under review. It was a method he'd learned by trial and error during his years as a jobbing painter.

Milo gave George a snack and settled him down in the back garden. He then began to work on the portrait of O'Malley. Milo pressed the blinds button so as to darken the studio. He didn't want sunshine pouring in and ruining his view of the colours. Gradation of tone was everything. He always sought a subtle union of colour nuance. He then got out the recent sketch of O'Malley, contemplated it for a second, smiled and throw it in the bin. He certainly wouldn't be using that!

Next, Milo turned on his computer, which loaded Windows 2055 onto the two-metre-square screen. He then ran a list of 'Art Inspiration Menus.' He was a great admirer of two earlier artists, these being the Dutch painter Rembrandt van Rijn and the French photographer Henri Cartier-Bresson. Standing across the room from the screen he told the computer to run through some portraits by both men.

Milo loved Rembrandt's self-portraits, particularly the very last of these. It was unflinching in its portrayal of an old man about to enter his final decline. It had a sort of dignified pathos. As in all Rembrandt's portraits the eyes seemed to expose the sitter's soul to the viewer. Milo loved that straightforward honesty. However, it wouldn't do for O'Malley. Oh no, he'd want something much more upbeat. And besides, the new president and the word honesty were rarely, if ever, found together in the same sentence. So, Milo chose instead the Kenwood House paining, where Rembrandt depicts himself in a white cap. He has a look of mature confidence in this picture. Self-assured, experienced, man of the world, even a little world-weary, as if life could hold no further surprises. That seemed a much better fit for O'Malley.

Milo stored this image in the work-in-progress folder labelled 'The O'Malley.' Then he turned to Bresson. His work, thought Milo, would evoke great dignity. The sombre faces of his subjects stared at the viewer impassively. They were more like gods than weak mortals. In particular, Milo liked a portrait of two black people, a man and a woman. They appeared knowledgeable and wise; they had gravitas. Yes, that old crook O'Malley would want some of that.

Having selected the two images, Milo needed to make a few changes. He instructed the computer to make the Bresson characters white Caucasian. In doing so it not only altered their pigmentation but also automatically adjusted their features in an appropriate manner. Milo could, of course, override the machine's handiwork but he knew from experience that there wasn't any point. It always did a better job. Similarly, he instructed the computer to tidy up Rembrandt's hair, darken its colouring (it was well known that O'Malley used the latest dye implants) and reduce the wrinkles to create a look described by Microsoft as 'mid-fifties male benign skin tone.' It was a facility hopeful men used when mailing their photos to dating agencies, a rather tacky business that Milo found pleasing to associate with O'Malley. By the time Milo had finished the portrait all this would be lost under layers of oil paint, undetectable by Sotherby's experts, let alone a philistine like O'Malley.

Having concluded the preparatory stages to his satisfaction, Milo began work on O'Malley himself. He uploaded about twenty images of the great man. Although taken over a period of ten years or so, they all had one thing in common; that wretched smile. More of a grin really. It reminded Milo of that other old humbug, Tony Blair. He secretly hoped that O'Malley would come to a similarly sticky end. It was obvious that the grin couldn't go into the picture. It just wasn't done to have the nation's leaders smirking in their official portraits. Not dignified. And besides, how could our elected representatives possibly concentrate on their legislative duties with a larger-than-life-size face of O'Malley constantly leering at them? Milo decided that it was in the best political interest of the country to avoid the grin.

Therefore, his next task was to instruct the computer to use its own creative judgement to produce a dignified image of O'Malley, minus the smirk. It took about five seconds, showing that even the computer found the task daunting. However, as it was probably beyond the achievement of any human being, Milo was well satisfied with the result. O'Malley was beginning to look like the leader he probably pictured in his own head.

At this stage the portrait looked like one of those old digital photographs. But that would soon change. During a lucrative consultancy Milo had worked with Microsoft to help them develop the software he was now using. Firstly, he instructed the computer to meld (a word Milo himself had suggested to Microsoft for this process) the Bresson male face with that of O'Malley. Excellent, thought Milo, now we're getting somewhere. Then he melded the Rembrandt with the Bresson-O'Malley figure. The machine was able to infuse the O'Malley template with the qualities of the pictures created by the two old masters.

Now came the tricky part. Milo pulled down two other functions called 'Light Magic' and 'Doppelganger.' The latter allowed him to give the amalgam portrait of O'Malley the painterly qualities used by Rembrandt. The result was spectacular. O'Malley now appeared not only as a dignified and interesting human being of great wisdom, but also looked as if he had just been painted by Rembrandt himself. Then 'Light Magic' lit the whole thing from a different angle. Milo began to feel excited. He repeatedly moved round the room contemplating the work from different perspectives. This was going to go down a treat with the selection committee, not to mention with O'Malley himself.

Milo allowed himself a break for lunch. There were important stages yet to tackle but as the work was going so well he decided to try to finish it today. Just before going down for lunch, followed by another short walk in the park with George, Milo got out the large canvas he had already stretched and framed for the painting.

The afternoon session began with Milo using a range of tonal software to make minute adjustments to the portrait. The machine was intelligent enough to do most of the work, sensing his line of thought and often anticipating his choice of colours. Gradually, over an hour or two, the work became a subtle, modern tribute to Rembrandt, albeit changing the patterns of his brush technique and using some stronger colours. At intervals of about ten minutes the computer checked the work-in-progress with every known portrait ever produced, constantly looking to eradicate plagiarism and ensure Milo's painting was fresh and original.

Finally, Milo attached the lightweight oil paint loom above the flat canvas frame. The computer's sensors then guided the electronic loom as its fast-moving sprays built up layers of paint. Its advanced design allowed it to both apply and dry the paint at speeds invisible to the naked eye. Reproducing the on-screen image of O'Malley took about another two hours, by which time the completed oil painting was not only finished but also varnished and dry enough to handle. Milo checked that the computer had signed and dated the work properly. He was tired after such a long day but the result prompted a heartfelt sigh of satisfaction. This was a fine painting, even if its subject was that old phoney O'Malley. Milo was so pleased he'd stuck to traditional portraiture for this commission, rather than adopting the new-fangled methods of some of his flashier contemporaries.

Catherine and the God Market

by Sheila Adamson

On Tuesday night Catherine answered the doorbell to find two aliens outside. It took her a while to work out how to react to that.

"Hallo!" said the alien on the left. "Can we interest you in a message of hope and gladness?"

"Uh?" she said.

The alien smiled brightly. At least, she thought it was smiling. It had a huge lipless mouth, which it was stretching widely; and huge owl eyes which it was blinking enthusiastically. It also had three arms, three legs and rather scaly grey skin. Presumably in an attempt to blend in, it was wearing a dark business suit. "Are you happy?" it enquired.

"Em..."

"Truly happy?"

Catherine felt herself edging backwards. Strangers weren't supposed to ask you questions like that. Of course she wasn't happy. What business was it of anyone else's, human or not?

"We'd like to tell you about true happiness," said the second, smaller alien.

"And eternal life."

"May we come in?"

Catherine's brain started to work. "Are you some sort of Mormons?"

"We are missionaries from the planet Vah," said the second alien. "We have come fifty-four light years to tell you about the wonders of the Divine Presence."

"Wow," she said faintly. "That's dedication."

"It is a privilege. To spread the Divine Word to a new world..." The first alien blinked rapidly, too emotional to finish.

"Well, I have to warn you," said Catherine, "we have a few gods of our own here already. Some people might not welcome you."

She wasn't sure she did. She and God had fallen out a long time ago and it wasn't an argument she was anxious to reopen. But she couldn't close the door on them. The sheer alien improbability of

34

them overrode normal considerations. It was all she could do not to stare – at the scales, the unnatural eye movements, the ingenious tailoring of the three-legged suits. Nevertheless, she didn't want to encourage them too much.

"The god market is pretty saturated already," she said.

The aliens made gentle, condescending noises. "You may believe you have gods. But they aren't real."

"No kidding?"

"No, no. It's not surprising. You recognise the gap in your lives that should be filled by the Divine, and seek to create theological constructs that serve the same psychological function. In reality, however, these are nothing more than extensions of your own collective unconscious."

"Oh," said Catherine.

"Sorry," said the first alien.

Catherine shrugged. She didn't believe in God any more anyway.

"But the Divine Presence," said the second alien, leaning forward to underline the point, "is real. That's the difference."

"Right," she said. "It's not a psychological thingummy. Not in the least."

"Exactly." The aliens smiled. "May we come in and tell you more?"

Catherine scratched her head. It wasn't as if she was doing anything. Only watching Eastenders and feeling tired. Trying to ignore the pile of ironing waiting to be done, the unanswered messages from her mother and the unpaid bills on the coffee table. Eating chocolate digestives and wishing she wasn't fat.

Her thirty-fifth birthday present to herself had been a year without dieting. She was nearly thirty-six and she thought she might continue. It wasn't as if there was anyone to care how bad she looked naked.

"Whatever," she told the aliens, stepping back from the door. "Come in. Sorry about the mess."

The aliens shuffled in daintily. They propelled themselves forward by revolving their entire lower bodies, which was quite unsettling to watch. Catherine swept up an armful of un-ironed clothes from one chair, looking round for somewhere to put them.

"We prefer to stand," said the second alien. It introduced itself as Menig and indicated its taller friend was called Ac.

"I'm not sure your furniture is appropriate for us," said Ac. "It must be strange having only two legs. Is it difficult to balance?"

"Only when I'm drunk," said Catherine, dumping the clothes. "Em... do you want tea? Coffee?"

They demurred. It seemed they hadn't been here long enough to establish what was safe for them to consume. That was reassuring. It wouldn't say much for her awareness of what was going on if aliens had been wandering about the planet for weeks without her noticing. Was she the first human they'd talked to? If so, it was something of an honour. She decided to pay them proper attention. She would even keep a straight face. Seating herself on the sofa, she invited them to enlighten her.

Menig set itself in a symmetrical pose and started to declaim. "In the name of the Divine, I bring you the Divine Offer. The Divine has agreed to offer its protection to this world and is prepared to make available the following services to all loyal worshippers. Firstly, access to prayer facilities with the standard frequency of replies. Secondly, entry into the prize draw for the daily Act of Divine Retribution. Thirdly, the chance to register as a Gold Class Adherent and apply for immortality. And most of all, the peace of mind of knowing all your spiritual needs are in safe hands." The alien smiled conspiratorially. "It's a very good offer."

Catherine was unable to form a reply.

Menig felt it should clarify a few points. "Divine Wisdom is provided without guarantee and the Divine accepts no responsibility for misuse. Acts of Retribution are non-revocable and non-negotiable. We will require your legislative bodies to make clear that Acts of Retribution stand outside the law and are not subject to appeals or suits of any kind. There may also need to be some other minor changes in relation to ensuring regular worship facilities."

"W-w-w...?" said Catherine.

"To qualify for this offer, you must register as a worshipper," Ac explained kindly. "It's very simple, but obviously the Divine needs to know you are part of its congregation, so regular attendance is required. We often find it helps to codify that right and duty in some form. You'll have to tell us more about your existing laws." It gave an almost shy smile. "I'm really looking forward to hearing about your planet. It seems nice. Incredibly busy."

"It's not nice," she said, finding her voice at last. "It's a pit."

"Oh," said Ac. "I'm sorry. You need the Divine then, don't you?"

Catherine could tell them a thing or two about that, if she wanted. There were times when you needed the Divine so badly it made you scream. But the Divine was never bloody there, was it? That was the point.

"And what exactly will the Divine do to make things better?" she asked.

"That depends on what you want," said Ac. "You can only pray and hope your prayer will be answered."

"Yeah. Right. Been there, done that. No reply. In what sense is your Divine any better?"

The aliens made that condescending, laughing sound again. "The Divine Presence is real. It does answer."

"It's answered you, has it?"

"Yes," said Ac. "Of course. The Divine is busy and we can't expect instant responses every time. But I have had three replies so far in my life, plus the calling to take up this mission."

"I've had two," said Menig. "But I don't often ask for guidance. The Divine is not to be taken lightly."

Ac glanced at its colleague. "I don't ask often."

Catherine interrupted. "You actually get answers? Real answers from God?"

The aliens chuckled. "What do you think we've been trying to tell you?"

And for the first time, with an impact that drove the breath out of her lungs, Catherine realised exactly what they were trying to tell her.

Once upon a time there was a woman called Catherine. An ordinary woman, not terribly good at some things – okay, most things – but, you know, a human being who imagined she might reasonably expect some happiness in her life. She met a guy called John who seemed to love her, so she let herself love him and they duly got married. They decided to have a family. As the baby grew in her womb she assumed that she was on the right track. From now on her mission was defined: to love her family. She wasn't terribly good at much but she would do this.

And then the baby was born, poor little Robbie, and nothing was ever right again. Three months just to get him out of the hospital and home, a sickly, wrinkled creature with confused, sad eyes. All the nights he cried and cried. All the days of watching, watching for signs of improvement. Back and forward to the hospital. All the sleepless years of worry.

You expect there to be someone to help you. At first she put her faith in doctors, who talked as if they knew everything. They opened and shut Robbie's tiny body over and over but they didn't know how to cure him. She looked to John and he was as helpless as she was. All the rest of her family could supply was an increasingly fatuous sympathy. Her sister offered to pray for them. God help her, by that point Catherine was desperate enough to pray herself. She started attending church again, became a regular. If she was good and did what God wanted, if she came every Sunday, gave money to the poor and was kind to strangers, surely God would answer. How could he not?

One day she tried to talk to the minister, Mr Howat, about it. She poured her heart out over tea in the church hall after the service while he stood frozen to the spot by her all-consuming need, his ginger snap crumbling in his hand. He waffled. Prayer wasn't straightforward, he said, it was about you looking within yourself to...

"Is God real?" she cut in. "Does he listen?"

"Yes," he said, "of course God is with you."

The doctors came up with another operation, another medical miracle. Desperate, their marriage bleeding to death, John and Catherine said yes. Robbie's heart gave out two days after the failed surgery. John said it was almost a relief.

There are some things that can never be forgiven.

Once there was a woman called Catherine who had run out of faith in anything. And then faith rang her doorbell.

"I have to see it for myself," she said shakily, after the aliens had explained their wireless prayer connection booth. "I ... I'm not sure."

"That can be arranged," said Menig. It cast a critical glance at her living room. "We will need a larger space."

"Where do your people worship?" Ac enquired. "Our initial analysis of your communications provided conflicting data."

"Well, it depends what religion you are. I used to go to a church nearby. St Andrews."

"You imply that you stopped."

She pulled a face. "It's like you said. It wasn't real. Why believe in it?"

"It's fascinating that so many people do," Menig remarked. "I look forward to theological debates with the masters of your religions."

Catherine laughed humourlessly. What would Mr Howat make of this pair? She'd had a few theological debates of her own with him, especially after Robbie's death. Even now, years later, the memory revived her anger. Apparently it was up to her to show strength in the face of tragedy. It had taken her a ridiculous length of time to understand that he was just making it up. He didn't know why Robbie had died, he couldn't see God's plan, and he couldn't explain anything. So why the hell did he insist on pretending?

A dark smile hovered on her lips. Let's see how he copes with a real God, she thought. "I'll tell you what," she told the aliens. "I'll take you to the church now. Tuesday night bible group will be just finishing. I'll introduce you to a Master of Religion."

Catherine drove the aliens to the church. They clambered with difficulty onto the back seat and said what a charming vehicle it was. Ac was particularly taken with the windscreen wipers.

Then they positioned themselves in the shadows opposite the side door of the church and waited for the bible group to leave. When at last she was sure Mr Howat would be on his own, Catherine brought Ac and Menig through the side door into the lobby.

Mr Howat looked slightly older than she recalled, his hair half gone and his eyes weary behind his glasses. He was locking up the meeting room, obviously about to go home.

"Hallo," she said. "I don't know if you remember me, but I used to come here."

Recognition, and a certain wariness, came into his expression.

"Catherine, wasn't it?"

"That's right. I've brought someone to meet you."

The aliens stepped forward. They were all smiles. Mr Howat gaped.

She explained the situation simply, and not without relish. "These guys have come from another planet. Apparently their god is real. Unlike yours. They thought you might like a theological debate."

"I beg your pardon?" said Mr Howat.

"It's a sort of God versus God play-off," she said. "They reckon the facts are on their side."

To be honest, now she was here she was starting to doubt the aliens' claims again. There was something about this building that drained faith from her. Every time she looked at Mr Howat she felt the bitterness flooding back. She wasn't sure she could handle being let down by another false god.

But if Ac and Menig really could prove it – that was different.

Mr Howat made a few noises similar to a Mini starting on a cold morning. Ac twirled forward diplomatically. "Please. We are not here to condemn you for your previous worship. We believe that all religion is a worthy striving towards the Divine."

"However," said Menig, shimmying up alongside, "we hope you will be interested to hear what we have to say."

And they went over it all again: the Divine Presence, Divine Retribution, the application for immortality. It was cold in the lobby. Catherine sat hunched on a hard wooden chair beside a pile of hymn books, rocking her knees to keep warm. Mr Howat leant against the wall, straining back from the aliens' eager gestures. He looked horrified.

"You make a contract with God?" he asked, pronouncing the word 'contract' with marked distaste.

"Certainly not," said Menig. "The Divine makes a contract with us."

"You could call it a Covenant, if it makes you feel better," Catherine suggested.

40

"The Covenant was different," said Mr Howat.

"Seems to me it's exactly the same," said Catherine. "Exodus. God offered Moses a deal. Worship me and I'll do great and terrible things for you. Wasn't that it?"

Menig interrupted. "Perhaps it would be easier if we showed you. We will construct the communication booth. Do you have a large space we can use?"

"The hall, I suppose," said Mr Howat. "But I don't know what you can show me. I don't need to be shown God."

Catherine led the way into the church hall. Without people it was a desolate room, a cheerless shed tacked on to the church itself, suitable for coffee mornings and bring-and-buy sales. It couldn't look less like a home for God.

Ac sniffed the air uncertainly and shrugged. "This will do."

The two aliens produced dark packages from their pockets. With a brisk shake the packages were unrolled to reveal a bewildering array of tools and strips of metal. Enthusiastically, Ac and Menig commenced assembly.

Mr Howat slumped down on a plastic chair. "This can't be happening."

"Why not?" said Catherine. "If you can believe in an invisible, intangible God you can believe in aliens, can't you?"

"You might think so," he said with a grudging half-smile. "But God isn't as intangible to me as He is to you. I feel Him all the time. His presence and love give meaning to our lives, to all our lives, no matter how humble. I can't prove it. But I feel it deep in my heart and it keeps me going. I wish you could feel it, too. I don't know how to convince you."

She scowled. Could he not hear how feeble he sounded?

"How are things?" he asked hesitantly. "Your marriage – did it get any better?"

"We divorced."

"I'm sorry." He cleared his throat. "So, no one new? No…"

"No man, no children."

"Ah."

"My fault, I'm sure," she snapped. "I should have prayed more. God would have sorted me out, wouldn't he? Oh wait – no, he doesn't exist."

Mr Howat gave her a doleful look. He took off his glasses and cleaned them ponderously.

The aliens were working quickly. Already they had constructed a thin silver cage, about six feet square. Now Ac was adding some complicated wiring while Menig clipped on small black spheres at strategic locations. It had the air of a magician's prop. Catherine felt another pang of doubt.

Ac let out a ball of gossamer wire, trailing it in a wide circle round the cage, then laid the ball down and switched something on.

All at once the cage was glowing. Not brightly, just a soft, bluish lustre. At the edge of hearing there was a deep hum.

"Right," said Menig. "Who's first?"

Once upon a time there was a man called Brian Howat. From an early age it had seemed obvious to him there must be more to life than mere facts. A baby senses colours and shapes but it can't see until it learns what the shapes mean. In the same way, people could see their cars and houses and boiled potatoes, and so imagined they could see their lives. But there was no understanding. They didn't know what their lives meant.

Like many young men he went through a spell of rebellion. At university, he moved away from his uncritical Church of Scotland upbringing and experimented with philosophy. It left him cold. All the cleverness of Sartre and Heidegger could do was strip man of his relationship with the universe, leaving him alone in a sea of unanswerable questions. If that was true, it wasn't a truth worth knowing.

One autumn afternoon he was walking back to his digs, considering what he should do with his life, when it came to his attention that it was a beautiful day. The trees scattered multi-coloured leaves on the pavement, while the sky was a fragile blue brushed with the softest of clouds. Around him preoccupied pedestrians stomped about their business without glancing upwards. What were they thinking? Here was the world, a hundred times more wonderful than anyone had a right to expect, and they didn't even notice? And a great truth hit him: God was around us, a million times more wonderful than we had a right to expect, and we didn't notice.

He felt humble and awed. He knew what he would do. He would make people notice.

Thirty years later, he was running out of hope of success. More and more he focused on small things: visiting the sick and the elderly, organising charitable donations. He tried to live a good life. God was there, every time a smile appeared instead of sadness. And every now and then a shaft of sunlight would catch him off guard; or the smell of his garden after the rain; and he would feel it again, that surge of joy it was so hard to persuade others to share.

God doesn't exist, people like Catherine would say. *Where is he? Show me.*

Brian wanted to say*: Look! See how huge and yellow the moon is tonight. See the glitter of frost under the stars. There He is! There!*

But although they saw it they couldn't understand it. And then they were angry at God and at Brian for their own failure to see, as if God was the one making them blind, not their own wilfulness.

Now two aliens were offering to make him see. He didn't need to.

It was only when Catherine walked into the glowing cage that Brian realised how dangerous it might be. What if these aliens were in fact some kind of horrible, body snatching cannibals? What if it was all a ruse? He stood up, a shout of protest hesitating in his throat.

Catherine eased her broad hips into the cage. Her pale belligerent face wore an expression he had never seen there before: hope. She looked five years younger.

"Think your question," the larger alien told her. "Close your eyes and concentrate."

The smaller alien gyrated round the device, nodding to itself. Catherine shut her eyes. Brian's heart was in his mouth. Stupidly, he cast around him for a weapon. All he could see were plastic chairs and church newsletters.

An astonished smile spread on Catherine's face. She opened her eyes. "It answered me!" she breathed. She laughed, then clapped a shaky hand to her mouth. "Dear God. It answered me."

The aliens exchanged satisfied glances. They arranged their arms and legs symmetrically and murmured, "The Divine honours us and we are thankful."

Catherine moved slowly out of the glowing cage. "That is amazing. Thank you, Ac. Thank you, Menig. Thank you so much." Her voice was trembling. She was on the verge of tears.

It must be a trick, thought Brian. A nasty trick played on a vulnerable woman. Anger started to creep up on him.

"You have to try it," she told him. "You really have to try it."

"What exactly happened?" he asked.

"Try it and see." Again she laughed, a semi-hysterical sound. "Sorry, but I can't stick around to watch. I have to be somewhere."

"What? Why?"

"Places to go. Lives to get. About bloody time." With a wild grin, she disappeared out of the hall.

Brian took a step after her, unsure it was wise to let her go alone. Menig called him back. "Your turn now! Don't you want to speak to the Divine?"

"I speak to God every day," he informed them coldly.

"Please Mr Howat," said Ac. "There are so many things we have to talk about, and how can we start when you haven't experienced the Divine as we do? How can you understand?"

The Divine wasn't something you could have piped into your head from a machine. It was something you had to reach for with your soul. Yet, curiosity tugged at him. After all, how could he persuade Catherine what she'd felt wasn't real unless he'd felt it too?

The irony of the situation was not lost on him. He didn't want the aliens' god, and he certainly didn't trust it. But he couldn't ignore it.

Was this walking into the valley of the shadow of death? Gingerly, he picked his way between the cables and wires to stand encased in the cage of blue light. There was no sense of heat from the shining lines around him, but the humming was deeper. He felt a sudden terror as if he was about to jump out of an aeroplane.

"Think your question," said Ac. "Close your eyes and concentrate."

Brian obeyed. The humming vibrated softly in his body.

"Concentrate on your question," Ac repeated.

What question? What did he want? He didn't want anything from God, just for Him to be there. Distant, mysterious and indescribable. Not answering questions on demand like a sideshow fortune teller.

Yet he sensed a presence in the back of his skull, a something waiting for him. Waiting for his request.

What are you? he thought.

And the presence opened up. His soul fell into the void, tiny next to the vastness around him. He couldn't think. He could only feel the scale of it, the power, the glory, there was no other word, the divinity of it. He pulled away in panic, horrified at his proximity. Man was not meant to be this close to God. It was like trying to live on the surface of the Sun. He opened his eyes and let out a strangled howl.

The three-legged aliens smiled at him with their impossibly wide mouths. "Did you feel it?"

Wordlessly, Brian staggered out of the cage. He sank into a chair and wept.

Catherine finally found a parking place. She didn't know this part of town well. After the message from the Divine she had hurried home, stopping only to check her A-Z and throw on a less slobby blouse. Now she was here she wished she'd also dug out some better shoes and put on make up. She brushed her hair hurriedly and licked her lips, then got out of the car. Taking a deep breath, she straightened her shoulders, sucked in her stomach and entered the pub.

It was no more than half full, an old fashioned kind of place with a mostly middle-aged clientele. Steve Harley was oo-la-la-ing quietly on the juke box. Catherine looked around.

There he was. The man the Divine had shown her, just exactly like the image in her head. Short hair, a lean, lived-in face, a dry smile on his lips as he listened to the story his companion was telling him. The companion – a florid man with a loud voice – burbled on and on; her man just listened, turning a beer mat over and over and smiling.

Yes, she thought, *he'll do.*

With considerable excitement, she approached their table.

"Hallo," she said.

The two men looked at her. "Hallo," said her man.

"You're Mike, aren't you?" she said.

"Yes." He frowned slightly. "Sorry, should I know you?"

"You will do. I hope." It was difficult not to grin like a fool. All her life this had been impossible. Finding a decent man among all the crap that was out there. But the Divine had shown her. She'd asked where she could find him and it had shown her, as clear as a TV playing in her head. This man, Mike, what he looked like and where he was. And she'd known it was true. There was no need to imagine anything, no need to perform acrobatics with your soul. The Divine was real and it knew the answer to her prayers.

So she'd come.

Mike didn't seem to grasp the beautiful simplicity of it. "Is this some kind of joke?" he asked. "Who are you?"

"I'm Catherine."

"Catherine," said Mike. "And?"

"And what?"

"And what do you want?" His voice was level, not unfriendly, but with a clear edge of *Get on with it then*. This was harder than she'd expected. The Divine had shown her where he was but hadn't given any clues what to say. She sucked in her stomach again.

"I think she's trying to chat you up," chuckled florid man, nudging Mike on the arm. "Could be your lucky night."

She felt herself starting to blush. No sensible words came to mind, no smooth line.

"Seriously, what is it?" Mike studied her closely. She really should have taken time for make up. But the Divine had led her here, so there must be a chance. She just had to say something to catch his interest, keep him talking.

"You wouldn't believe what I've seen tonight," she blurted.

Mike gave a restrained sigh. "Try me."

"Aliens! Honestly. I've just met two aliens."

"Jesus," said the florid man. "She's not one of your old patients, is she?"

"Don't think so," said Mike, his frown growing more concerned.

46

"Are you a doctor?" she asked. Wow, the Divine didn't believe in half measures.

"No. I work in community education."

"Oh," she said, nonplussed.

"Is that a problem?" The dry smile was back. God, you could fall in love with that smile if someone would let you.

"I'm just confused. He said …"

"I used to be a nurse." Mike held her gaze. "What about you, Catherine? What do you do?"

"I work in insurance." They weren't showing much interest in the aliens. An unpleasant realisation oozed into her brain. "What sort of nurse were you?"

"A community nurse. Spot the theme?"

"A mental health nurse," his friend put in helpfully.

Catherine swore under her breath. "Great. You think I'm nuts. Dear god, I've completely screwed this up."

She had. There was Mike, eyeing her with a mixture of puzzlement and sympathy, and she could tell that the Divine had been right – he could have been what she wanted. Except he thought she was an escaped lunatic. Why hadn't she stopped and thought? One short conversation with a deity and she was reduced to the intelligence of a six year old. Bloody hell.

"I'm sorry." Mortification was bringing tears to her eyes. "There is a reason for all this. It's just incredibly difficult to explain."

"That's okay," he said calmly. "No harm done."

Easy for him to say.

She ought to leave. She ought to quit now before she made things worse. Yet, since it was hard to conceive of them being any worse, she forged on. "You see, I've either just had the most incredible religious experience or I've been hallucinating so much it's scary. And either way, it's kind of knocked me off my stride. I do normally act a bit more like an adult."

"I see," Mike said warily. His friend was making warning faces at him, trying to cut short the conversation.

"How do you feel about God?" she asked.

"Not keen."

"Even if you could meet him?"

Mike's lips twitched. "You should never meet your heroes."

Ah, a cynic. She wondered if he'd been let down too. She'd give anything to know him well enough to ask.

"Listen," she said desperately, "this is what happened. I met two aliens and they let me talk to God. I know it sounds crazy. But why else would I say something so insane unless it was true?"

"It depends," said Mike, "what you want me to do with this information."

"Come with me and see what I'm talking about. Either you'll be as amazed as I was. Or there'll be nothing there and I'm as mad as you think. In which case I'll give you the car keys and you can drive me straight to the hospital. I promise."

He raised his eyebrows but he didn't say no.

"Or else I'm just trying to chat you up but going about it in a really bizarre and imaginative way. Do I get any points for that?"

"It makes a change from 'Get your coat, you've pulled'," he admitted.

"Mike, for God's sake," said his friend.

"I can have you back here in forty minutes," she pleaded. "What do you have to lose? I'm not an armed robber. I can't hurt you. All you'll miss out on is the end of this guy's fascinating story. This is a better story. Much better."

Once upon a time there was a man called Mike, who trained as a mental health nurse. He'd seen what happens when the mind goes wrong. The health service fretted about cancer and the price of drugs but what astonished him was how much misery we caused ourselves. The front line wasn't hospitals. It was inside our own heads.

We lived in a world of plenty where Neil Armstrong could walk on the moon and some people daren't go to the shops for a paper. The more possibilities modern life offered, the more ways people found to destroy themselves. It shocked him that it didn't shock people more.

Mike imagined he could make a difference.

But you know the old joke about psychiatrists and light bulbs. What happens if the bulb doesn't want to change? The psychiatrist buggers off and leaves the community mental health nurse to manage the bulb's medication. Most of Mike's clients weren't being healed, merely maintained. All he was there for was to keep them going.

For eight years he did his best. There were occasional victories, and he appreciated them wholeheartedly. More often, there were defeats. He didn't blame his clients, how could he? He knew how exhausted they were. Of course it felt easier to go down than up.

What he couldn't stand was the dependence. It started small, just a niggle, the number of clients who had got out of the habit of taking responsibility for their own happiness. They had a sick line from the doctor and a cabinet full of pills so obviously they couldn't be expected to sort their own lives out. So they sat at home waiting for Mike to deal with this, and the social worker to handle that, and the council to fix the other. They clung to rules and relied on official reminders. It was all perfectly understandable. Just infuriating.

But, he realised, everyone was the same to an extent. It started to obsess him, the tiny ways people were always relying on someone else to do things they ought to be doing themselves. Lazy husbands waiting for the housework to get done. His mother waiting for his father to renew the car insurance. People in the office who said, "I don't have time for that, X should do it." Where X was some other part of the NHS who probably didn't have time either.

It started to affect his personal life. He and his girlfriend had the kind of arguments that were never about what they seemed. It wasn't clear what they were about. She said he was making life too complicated. He said he wanted to make it simpler.

Meanwhile, Mike might think he was on the front line but nobody with money did. They were always short staffed and under-resourced. He found himself waiting for someone else to sort that.

He tried not to give in to the blame culture. He cultivated philosophical approaches that would protect him from expecting more than life was likely to offer. It turned out there was a fine line between self-containment and emotional distance. His girlfriend started seeing someone else. He hadn't expected that. Grimly, he worked harder on his philosophy.

If he wanted a better life, he would have to create it himself. He made the decision to leave nursing and retrain, and was glad of it. Pushing himself to learn new skills increased his self-reliance. When something needed doing, he did it himself. The philosophy came to feel like a comfortable second skin, not an effort. He was fairly happy.

Sometimes he missed having a woman, but not often. After all, it wasn't as if he needed anyone. And deep in his subconscious, he dreaded being needed by anyone else. He knew how much it would annoy him.

His one problem was that as time went by all his good friends got married and had children, leaving only the boring ones free to go to the pub on a Tuesday night. It had been a pretty dull evening until the madwoman turned up.

Even as Catherine led him to her car, he wasn't quite sure why he had agreed to come. In her favour were two factors: she didn't seem psychotic; and she knew his name. She said the alien god had told her.

Now he was alone with her she had become more defensive. He sat in the passenger seat and she pulled out into the road, concentrating on her driving and barely glancing at him. "It's best I just show you," she said. "When we get to the church you'll see."

It was a Presbyterian church, he gathered, from her increasingly curt answers. For some reason that tickled his fancy, an alien invasion in the least imaginative of all religions. He smiled and she thought he was making fun of her, stiffening further.

He began to consider it more likely this was an elaborate con. Odd. If they wanted to lure him, wouldn't they use someone prettier? Catherine was defiantly frumpy, non-sexual. Perhaps that was the intention, to make her seem less threatening. Yet there was an edge of desperation to her that jangled his nerves. Surreptitiously, he kept an eye on their route in case she smuggled him down some dark alley.

She parked outside a solid grey church. It looked quiet and normal.

"I hope they're still here," she said, hurrying out of the car. "They're on a mission from God, after all. Got billions of souls to convert. This way." She strode towards a side entrance.

He followed. He still had no idea what to expect.

What met his eyes once he was in the church hall was the following scene: a six foot tall cage of thin silver rods, being examined by a three-legged alien, and another three-legged alien hovering anxiously by a hunched figure on a chair. As Mike moved closer he saw that the hunched figure was a balding minister with his face buried in his hands. The minister was curled motionless as the large alien fluttered helplessly beside him. "Catherine! I am glad you are back."

"What happened?" she said.

"Mr Howat communed with the Divine Presence. He has not spoken since. I don't understand. Menig is checking the booth."

"It all seems in order," the other alien called. "It must be an emotional reaction. Not every species is the same, Ac. Remember they warned us of this in training."

Mike stared. At first all he could think was that it was true, these really were aliens. They had to be. Their every movement was impossible. That meant Catherine hadn't lied.

That meant the aliens had given her his name. He felt slightly scared again.

He studied her in a fresh light, wondering if he should apologise. She was crouched by the minister, gently shaking his arm. "Mr Howat?" she was saying. "Are you all right?"

"No," said the minister in a muffled voice.

Mike moved to sit on his other side. His eyes met Catherine's. To her credit, the words *I told you so* didn't cross her lips.

Mike touched the minister's elbow. "Mr Howat, my name's Mike. I'm here to help. Can you tell me what happened?"

"I touched God," gulped the minister. His shoulders started to tremble. "Lord forgive me!"

Catherine looked up. "Ac? Do you know what he saw in the booth?"

"Oh no!" The large alien sounded shocked. "Any communion with the Divine Presence is private and personal. It is between him and the Divine."

"Let me get this straight," said Mike. "That thing over there – you can go into it and talk to God? Direct?"

"Yes, that is its purpose. Would you like me to explain the Divine Offer?"

"Not really." Mike was busy making sense of it, putting together the pieces. "Catherine, you've been in there?"

"Yes."

"And what did you feel?"

"I felt God – or something – something amazing." She dropped her eyes, failing to hide an embarrassed flush. "I asked for ... it doesn't matter what I asked for. But it was listening."

"I think it does matter what you asked for," he said doggedly, "if the answer was my name."

"Please don't," she said in a small voice.

Mike swore under his breath.

"We shouldn't ask God for anything!" Mr Howat suddenly announced, lurching upright. "God is not our servant!"

Catherine bristled. "Hey! You lot started it. It's the church who goes on about what God can do for us. If he can't do anything, what's the point?"

"God doesn't *do*. He *is*." Howat jumped to his feet. "He *is*. That's all we need to know. We need to know there is more to life, beyond us, around us. We need to feel the joy of God, just out of reach. And it doesn't matter if there is mystery and uncertainty, because God understands! That's all we need! The rest we have to do ourselves."

"But we can't do it all by ourselves!" Catherine cried. "How can we? It's too difficult."

Mike shook his head. "You're wrong. We do have to do it by ourselves. Sorry, but that's the one true thing I know."

"Oh, now everyone's an expert." She folded her arms and glared at him.

He shrugged. "It's just common sense. If we leave control of our lives to someone else what can we achieve? How can we become better people? If God actually did go around answering prayers and performing miracles it would make us too lazy to try and improve the world ourselves."

"If he wants to play it that way, God shouldn't have made the world so awful in the first place! Why does he let volcanoes and earthquakes happen? Why does he kill babies? How does that make us 'better people'?"

God doesn't do these things, Mike was on the point of replying, because he doesn't exist. Then he remembered the aliens' booth.

"I'll ask him," he said.

The aliens waved their hands frantically. "The Divine Presence has not yet taken this planet into its congregation! The Divine cannot be held responsible for any previous incidents!"

"Oh. Handy get out clause." Mike studied them. "So what happens in future? If we sign up for this will the volcanoes stop?"

"The Divine will consider requests according to its normal protocols," said the smaller one, Menig. "Not all communions are answered. The Divine may consider a request to be out of keeping with the Divine Will."

"All requests are heard, though," said Ac. "Please. Try it. I think you will be reassured."

"I don't know." He needed a moment to think. All his instincts said they didn't need a God, of any sort. Especially not this sort – a Deity on Demand, 24/7, customer focussed machine. It wasn't religion as he knew it. It was science fiction.

The trouble was, it wasn't mysterious enough. He laughed to himself. Perhaps Howat was right. A God who wasn't out of reach didn't feel very God-like.

The minister was pacing in a corner of the hall. "God doesn't do, He is," he muttered. "God is in the volcano just as He is in the snowflake. Why can't you see that? God is in you, but you have to find Him."

"You make it sound like a game of hide and seek sometimes," said Catherine. She rubbed her eyes. "We're going in circles. I don't understand why neither of you are excited about this. For the first time we have a real, actual God willing to help us. Isn't that good?"

"We should help ourselves," Mike said stubbornly.

"It's the God inside us that's important," insisted Howat. "How we react to His presence, how we live our lives. God could give you a hundred gifts, but would that change you?"

"I'm sorry, Catherine," said Mike, "but I have to know. What did you ask for, that made you come and find me?"

"Why do you have to know?"

"Because I don't think you got what you wanted. Did you?"

"I think I asked the wrong question."

He hated pursuing this, but he was sure it was relevant. "What question did you ask?"

"Oh for God's sake! If you must know, I asked where I could find a man I could fall in love with." Fury gave her face a glow that was almost attractive. "Yes. I know it's petty. And I obviously forgot to check that the man in question could fall in love with me. So I screwed up and embarrassed both of us. I'm sorry, all right?"

"Well," he said, taking a deep breath, "I don't know if I could fall in love with you or not. To be honest, it's not a good start. You see, where you've gone wrong - it's not the question you asked or maybe even the answer. It's what you've done with the answer. I mean, you haven't given me any time to get to know you – "

"Yes, I did spot that!" she interrupted. "No need to rub my face in it."

"But what it boils down to," he said, "is that in the end a God can only do so much. You have to do the rest. There's no escape from that."

There was an uncomfortable silence. Catherine hugged herself, avoiding his gaze. Howat sat down abruptly, looking worn out. He cleaned his glasses, then replaced them and watched Catherine intently. It was as if they were all waiting for her decision.

Once there was a woman called Catherine. She watched the news and saw the wars and disasters and there never seemed to be anything that could be done. Wasn't there a role for the Divine there? And was it so wrong to ask for a little help for herself? She wasn't as strong as Mike. Not everybody could be perfect. That was why we needed gods.

But he was right about one thing. She'd taken her divine answer and squandered it, like a tramp spending a fiver on Buckfast.

Just once she'd like to meet a god who didn't make her feel more useless than when she'd started. Why had she been so stupid? They hadn't given her time to think. She should have asked for something bigger, something less personal. A cure for cancer, something like that. Instead all she'd been able to think about was how unhappy she was, as if a man could step into the gap in her life and provide all the answers. The more she thought about it, the more surprised she was the Divine had answered her at all. Unless it was the Divine idea of a joke.

Divine comedy. Ha. That was all they needed.

She looked at Mr Howat. His idea of God was too nebulous for her. Everywhere and nowhere. Nothing solid you could rely on.

She looked at Mike. His world was so solid it had no soft edges. She wasn't sure she wanted that either.

She looked at the glowing cage. God – or something very like it – was there. In touching distance. And it still didn't help.

She wanted a life. She wanted her baby back. Not even the Divine could do that.

Tears filled her eyes. All she could see was Robbie, his little arms reaching jerkily for her. Reaching out for help. All she'd been able to give him was love. And sometimes love wasn't enough.

Catherine bowed her head and sobbed. After a moment, an arm came round her. There were voices: Mr Howat ordering the aliens to leave; Ac and Menig protesting; Mike arguing them down. She couldn't bear to look. There was a lot of shuffling and clinking as they dismantled their cage and took God back out of her life. Perhaps Ac and Menig could find someone who would make better use of the Divine. It was wasted on her.

She cried for a while, because that was how she felt, and she was beyond pretending. At length, she noticed a hand shaking her shoulder. She raised her eyes to see Mike studying her.

"They've gone," he said. "Are you all right? Do you want me to take you home?"

"I suppose I ought to manage by myself. You know. If I want to become a better person."

He allowed her a hint of a smile. "Just this once I'll stretch a point."

Howat ushered them to the side door. Outside the moon was up, large and yellow above the roof tops. Catherine gazed at it wistfully. Mike tugged her arm and led her towards the car. She looked back to see Howat silhouetted in the doorway, staring at the night sky.

There was something important she needed to work out, a truth about what had just happened that she was on the verge of understanding. What they'd lost and what they needed and what they wanted, and how none of those three were the same. And what maybe they'd had all along. She could feel the truth on the brink of her mind, or somewhere in the ache of her heart and the moonlight.

"Come on," said Mike. "You need a drink."

And it was gone.

Rudy

by R D Gardner

Rudy came to me again last night. He came at two o'clock in the morning, sitting on the edge of my bed, blond and smiling in his artistically razored denims.

"Paul, you've got so old!"

He doesn't need a lamp to see me by, but I switched it on anyway: it made him more substantial, counteracting his own bluish light, that glows without illuminating anything but himself. For a moment, I imagined I could feel his weight.

"I'm seventy-eight, Rudy: don't you remember?"

"Of course I remember. I *remember* everything – but sometimes I wonder if you remember me."

"Every time I look towards London I remember you, Rudy."

I had been to London the previous evening, and Rudy had been very much on my mind. The blackbirds were whistling up the spring twilight as I left, the sky behind me the deep, translucent blue of Bristol glass, but over London, the sky was an appalling, poisonous orange-green, in which the brilliant white lights of the high-altitude aircraft circled slowly, like the malevolent satellites of an inhospitable planet. Road traffic was heavy enough to keep the border holograms constantly triggered, spelling out '*London: The Beating Heart Of England*' in letters of insubstantial fire, although there was no sign of the animated Dick Whittington figure that should have capered above them. Border holos had been a real hazard when people still drove their own cars: I'd once ended up in the ditch, driving north and paying too little attention, when a head and torso clad in Lincoln green had suddenly filled my peripheral vision, cap feathering the sky, proclaiming '*Welcome to Nottinghamshire – Robin Hood Country*'. I haven't driven north now since Hull went down: I can't face the sight of that tall bridge in darkness, the river lapping at the powerless flood-gates, and the scattered fires burning where a vast web of lights used to be.

The absence of Dick Whittington frightened me. It might have been an ordinary fault, something as simple as a vandalised projector, but I felt a tremor at the foundations of the world. After that, there was nothing that wasn't ominous. If traffic at a junction was stopped for longer than seemed reasonable, or an advertisement seemed briefly to ignore the passers-by, I envisaged tiny holes fraying unnoticed in the colossal, infinitely detailed web of Rudy's attention. I read auguries of London's fall in the erratic swooping of a razor-winged anti-pigeon drone. Maybe this was how it had started, when night and chaos swallowed Hull: the three crowns at the roadside flickering and going out, people kicking the boxes and grumbling about... what had her name been? Bridget, Beatrice? She was newer than Rudy, years newer, but they'd installed her in a hurry and on the cheap, wanting her up and running before the next council elections, and they'd maybe cut a few corners on the psych reports. We were lucky that Hull still had an independent telecomm network: it could have been a whole lot worse. If Rudy goes down... well, Scotland will probably survive.

I'd been quiet too long: he was frowning. Think of something to say, Paul, and quick.

"How's your 'train set' coming on, Rudy?"

I really stressed the inverted commas in '*train set*'. Rudy hasn't been at ease with metaphors since he came on-line, and he gets worse with time. It was still a moment before his face lit up.

"It's terrific! The Livingstone Line's nearly finished, it'll be ready by September..."

He went off into a singsong recitation of the stations on the London Underground's new Livingstone Line, rocking slightly back and forth to the rhythm.

"Do you remember how we used to watch trains, Paul?"

"We used to stand on the railway bridge..."

"Yes, it was made of iron, and covered in layers and layers of grey paint, so thick you could hardly see the shapes of the rivets, and it had a special kind of smell when the sun heated it, rust and dusty paint and old, old oily dirt, and when the trains went underneath we'd drop stones and try to... try to hoosh..."

An animated scene had appeared where Rudy had been sitting: two boys on a railway bridge, playing Glaswegian Poohsticks with bricks and glass bottles.

58

"We didn't use to drop stones, Rudy. We didn't drop anything: we *watched* the trains. We wrote down their numbers. Sometimes people waved."

Slowly, Rudy's projected image faded from the over-bright colours of memory to the pixelated monochrome of secure-cam footage, the styles of the late 1990s modernised themselves, and the boys' faces became those of strangers.

"Did you catch them, Rudy?"

He reappeared at the foot of my bed, as though my voice had changed the channel.

"Oh yes! Four months' community service for endangering the operation of the railways, and two more for damage to the environment and failing to recycle glass vessels. They're doing squirrel patrol on Hampstead Heath."

"That's a bit harsh, isn't it?"

He shrugged. "They're young, they've got good reflexes – and we do give them protective clothing, you know."

For a moment, it was really Rudy there, quick and sardonic and twenty-six years old; then he slid away on another long orbital curve, reciting the year's proposed costs for the upkeep of the London parks, right down to the prices and varieties of the bedding plants in the Duchess Camilla Memorial Garden. If he only had proper company in there, wherever 'there' is for him, I don't think he'd get like this, but there's nobody else now who really talks to him: people interface with him all the time, but they never converse. The entire population of London calls him 'Rudy', but it never crosses their minds that he once had a surname; I doubt if fifty of them know what it was. He exchanges information constantly with the other *Urbes*, of course, and maybe they converse, in their way, but I can't imagine that it helps. If anything, it probably makes them all worse, reinforcing nothing but what's least human about them, the memories of flesh and sunlight and things that can be touched with living hands fading faster than ever as they drag each other spiralling into the dark.

Flowers. Tell him something about flowers.

"Weren't those the flowers Julie wanted for her wedding? She made such a fuss about getting them, and when she actually saw them, she ran up and down the aisle screaming because they were just the wrong shade of pink to go with the bridesmaids' dresses!"

"Did we go to Julie's wedding, Paul? Whom was she marrying? We never found out, did we – the deaf man stood up and stopped it."

"Of course we went to Julie's wedding: you were Best Man. She couldn't decide between us, so she tossed a coin and lost it. It was a five-pound piece, and we took the front room apart looking for it…"

"I remember! We found your wallet down the back of the sofa, and we found that *Time and the Concorde* album you'd blamed Richie for borrowing, but we never found the coin, and Julie cried – she cried an awful lot while she was planning the wedding, and shouted at everyone. Didn't she want to get married? Dad gave her away, didn't he – was it an arranged marriage?"

"Oh, Rudy." I didn't know where to start. One moment his memories were sharper than mine, the next he was patching them together with a kind of cultural clip-art: call up 'weddings' and pick an image, any image, none with more significance than any other. Nor could I get it out of my mind that right now, somewhere in London, the lights might be going out. Holo-images wavered above my bed: a few frames from 'Four Weddings and a Funeral', with cartoonish masses of pink flowers superimposed on the church interior; Julie weeping at an altar in a red and gold sari, a caste mark on her forehead like a pink petal.

"You know better than that. Julie chose Patrick all by herself: she brought him home from university one day – 'This is my fiancé, he's studying Environmental Regeneration' – and Pat looked as surprised as we were. I think she must have been planning her wedding since she was five. It gives you a lot of stress, organising the day that's going to redeem your existence on this planet: if it could only be made perfect, she'd live happily ever after."

The holo-Julie appeared for a moment in the cream and lilac wedding dress that had caused so much grief, then dwindled: Julie as a child of six or seven, a tattered net curtain draped over her head, trailing a doll bridesmaid as she married her biggest teddy bear. Then I jumped in real shock as Rudy reappeared with a child on his lap: Julie's daughter Summer, maybe two years old, bouncing horsey-horsey on Uncle Rudy's knee.

60

"This is the way the ploughboy rides," he sang, "hobble-de-dee, hobble-de-dee, this is the way the ploughboy rides... and *down* into a ditch!"

He tumbled the phantom child from his lap, and she vanished before she hit the floor.

"You're not supposed to *really* drop her." I said reproachfully, and he looked stricken.

"No wonder I wasn't allowed to have children."

"That had nothing to do with it, Rudy! You'd have made a great daddy – Summer and Rowan loved you! Neither of us was allowed children, but it was because of our jobs – you must remember child-free contracts, people sign them with you every day! You don't want valuable professionals drifting off on parenthood leave, taking time off whenever the kid gets a cold, turning up late because somebody else's kid gave the school bus a virus and it forgot to pick anybody up – yes, I always thought it was you who taught Summer how to do that – and then rushing off to school sports day when everyone else is working overtime. It's unprofessional, and bad for workplace relations. Julie and Pat were unbelievably brave: they both had a real chance of rising high enough to afford a full-time nanny, and then they could have had jobs *and* children, but they refused to do that. They were prepared to go to the Estates, but we talked them into taking our money. We always knew we weren't likely to have our own children, so they let us make Summer and Rowan a little bit ours."

"I never thought about having actual children – you know, all that selfish-gene stuff. If we could only have achieved real artificial intelligence, we'd have left the world something that would never have died."

"But you're already immortal, Rudy. You've got the whole city of London for a baby, and I hate to think how often it needs its nappy changed..." Bad analogy. I'd tripped an errant fragment of *Urbs* memory, and I got told a lot more than anybody needs to know about what the citizens of Kensington and Chelsea throw away.

I had always suspected that frustrated paternity – the desire to leave something behind to bear his name – was part of what drew Rudy to the *Urbs* Project, when it became clear that no artificial intelligence they could even envisage creating would be capable of automating a city. The Project approached the problem from the other end – why go to the unimaginable trouble and expense of building a replica human brain, when millions of real ones are produced by unskilled labour every day?

First catch your brain. However readily your subject had donated his corpse to science, the operative word is *corpse*. Maybe still warm, maybe even still breathing, but clinically dead – brain dead – and once that light's out, as the man said, there's still no relighting it. At most, Rudy and his fellow-boffins could coax a couple of candle-power out of the remains: they stayed drunk for a week after they taught one to operate a set of traffic lights but a computer that measured its memory in *kilobytes* could have done that. Dead brains got them nowhere, living brains were out of the question, but they didn't give up: they found a way to combine the two, copying every detail of an active human brain to one they'd prepared earlier, something they hadn't exactly made and hadn't exactly grown. Cut-and-shut artificial intelligence: the *Urbes*.

The first *Urbs* to enter public service was the most desperately needed one. It seems criminally irresponsible to field-test a radical new invention by letting it loose on London, but they had no choice: the city was being pulled apart by various localised automation schemes, and if they had taken a few more months to try an *Urbs* out in Welwyn Garden City or Milton Keynes, London might well have been beyond reconstruction. It was an epically challenging task, and Rudy imprinted the London *Urbs* with the best brain he could find: his own. It's been there ever since, keeping the streets lit and the traffic flowing, culling the pigeons and landing the planes, giving numbers to the newborn and deleting those of the dead. It answers to Rudy's name, because that's the name it thinks it has: at the root of those infinite archives is the crumbling, half-buried labyrinth of Rudy's memories, and when it wants to interact with its mortal charges, it wears his face.

"… a red silk dress, cut in pieces…" Rudy's litany tailed off. "Paul, when's my birthday?"

"Well, you're a lucky man, Rudy: you've got two. Your physical birthday was on February the fourth, and you came on-line

62

on the first of September, which is really another birthday. We had a party for you once, but the other people in the pub didn't take kindly to your overriding the holo-projector so you could join us, and when we explained who you were, they went ballistic because they wouldn't be able to get home: they couldn't understand how you could be projecting into this pub and running the Underground at the same time. There was a bit of a fight, and you panicked and sent the police, and we never repeated the experiment."

I should have known that he wouldn't be able to recall any of that. I got a brief replay of a fight in a pub, but it was a dockside pub in Southampton – Rudy's twenty-first birthday, when we should both have been old enough to know better. Then another party, one I hadn't been at: an office, archaic computer terminals, young men raising plastic cups. Young men in jeans, sweatshirts, combat pants; some in white laboratory coats; one blond, with long hair pulling free from a loose ponytail. There was a wild hilarity in the air, an edge of hysterical release in their laughter that had nothing to do with drunkenness: they were celebrating the end of a momentous task, achieved against tremendous odds. I was looking at the first thing that Rudy London had ever seen.

"I've got no other memories of him, Paul, but then I never remember seeing you: I don't save it, and I can't believe how much you've changed. Does he come to see me often?"

I have to tell him this every time, and every time he forgets. No-one bothered to inform him officially – it's outside his authority – and as a provincial I don't have the right to command him: I can't give him new information and tell him to *save*.

"He's dead, Rudy. Fundamentalists blew his laboratory up, claimed that only God had the right to create intelligent life – killed him and three of his colleagues. Rudy's been dead for fifty years."

I was already getting tired, and I knew I would have to keep this up all night. I never understood the finer points of his condition, but in effect Rudy London – the *Urbs* – is like a set of infinitely complex programs on those old-fashioned computer hard drives. With time and a lot of use, bits of information ended up in the wrong places, got duplicated unnecessarily or accidentally erased; errors crept in and replicated, dead space appeared, and eventually your computer would start acting up and you'd defrag it, letting it sort through the mess and tidy everything into properly organised compartments. It happens to human minds and memories too, but we defrag ourselves all the time, just interacting with each other: you're doing it every time you clock on at your office and join the discussion of last night's football match or holo-soap, resetting yourself to Default Human. Without this constant recalibration, you start to drift, and don't realise that anything's wrong until your *Urbs* sends ECO-SWAT round to deal with your performing cockroaches. The *Urbes* aren't like that. I don't doubt that they defrag their files all the time, the masses of data that they process every day tucked away as neatly as bricks in a wall, but that action in itself must erode their residual humanity, and there's nobody there for them, no norm for them to reset to apart from each other. That's when Rudy comes to me, trailing the clotted and tangled fragments of recollection like handfuls of wool pulled from a barbed-wire fence, and I sit up all night with him, carding and combing them, spinning chaos into order, weaving the ragged edges of his memory together – and the Underground keeps on running, the London Stock Exchange keeps on ticking, and the big silver birds keep on circling over Heathrow.

Nobody anticipated that this would happen. They were surprised when the *Urbes* remembered who they had been and insisted on being called by their names, but thought little of it: it made for a friendly front-end to the awesome inhumanity of their creations, something the proles could interact with. Then Beatrice Kingston-on-Hull, that cold, solitary, controlled woman, became distracted, forgetful, endearingly eccentric... and fragmented into madness. They had to cut the cables to shut her down – they blew up the pylon lines and blacked Hull out for good. I doubt that anyone will ever dare to restore the power.

After Rudy had gone, I went to London again. I watched the hard perfect arcs of the raptor drones picking off careless pigeons, and felt vaguely saddened by the darting, driverless black cabs. Rudy has all the Knowledge now, but he doesn't know that I'm an old man; he can't count how few of us are left who remember who he was. The border holos were complete again – Dick Whittington with his faithful cat at his heels, forever young, forever turning towards London, my brother's face glowing in the morning light.

Twice or Forever

by Charlotte Bond

The sun was hidden behind a bank of cloud spanning the entire sky and the new buds on the trees were still huddling in their brown casings as Elizabeth threaded her way among the crumbling headstones, trying not to trample the new grass underfoot. She knew she wasn't alone in the graveyard when she saw the head of a gravedigger bobbing up and down in a deepening hole.

Elizabeth's feet carried her to the same spot as they had done for two hundred and ten years, as she pulled her coat tight against the spring chill and tried to keep her blonde hair out of her eyes.

Carefully dividing the scarlet tulips into two bunches, she laid one on each green mound in front of her. Bending down, she cleared away the moss caking her father's headstone and wistfully traced her finger over his name. She looked over at her mother's grave, suspiciously free of lichen; it made her smile to think that her mother's fastidious cleaning habits had apparently imbued the very ground she was buried in.

She glanced around the graveyard, hoping rather than expecting to see her brother, Robert, coming to share her remembrance. Her gaze fell upon the elderly gravedigger who was leering at her unpleasantly and she turned away. With the face and body of a twenty-two-year-old, her two hundred and seventy year old mind had come to expect the stares, even if she didn't welcome them.

It was at times like this that Elizabeth missed her old life acutely. She had always been grateful that her family had been wealthy enough to buy the Treatment for her and Robert, and yet she remembered when the houses in the city had been made of quarried stone, not reconstituted plastic blocks. She remembered being able to walk down the street without having to dodge the mecha-cleaners which buzzed around at ankle height. Her annual visit to this place provided a moment of tranquillity away from a world tainted by the uneasy peace which comes when a society is divided at the most basic biological level. Elizabeth realised that she reminisced more frequently these days, but she reasoned that, when you are immortal, life inevitably becomes repetitious.

Her offerings made, Elizabeth got up and made her way back home as dusk began to gather around her. As she stepped beyond the dilapidated gates of the graveyard, she glanced nervously at a group of three men who sheltered in a shop doorway. Two of them were talking, stamping their feet in an effort to keep out the cold; the third, wrapped up to his nose in a cornflower blue scarf which stood out against the grey surroundings, was watching her. A shiver ran down Elizabeth's spine – there was no way of knowing whether his attire was to defeat the cold or obscure his identity, there was no way of knowing whether he was a citizen or a Protestor. What she was certain of though, was that the Protestors were indiscriminate in the hostages they took on their twilight raids and she hurried home nervously. The tension in her shoulders only eased when the security gates of her road swung shut behind her. She felt a little queasy but it wasn't until her palm was on the key-lock of her door that the nausea built exponentially and she barely made it to the sanitary unit before she vomited. When the convulsions were eventually over, she took several deep breaths and then drew herself a hot bath to soak away the melancholy of the afternoon. Elizabeth had just started the organic protein generator for dinner when she heard Robert halloing as he let himself in. His embrace was affectionate but restrained and Elizabeth felt him wince when she hugged him back.

"Everything okay?" she asked, concerned at the sallow skin which seemed to hang off his cheekbones more than it had done last week.

"I'm fine, Libby," he lied, pouring himself a glass of synthol and slouching at the breakfast bar. "Just a little nervous about whatever filly you are going to try and set me up with tonight." His eyes twinkled in their sunken sockets.

"I wish you wouldn't refer to my colleagues like that," Elizabeth replied with a mock scowl, "nor derogate my efforts to find you a new girlfriend. It's been long enough and I think you'll really like Heather."

"What," scoffed Robert, "like the last three you were positive I'd like?" Elizabeth's scowl was for real this time as she handed him a bowl of reconstituted salad.

"Be useful and take this through to the dining area."

"I just don't see," said Heather, her girlish pout emphasised by her deep red lipstick, "why you don't think everyone should be Treated. How can you hold such an opinion when you're a doctor yourself?"

Elizabeth sighed. Robert's instant attraction to petite, flirty Heather with her waterfall of auburn hair had been evident; yet her temptingly kissable mouth had lost its appeal when the opinions came tumbling out. Elizabeth glanced at Bret, Robert's colleague and old friend whom she had invited to even the numbers. As ever, he wore a wry smile of amusement.

"I am certainly a doctor," Robert replied coldly, "and you're evidently very new to the Treatment." Heather tossed her waterfall defiantly.

"I completed the Treatment six months ago, and it was the best decision I ever made," she said proudly. "I used up every penny of my inheritance to pay for it, and I think everyone should have it." Heather turned her dazzling smile on Elizabeth. "And how long ago did you have the Treatment?" Elizabeth glanced hesitantly at her brother before answering.

"Both Robert and I had the Treatment over two hundred years ago," she replied with a brief flash of gratification at Heather's disbelieving expression.

"Right at the beginning? Wow," breathed Heather. "And you don't look a day over twenty-two."

"That's because she isn't," Robert said curtly. "Her telomeres are in the same condition now as they were when she was twenty-two, as they will be when she is five hundred and twenty-two and forever." Heather was rapt.

"Telly-whats? What are they?" she asked. Elizabeth could see anger stiffen Robert's features.

"You mean no one explained the process to you? Didn't you ask before you signed away your body and your life?" he said. Heather gave off a delightful peal of laughter.

"What does it matter how they do it?" she beamed. "Immortality is worth any price and any process. But I'd like to know, all the same," she added anxiously, aware she was losing her audience. Robert leaned forward, his voice pitched as if talking to a child.

"Telomeres are biological buffers," he explained. "Every time your chromosomes replicate to make new cells, the telomeres – the bits of DNA at the end of the chromosome – aren't replicated fully; they become shorter. When they run out completely, your DNA unravels so the cell either dies or becomes cancerous."

Elizabeth had heard this spiel from her brother many times before. Bret poured himself another glass of synthol and settled back to enjoy the ensuing fireworks while Elizabeth surreptitiously turned the atmosphere setting to ambient. She had a bad feeling about this conversation.

"So, they're a bit like those plastic tips on the ends of your shoelaces?" asked Heather. Robert looked taken aback.

"Yes," he said, impressed. "That's a good analogy." Heather beamed triumphantly as he continued. "The Treatment activates the enzyme telomerase which can replicate telomeres exactly so they never wear down. It's already in your cells, but dormant."

"So," said Heather, her pink nose crinkled in concentration, "because your cells don't age and die, neither do you."

"To put it simply, yes," replied Robert.

"So that's why I had to all those complex genetic tests?" she concluded. Robert nodded.

"Sort of. You need a very specific gene structure for your body to accept the Treatment," he said. "It was found early on that only those who had a high ratio of cancer-controlling genes would be able to survive the genetic treatment. You see, telomerase is active in cancer cells too, so turning it on in normal cells makes them either immortal, or cancerous."

"Ooo," whispered Heather with a sense of morbid fascination. "That's what happened to the Unfortunate, isn't it? They turned into huge cancerous blobs." Robert's expression hardened imperceptibly and Bret shifted uncomfortably.

"Some of them, yes," he said, hastily moving the subject on. "Another trade off is that the Treatment renders you unable to have children."

"It might not be completely impossible though," Elizabeth interrupted. Robert glanced her way.

68

"I wouldn't want anyone to hold such false hopes," he said brusquely. "No one knows why a foetus turns cancerous before the pregnancy has reached its fifth week. Some say we can't pass on our genetic information properly, others think a foetus needs apoptosis to develop properly. The Church denounces it as a curse."

"It doesn't matter anyway," said Heather through a mouthful of vegetables. "Who would want to be burdened with squalling brats anyway?" Elizabeth remembered thinking something similar herself until very recently, before circumstances had challenged her ideology.

"Undergoing rigorous pysch-tests is part of the selection process," Robert said, "to ensure you can cope with immortality. Some people just go insane."

"Too true," interjected Bret.

Robert paused to take a drink before continuing: "The need to have a specific genetic structure can cause other problems too; it means that parents may not be suitable when their children are. Maybe not even brothers and sisters."

"What about you two?" Heather asked. Robert smiled fondly at Elizabeth.

"It might help if you're non-identical twins, I suppose," he replied. "But it doesn't always work like that, we were just extremely lucky. Some people end up being all alone if they're the only one eligible in their family. Facing that prospect for centuries is enough to drive anyone crazy." Heather snorted in an unbecoming display of scorn.

"How can you ever be alone?" she asked. "There are hundreds of Treated these days. You could always go live on that island they clubbed together to buy."

It was Bret who answered, his voice soft and thoughtful. "Most of us prefer to stay in society," he said. "With the inevitable wealth and additional experience we gain from our longevity, we can invest in longer term projects than most others would be comfortable with. We at least will be around to see them to a conclusion." He shrugged. "It's a way to give something back, I suppose, perhaps even bring society back into harmony."

"Like helping those who genetically qualify for the Treatment but don't have the money?" suggested Heather.

Elizabeth intervened, seeing a flare of impatience in Robert's face. "In some cases, yes," she said carefully. "But there are also those who protest that the Treatment is wrong, that immortality is against nature and that the Treated are nothing more than freaks."

"Well, *they're* the freaks if you ask me," said Heather with a pout of disapproval. Elizabeth saw Robert draw breath to retaliate but Bret got there first.

"Shall we move to some more comfortable seats?" he asked.

"Absolutely!" beamed Elizabeth in relief. When they were settled more comfortably in the seating area, the conversation moved back to more mundane matters but Robert refused to let the subject drop.

"I used to be like you, Heather," he commented at the first pause in the conversation. Heather looked at him askance. "I thought it would be a better world if everyone had the Treatment, but I've learnt that with struggle, with sickness even, comes hope. The human spirit needs something to strive against to rise out of mediocrity to greatness."

"But we have achieved great things since the Treatment," Heather exclaimed. "It's like Bret said earlier." Heather flashed him a smile and Elizabeth was surprised to see Bret's cheeks flush slightly. "With our longevity, we can accomplish all sorts of long-term projects that we would never attempt before. And besides," added Heather, draining her glass with a flourish, "who would want to die anyway?"

"I would," said Robert in a low voice. Heather paused, her glass mid-way to the table. Elizabeth felt a knot tighten in her stomach and she forced herself to try and relax. She glanced at Bret who seemed to be deliberately avoiding her gaze. Robert was looking intently at her.

"Why on earth would you want something like that?" asked Heather teasingly, evidently believing he was playing devil's advocate. Elizabeth knew that was far from the truth. She knew that what was coming would be the explanation for his silence these last months, for the tension which had arisen because a secret had hovered between them.

"Many reasons," Robert said evasively. "Because I've been living a life without meaning. Because I've no relatives left alive except Libby, because I've amassed a small fortune with no one to spend it on. Because I miss mum and dad who've gone where I can't follow. And it's not as if I can have children to soften the loneliness either." Elizabeth felt her stomach lurch as if something had punched her from inside. Her arm instinctively encircled her belly, but Robert misinterpreted her action. "I'm sorry if my blunt words upset you, Libby. I'm just trying to make you understand how empty I feel my life is."

"It's got me in it," said Elizabeth, her despair oscillating to anger and back again. "And I don't want to lose you." The pain of betrayal was clear in Robert's eyes and Elizabeth pressed further, wanting to hurt him as much as he was hurting her. "You were the one who talked me into having the Treatment. You said it was the best for both of us, you said we could be together and support each other." Tears shone in Robert's eyes but his mind was made up and his voice was controlled.

"I know, and I can't say how sorry I am, how wrong I was. Libby, I've been alive for almost three hundred years. I've seen all that this life has to show me and I want to see what lies after it."

"What if there's nothing?" said Elizabeth, desperation mounting. Bret was still looking away but Heather was watching their exchange open-mouthed, the philosophical sentiments evidently beyond her grasp.

"Come on now, Libby, you were always the one trying to drag me to church. You were the one who was convinced there was something more than this."

"Yes!" Elizabeth said, raising her voice and clenching her fists in anger. "Yes I did, and you were the one who talked me out of it! You convinced me that I might be wrong, you sowed enough doubt in my mind about my faith to make me believe the Treatment was the best thing for us." Pain shot through Elizabeth's palms as she dug her nails in with the effort of not screaming at him. "And now you're saying you were wrong after all? After all we've been through? That you're going to leave me all on my own? Alone?!" she spat out the last word.

"Do you remember Eve, Libby?" he asked softly. Elizabeth felt the colour drain from her; she didn't think she could ever forget Eve. Her face swam through Elizabeth's mind: her skin was flawless, her hair falling in thick chestnut waves to her shoulders and yet her eyes were sunken, tired and full of pain. Meeting her gaze was like looking through two holes in heaven into the deep heart of hell.

As Elizabeth banished this recollection, another forced itself into her consciousness – Eve sitting in a hover chair, Robert gently peeling down her surgical gown to show Elizabeth the monstrosity underneath. Beneath Eve's alabaster skin, a multitude of swellings clustered on her neck and her arms. Her breasts were smooth, round and pert but surrounded by lumps which moved like a bag of marbles when she breathed.

"Yes, I remember," said Elizabeth in a subdued voice. "You said she had Hodgkin's Disease."

"That's right," said Robert. "The symptoms didn't appear until the last stage of the Treatment when it was too late to reverse it. Her increased levels of telomerase meant the cancer spread quickly. Eve has been forced to live like that for decades." Elizabeth glanced at Bret, hoping he would interject and move them off this subject, but his eyes were fixed unwaveringly on the floor.

"That's silly," scoffed Heather. "It's only cancer. That can kill us too, and just as quickly. Why hasn't she died yet? She shouldn't live so long." Robert wore the same mask of anger as he had done that day he'd taken Elizabeth to meet Eve at the Rest Home.

"Eve is useful to the company who distribute the Treatment. What better way to understand your product than to pick apart your mistakes to see what went wrong. For years they've been pumping her full of anti-cancer drugs, slicing out the more virulent tumours. keeping it at bay enough for her not to die but sufficiently prolific for them to study its effects. The last barrier to perfection of the Treatment is our susceptibility to cancer, and to them, no cost is too great for its eradication." With these words, his face became a sneer of disgust, hatred even, and Elizabeth was once again aware that there was a whole side to her brother she had never seen in their centuries together.

"Well, alright," conceded Heather reluctantly, "maybe someone like her would want to die. But why on earth would you want to?" Elizabeth felt she already knew the answer but she refused to believe it, even when Robert undid his shirt to expose the red lumps which protruded from under his arms. There were smaller swellings clustering at the base of his neck as well.

"I think we should go," said Bret tactfully but his words were lost on Heather who stared at Robert with undisguised fascination. He had to forcibly guide her to the front entrance and out.

When Elizabeth heard the door slide closed, she realised Robert expected her to say something.

"And here's me thinking all your long hours and missed visits were because you were a Protestor," she said. Robert gave her a weak smile. "I don't suppose –"

"No," he broke in, then smiled apologetically. "I've been through the options a hundred times and found no solution except this one. I'm counting on you loving me enough not to want me as a monstrosity in a wheelchair. I don't want to be wheeled in and out of my rest room to be prodded and jabbed in advancement of a vain social cause."

Elizabeth sat there, speechless, as the hopeless inevitability of the situation pressed down on her soul: she was going to lose the one thing in her life which was irreplaceable. What was really bitter though, was her knowledge that he was right. They weren't alive, just living from day to monotonous day with nothing to define the passing of the years. Even in her despair, Elizabeth knew Robert had made the right choice, even if that choice left her completely alone.

Not completely, said a small voice at the back of her head, and Elizabeth wrapped her arms protectively about her stomach again. She wondered whether maybe she did have something to strive for now, or whether she was just transporting a lifeless mass of toxic tissue. Robert was looking at her expectantly.

"Of course," she said, drawing herself back into reality. "I would never see you suffer if by any action I could prevent it." She swallowed nervously. "When will you... do it?"

"There's a secure termination facility nearby which has agreed to take me," he replied. "I said I'd prefer decapitation – it's quicker, less messy too." Elizabeth tried to ignore the images his words conjured in her mind.

73

"Yes, but when?" she persisted, but Robert's response was pre-empted by the buzz of the hailer. Elizabeth started with shock.

"Tell me that isn't them at the door now?" she said imploringly, but Robert could only look away guiltily.

Elizabeth walked slowly to the door in a dream-like daze. She glanced at the ident-screen which verified that two government officials were waiting outside; the door slid open to reveal two unsmiling faces.

"Just a moment, please," Elizabeth said, unsure of where the words had come from. It didn't sound like her voice. Robert came up behind her, hastily stuffing his phone in his coat pocket. He seemed to change his mind and gave it to her.

"No one's going to be calling me on it now," he explained with a shrug.

Elizabeth found herself being guided out and belted into an autocar. When it moved off, she stared out at the blackness passing beyond the window, so oppressive and unnervingly close, restrained only by a thin pane of glass. As the autocar glided smoothly through the security gates into the city, a flash of colour caught her eye and Elizabeth turned in her seat to see a man, muffled by a cornflower blue scarf, standing by the gate. She watched his immobile form until the autocar swept around another corner and he was lost from view. She began to speculate on his appearance but grief and exhaustion soon drove all thoughts from her head. Finally the autocar glided to a stop and the cabin fell silent as the whirr of the mechanics ceased. Elizabeth stepped out of the vehicle and found herself in a government compound, its central feature a squat concrete block which bore no resemblance to the picturesque government hospitals that appeared on the Media.

An ugly building for an ugly purpose, she thought. They were met at the door by a man in a white coat, his thick-rimmed glasses perched high on his hooked nose.

"ID," he barked gruffly and they held out their wrists automatically. Elizabeth gritted her teeth against the rude jab of the blood recognition system and looked over the inside of the building. Beyond the thick metal doors was the largest panel of IDS controls and defence systems she had ever seen. She looked apprehensively at their guide.

74

"Protestors," he muttered by way of explanation.

"It's all to keep people out then?" Elizabeth replied apprehensively and the man gave her an appraising look. Robert's grip on Elizabeth tightened protectively.

"But you will look after my sister when all this is over?" he said anxiously. "Make sure she is safe; it was part of the agreement."

"Oh yes," said the man, winking at Elizabeth. "We'll take care of her. Follow me, now."

Elizabeth's unease increased as they made their way down some steps into a high-ceilinged corridor where their footsteps echoed harshly. Elizabeth's eyes were straining in the dim light which just seemed to seep out of the walls and she was fighting down nervous apprehension at every step.

Their guide led them through a door bearing the glowing moniker 'Waiting Room'. The room beyond was bland and beige except for one long wall which was made of glass and opened up a view into the adjoining operating theatre. Elizabeth stared at the blades of surgical instruments which glinted cruelly in the light, arranged carefully on top of cold metal tables. In the centre, drawing the observer's eye, stood an upright bed with restraints hanging from it. Elizabeth began to feel nauseous again as three figures dressed from head to toe in surgical green entered and began busying themselves with preparations.

"I'll give you both a moment," said the man in white as he left the waiting room. Robert and Elizabeth looked at each other awkwardly, unsure of how to spend their last moments together. Robert walked forward and took his sister's hand tenderly.

"Eve told me something quite profound," he said. "You only live twice."

"That's just the title of a classic movie," Elizabeth retorted.

"It's so much more than that, Libby," he said gently. "It's one of Basho's haikus: 'you only live twice, once when you're born and once when you stare death in the face'. Don't you see? By living forever, we are denying ourselves that last vital experience of life. So, in a way," he added, planting a kiss on her cheek, "I'm actually quite lucky."

Before Elizabeth could reply the man in the white coat returned and led Robert out of the room. Elizabeth pressed her hands and face against the glass to see Robert enter the theatre next door. He took his eyes off her only once to glance down at a clipboard they handed him to sign something.

Signing his life away, Elizabeth thought bitterly. She was vaguely aware that the white-coated man had returned, but she gave little thought to his presence.

Her brother wore a sad yet resolute smile as they strapped him on the upright bed and adjusted the fittings for his wrists, ankles, waist and forehead. As they lined up the laser wire in front of his throat, Elizabeth saw his eyes were full of fearful excitement and her incomprehension of what he was experiencing made her feel that more separated them than just a pane of glass. He wiggled his little finger at her, simulating as much of a wave goodbye as his restraints allowed. Elizabeth waved back.

"You might not want to watch," said the man behind her.

I will watch, she thought fiercely. *Right to the end.*

The doctors in the other room fired up the laser wire which glowed hot and red, recalling to Elizabeth's mind pictures of souls burning in a fiery scarlet hell she had been shown as a child. An anguished panic washed over her as the realisation dawned that, without doubt, she would never see Robert again. Hoping to halt the inevitable, Elizabeth started to yell, to bang on the glass, never realising that it was soundproof and that her brother could not hear her pleas for reconsideration.

"Don't worry," he mouthed soundlessly as the medic stood back and the automatic arm of the laser rushed towards his throat, severing his head from his body in one clean, swift movement. For a moment, his look was one of surprise, then any thought or feeling behind his eyes slowly faded. Elizabeth watched the strain of life seep out of his muscles as darkness and dizziness encroached on her vision until everything faded to black and she slid senselessly down the glass.

Elizabeth came round from a deep nauseous darkness to see squares. Her vision blurred again as unconsciousness threatened to reclaim her but she fought to focus her eyes in the unforgiving neon brightness. As the world materialised around her, Elizabeth realised she had been laid out on a row of chairs and was staring at the tiles of the ceiling. There was the muffled blare of sirens from the other side of the door.

Gingerly, she sat up to get her bearings, momentarily confused. She glanced to her left and recollection flooded her mind as she saw the operating theatre – clean, shining and empty.

"Feeling better, Elizabeth?" asked the doctor sitting opposite her. With his surgical mask removed, Elizabeth could see the kindly smile he wore beneath his salt and pepper beard. His face was a riverbed of wrinkles, tautened by his slight frown of concern.

"A little," she admitted dazedly. "What's all that noise?"

"Oh, that's just the perimeter alarms," the doctor replied. He held up a hand to dispel the anxiety which spread across Elizabeth's face. "The Protestors are always trying to cause trouble, but their raids never penetrate into the building itself. Well, not often. But you shouldn't worry, Elizabeth," he insisted. "You must take it easy, especially with your condition."

"Condition?" asked Elizabeth, glancing at the door.

"Your pregnancy," the doctor replied, scrutinising Elizabeth's face.

She kept her visage carefully impassive.

"The mediscan picked it up," he explained. "You're a very special individual."

"Special?" asked Elizabeth, glancing at the door again.

"Certainly," the doctor continued, leaning back in his chair, composed and relaxed while Elizabeth's muscles were tensed for flight. "Never in my career of studying the Treated have I seen any of them carry a pregnancy as far as you. Your bloodscan showed you're well into your twelfth week."

His eyes sparkled with greed as he got up and moved over to open a surgical box on the table behind him. Elizabeth sprinted for the door but the key lock was dead to her touch.

"There's no need to be distressed," the doctor said calmly. "This won't hurt – I'll make sure you're soundly asleep before I take the foetus out."

"Take it out?" choked Elizabeth. Adrenaline coursed through her as she watched him fill a syringe with pale blue liquid.

"Of course," he continued, turning to smile pleasantly at her. "If we leave that thing inside you, it's only a matter of time before it turns cancerous, and that would be such a waste. You don't want your baby to die, do you?" he asked. His voice lowered into menace. "And you don't want to be full of canker, do you, just like our poor little Eve?" Elizabeth pressed herself against the door as he walked towards her. "But I'll look after it for you, grow it in a biotube, take better care of it than your biological system ever could. If it's strong enough, I can clone it, then I'll have hundreds of specimens to work with. You could even keep one yourself, see if you can raise it as a normal child. Depending on how well you cooperate now, of course."

"No!" cried Elizabeth, as he reached out to restrain her. "I won't let you!" One of his hands tangled in her hair and forced her head back, exposing her throat. Elizabeth had to use all her strength to hold back the syringe. They grappled and fought so intensely that neither of them registered the click of the key pad releasing.

Elizabeth fell backwards into a firm but surprised grip while a dozen rougher hands pulled the doctor off her, sending him careering to the floor with a bloody nose. All was noise and confusion as seven figures surrounded and herded her down the corridor. She tried to make out the faces of her rescuers, but they were shadowed in the dim emergency lighting. The cacophony of the sirens was excruciating now and Elizabeth's ears still buzzed painfully when she emerged into the night air. She was hurried across the compound where the door of a waiting autocar was opened for her. It was only as she was bundled inside that it occurred to her that whatever she was being taken towards might actually be worse than where she was fleeing from. She squirmed to get out of the vehicle but the door slid shut and locked her in.

There was only one other occupant in the autocar – a young man with sandy hair, freckles and a serious expression. A cornflower blue scarf was neatly folded on his lap and Elizabeth felt her stomach lurch.

"You're that Protestor, the one I keep seeing," she said icily, her hand groping for the door release.

"Yes I am," he said softly, a smile skipping across his lips. "I'm Mark, and you're Elizabeth. Your brother called me earlier. He said you might need some help."

Elizabeth stared at him, stunned for a moment, then she wept with relief.

It was the same corridor that she remembered but now people were running down it and screaming, being rounded up by Protestors while Elizabeth went up it with a calm and measured stride. She had been told not to go on these raids at such a late stage in her pregnancy, but she had become addicted to the adrenaline they incurred. She couldn't remember feeling as alive as she had done in the last three months. Obviously she would give it up for the birth, just as soon as she had done this one last raid.

Elizabeth walked through the battered door to see three orderlies kneeling on the floor, heat-guns pressed against their temples; one of them was whimpering softly. Elizabeth looked towards the patient seated by the window, wrapped up in a thick rug despite the heat of the day. Weary eyes looked up and met Elizabeth's with a smile of recognition.

"Hello, Eve," said Elizabeth, returning the smile. "Want to feel alive again?"

by Clive Gilson

You wake up with the subliminal turn of engines in your head. Shifts are changing. Hot bunking. Space is at a premium, the notion of which loses its humorous appeal after a few days and nights on the ship. Not that you can tell day from night here. There are no windows in the pressure hull. There is nothing to see. Starshine seen with the naked eye burns retinas to a crisp.

Alarm bells ring. Strange-looking men appear, poking their hands through the bunk curtains and nudging you awake. You pull back the curtain and see a gaunt face covered in stubble and grime. We live in a world where time is measured as twelve hours on and eight hours off, an endless rotation of bodies filling spaces too small to be invaded. Life on board is about orientation. You learn quickly not to sit up. The bulkhead above the top bunk dents your skull so after a couple of days nursing a headache basic instinct cuts in. One man rolls onto his front, swings his legs out of the bunk and another man climbs into the stinking warmth of the bed. You're so tired that you're asleep before your head hits the pillow. This is daily life on K-Forty-Seven. A hunter-killer, Seventh Fleet, on convoy duty at the edge of the Kulper Belt. All at sea in the bad lands, at the edge of the world, to coin a phrase, where the Outlands meet civilisation.

Get a profession, my parents said, something safe, a way to earn a living without venturing off-world. Journalism is my bag. Two years as a cub-reporter on independent network news and the bastards introduce conscription. I have a profession, a track record. I spent two years drinking and screwing my way around navy posts, two years of reporting on ship movements, tragic losses and heroic returns. When the call-up scheme came the recruiters smiled sweetly and told me to join the fleet newspaper. My first assignment? Embedded on a glory ship.

You have an image in your head as a kid; shiny surfaces, flashing lights, metallic voices and red shift. Science fiction. Sure, the big guns, the capital ships, they look impressive on the surface, and complex systems do have a beauty all of their own, especially when they ride across the skies in vast tonnage, but the reality of war is never like the films. This is the cutting edge, the exposed blade, serrated and notched, unsheathed and bloody.

I am, technically, a junior officer, one of five on board, which makes the mess a little cramped. Usually a K-ship runs a crew of fifty including four commissioned officers; the Captain, First and Second Watch Officers, and the Chief Engineer. They get their own cabins, while the rest of us make do with bunks slotted in around machinery that never sleeps in its effort to keep us alive. The designers of this bucket made some allowance for the necessities of life, though, and the heads are clean and sufficient, although showers are rationed to one per man every four days. Grey water. Nothing beats the simple luxuries.

The officers' mess is in the central section of the ship, under the main control room, and breakfast is already underway when I swing myself through the pressure-door bulkhead. Silence. The Chief is concentrating on shovelling soup into her mouth, and the Captain is reading through daily orders. Lewis, the Second Watch Officer has already eaten and hit the sack. Dewey, our good 'ole home boy Yank First Officer is on the bridge. You have to be thankful for small mercies in a place like this and elbow-room is definitely one of them. As I slide into the space recently vacated by Second Officer Lewis, the replicator panel is already rising at the far end of the table. The soup is hot, but that's about all you can say in its favour. Food is basic out here, full of the necessary proteins, carbohydrates and vitamins needed to sustain a body, but hardly a highlight of the day.

The Captain, generally referred to as the Boss, looks at me and grins: "So, Newbie, sick and tired of all these drills?"

We've been on patrol for six weeks without a sniff. To keep the crew on their toes the Boss has had us on crash drills, attack drills and emergency manoeuvres almost every shift. You can tell when he's planning something. There's a look that passes between him, the Officer of the Watch and the Chief, a wry little smile that marks the moment when the alarm is sounded and orders are barked out across the ship's communications system, "Cloak! Run silent! Brace for impact!"

He folds the daily orders, tucks them into his jacket pocket and slides out from the table, heading for the bridge at the prow of the ship. Before he disappears forward through the next pressure hatch he turns and says, "We'll see whether you've got the stomach for the navy, eh?"

The Chief wipes the last of the soup out of her bowl with a hunk of synth bread and sucks it dry before putting it into her mouth. She raises an eyebrow as she too leaves the mess, muttering "poor sods" to herself as she goes aft to check on her beloved field generator. I don't know if she means the enemy or the crew. That's it, the sum total of the morning's conversation, so I finish my soup alone, feeling the heat of the liquid settling in my stomach as the butterflies start to rise. The excitement of the chase. God alone knows what the kill will feel like.

By the time I've finished my breakfast the hum from the engines has risen in volume, and so has the general buzz in the atmosphere. The sound of boots on the raised metal gangways is more urgent than at any time since I came aboard. You can hear an edge in every conversation. Faces that have been showing signs of fatigue and boredom are harder and more focussed. I can hear the Chief up in the control room running through systems checks. A couple of ratings from the previous shift have taken up station by one of the heads to make sure they don't get left out of the action. Like a choir boy at his first Sunday morning service, I straighten my uniform jacket before seeking permission to enter the bridge.

"Permission to come for'ard?"

A look. Dewey grins. "Granted." New Orleans. That unmistakable southern drawl. I have adopted a small space by the navigation workstation, somewhere that I can perch and watch the crew in action without getting in the way. The bridge is wider than the main concourse, filling nearly the whole width of the ship on the forward deck. The Boss sits in the command chair amidships, surrounded by consoles and touch-screens showing tactical and status data for key operational systems. To his rear the Chief will take up station at the main engineering control. To his left and right are the navigation and weapons systems operators and in front of him is the main helm. Behind us and along the ship's length operators and engineers man sub-controls, engines and workstations dedicated to the art of concealment and death.

Dewey takes a couple of paces towards me and leans into my cubby hole. "Convoy five hours dead ahead. Fat and slow."

The Boss sits impassively in the command chair watching figures and tactical displays spin and fall. "Port one-four seven, vertical twenty."

Dewey breaks off from our brief conversation and repeats the order to the helmsman: "Port one-four seven, vertical twenty."

From the helm comes a direct reply as the new co-ordinates are entered onto the touch-screen console. "Port one-four seven, vertical twenty. Aye, Sir."

This bit is like the old films. The hum from the field generator bursts through the soundproofing under our feet and we can feel the ship being hauled through space by the energy field that encases us, providing motive power, defensive shielding and, if invoked, our cloaking device.

The Chief enters and reports. "All systems A-one, Captain, ready for deployment."

The Boss turns in his chair, looks at Dewey and nods. "Cloak!"

The Chief sounds an alarm and we hear the computerised communication bounce off the thick metal walls of the hull. The lighting code shifts to pre-attack blue. While I try to adjust to the subtle change in the ambient lighting, First Officer Dewey relaxes and leans against the bulkhead from behind which I am recording the activity on the bridge and making my notes. "*D-E-W-E-Y*. Make sure you get that right, Newbie. I want the girls to know what a hero I am, get my drift?"

The Chief snorts audibly in the background. There is a new sense of urgency about everyone's movements, and I ask Dewey about the attack.

"You gotta remember, this baby is built for speed. Basically it's one fucking big engine and we're riding piggy-back. The convoy is making mark one, one point five. Anything else would take twenty, maybe twenty-four hours to make contact. We, on the other hand, will be sitting right up their pretty little touche in under five. That's why we're cloaking now. At this speed we'll show up on their far-scans way before we get in range. So what we do is go hell for leather until we're about twenty thousand clicks out, tucked up in our own little world, and then we slow it all down and ease in underneath their exhaust signatures. They're freighters, you know, old tech, atomic ion drives. Perfect cover if the cloak is working properly. Bit of cat-and-mouse with the escorts, but we get right in and, depending on the landscape, we do them one way or another. Then, Newbie, then you'll see just how good the old man is. When their escorts get over the shock they'll be pretty mad."

I nod and blow out my cheeks. It's all recorded and filed.

"And if I were you I'd get your reports bedded down snugly in that little black box of yours. If the Boss fucks up, your little bag of tricks is about all that'll be left of this old girl." He pats the bulkhead above my head, grins and returns to his station next to the Captain, who has been listening in on our conversations and is grinning at me too.

My finger trembles on the record button and I struggle to hold it down. The peace of the bridge, the peace that wraps itself around me in the hum of the engines is shattered and the cool blue light suddenly turns ice cold. I feel sick and make my excuses, saying something about the report, gulping in stale air as I stumble back to the officer's mess. On the way a couple of time-served ratings wink at each other as I pass. I hear something about sorting the men from the boys and try to smile but I can feel it only as a grimace, as a death mask. As the Captain said over breakfast, we'll find out if I have the stomach for a life in the navy, and given the cold sweat pooling under my armpits, I pray to God that the machines break down before we get anywhere near the killing zone.

The Chief, damn her soul, makes sure that the machines work perfectly. I spend thirty minutes with my eyes shut, and then try to shock my body back into some sort of shape with two thick, black espressos. I start to feel stupid and ashamed of myself. I'm in two minds about whether I should report back to the bridge when Lewis pokes his head through the doorway from his cabin and tuts. He joins me over a third coffee, complaining that he can't sleep with all this bloody noise. His body odour mingles with the bitter smell of strong coffee.

I am the first to speak. "What's happening to me? It's all confused. White noise. Mostly all I can hear is the blood pumping in my temples."

84

Lewis stirs sweetener into his coffee slowly. "Too much caffeine. Don't worry. It gets to us all. My first time out in one of these, K-Ninety-Four, a Type One, I had to change my trousers after my first counterattack. Pissed myself. You won't believe the punishment these old girls can take. Mind you, the Type One was pretty basic. No cloaking. Pure, raw speed. In, kill, and get the fuck out. It was okay in the early days, but the Outlanders worked out how to deal with us. This little baby, though – she's tough. This is our third patrol." He runs a loving hand over the alu-steel wall. "The Type Three. Twice as fast and you can't beat the field generator. State of the fucking art."

My hand reaches instinctively for the recording device. "What I don't understand is why it's so cramped, so basic?"

Lewis sips hot coffee and mulls it over for a few seconds. "The exigencies of war, my friend... or, to put it another way, we're losing, we haven't got the time. K-ships might make the difference if we can build enough of them quickly. So, what's important? Crew comfort or tonnage destroyed? The equation is simple. Make the machines and strap the fewest number of men into them to get the maximum bang for your buck. You do know, don't you, that sixty percent of crews don't make it through a three year tour?" From his jacket pocket he pulls out a hip flask. "Take a shot and get back up there."

The Boss spots me on the threshold of the bridge before I have time to request permission to enter and waves me into the room. As he does so I am met by a sea of faces, most of them leering at me. Initiation. The Boss nods a couple of times. "Our new boy has balls, ladies and gentlemen!" He laughs dryly and resumes his watchful surveillance of the tactical displays. I settle into my cubby hole, feeling a wave of embarrassingly warm camaraderie wash through me.

The ship burns with expectancy. The engines purr as we hurtle through black space, cocooned within our field, a field that, to anyone on the outside, looks just like any other patch of emptiness. It takes three massive computers controlling a series of field generation blisters on the outer hull to mimic the full expanse and density of empty space. Nearly one third of the ship is dedicated to the field control system. The rest of the ship comprises the field generator itself, the weapons systems and one long, thin deck on which the crew exist for months at a time.

Over the next three hours we close in on our prey, and as more thick black coffee does the rounds, I begin to see why the crew draws so many parallels with the old stories of the wolf packs operating in the Atlantic at the beginning of the technology age. Names and designations. Terminology. The whole kit and caboodle.

A succession of manoeuvres, of course-plots and subtle shifts in our field engagement, lead us to a point where we begin the attack run. The Boss grows visibly paler as we approach the twenty thousand click point, as though he is replacing the blood in his veins with iced water. Behind him the Chief is scanning the filed status monitors and barking orders back to the control room, trimming the ship and balancing every system to give us the best advantage that she can. Calm and efficient. Orders: "Ahead one point six."

"Ahead, one point six."

"Ahead, one point six. Aye, Sir."

The ship decelerates rapidly and I can feel basic Newtonian force acting on the contents of my stomach despite the corrective action of the internal dampers. The Boss lines us up. "Chief, have you got a handle on the exhaust signature? The big mother, third left of the main group, dead ahead."

"Calculating. Got it. Aligning shields, give me a second… ready on your mark."

"Number One, get us to the edge and feed us in nice and slow."

It begins. We tag onto the wake of the convoy and gently merge our cloak with the exhaust signature of the heavy metal in front of us, using near-scan to keep a weather eye on the escorts, which number three destroyers and two fast pickets on flanking duty. Twenty thousand clicks becomes fifteen, then ten, seven, six. Five thousand clicks puts us in effective range and the Boss calls up tactical weapons display, relaying orders to the weapons operator, who enters tactical options into the command system to plot targets.

Four thousand clicks. The walls start to close in on me as the bridge crew work silently and efficiently, every one of them focussed, running on adrenalin and the certainty born of hundreds of attack drills. I can feel the heat rising and, looking down, I can see wet patches blossoming on my shirt underneath my open jacket. Running my finger round my collar simply distributes the heat more evenly. The liquid on my body has drained my mouth dry. My tongue feels like old shoe leather. Looking around the bridge I am comforted by the fact that everyone else in shirt sleeves is as damp as I am. Still no firing plot. Three thousand clicks.

"Shit."

The Boss leans forward.

"Run silent!"

Lights shift to red. Unlike ancient submariners, silent running means that all external scans and counter-measures are killed. Sound is immaterial. We exist within our cloak, blind, with our ears cocked for the sound of heavy footfalls over our shoulder.

"Destroyer peeling off and dropping in behind us," Dewey explains. "Thing is, we don't know if it's seen us or if it's routine. They drop back in rotation every couple of hours to see if anyone is following. Standard defensive tactics."

I struggle to make my mouth work, swallowing to force the glands in my mouth to produce saliva. My heart is thumping in my chest. "How do we know..."

"If you see a very bright white light then you're dead." He laughs out loud. "Only way to know for sure. If you're still looking at me in ten minutes then chances are they're none the wiser. Tick-tock, tick-tock." The bastard is grinning like a Cheshire Cat.

A kilometre is an arbitrary measure of distance out here. The destroyer remains on station at the head of the convoy for twenty minutes before swinging back out into a standard defensive position, during which time we drift underneath the boardwalk, crawling ever closer to the tight little knot of ships bobbing around at the edge of the solar system. I can't take my eyes off the ship's chronometer. With every minute watched I feel the weight lifting from my shoulders. I yawn. Nerves. Embarrassed again.

Warfare at this distance is a strangely quiet affair. Commands are almost whispered on the bridge. We manoeuvre slowly to protect our cloak of invisibility, careful not to distort the empty view of the universe that our enemy is watching so intently. One false move, one sudden jerk or jolt and the reflective patterns woven by our cloaking shield will fluctuate, breaking us out of the weave in the minimal time-lag between the generation of our computerised simulation and our physical reality.

The Boss strokes his stubbled chin and checks the tactical displays for the thousandth time this morning. He knows the game inside out but he wants reassurance. "Weapons, give me firing patterns."

"Range five-forty clicks. Too close for field burst. Torpedoes armed and ready. We'll have five seconds from reveal, two full patterns of eight, then, this close, we'll have to crash."

At the answer the Boss lets his head fall so that his chin rests on his chest. He rubs his eyes with the palms of his hands. He turns to look at Dewey. "What do you think?"

Dewey is tense and watchful. "We could drop back, manoeuvre around them and burst from a safer distance."

"We could. Nav?"

The navigation officer checks readouts on his screens. "Too close to the Belt. Field echo would be too strong." He points at a series of markers on the near-scan monitor. "And the escorts are on permanent defensive rotation. Too many variables."

"Damn bloody escorts. They're getting too good, eh? I don't fancy torpedoes from this position. Five seconds is enough for a fix. We're too exposed back here."

The bridge is silent save for the hum of cooling fans and the quiet ticking of the digital chronometer on the wall above the firing position. The Boss fixes me with a cold look through tired eyes and speaks softly. "Is the cloak good, Chief?"

She mumbles affirmative.

"Make bloody sure it is. Inch us in, Dewey, right into the middle of the hen-house. Nice and slow, I don't want any unexpected interference with their field."

The manoeuvre means weaving in and out of the shadows. The convoy occupies approximately five hundred cubic kilometres of space, with the freighters running in fixed but staggered positions as we glide into their midst like a fingersmith. The Boss is going to pick their pockets clean. With nothing but near-scan stealth and a mixture of intuition and long years of experience it takes half an hour to reach our ideal firing point, a position right at the heart of the convoy, a position that makes the destroyer's response to our attack all the more difficult because of the freighters all around us. The air on the bridge is stifling now that the pressure doors in the bulkheads have been sealed for the attack. I have splitting headache.

First Officer Dewey has to wipe sweat from his forehead with his shirt sleeve as he reports that we are ready to commence the offensive.

"Right," says the Boss. "Torpedoes. Lock targets. Two patterns of eight. On my mark. Ready, Chief?"

The Chief is standing by her console, her hand poised over the controls at the engineering station.

"Display code red!"

"Code red. Aye, Sir."

The Boss is hunched forward over the tactical display. "Cloak!" The sound coming from under the floor panels lowers in tone. "Pattern one, away!" The ship shudders. "Pattern two, away!" It's like being at sea in a small dinghy in a heavy swell. "Deep scan!" A pulse of sound bounces off the outer field. "Cloak!" The hum rises half an octave. "Damn you, Dewey, get us out of here!" The dampers are on full but we are all slammed to port as the ship starts to corkscrew, picking up speed. The engines scream as they generate field energy hauling us down into the vortex.

Disorientation. The world around me becomes a riot of red lights, flashing crystal displays, alarms and shouts. It takes a few seconds for me to realise that I am holding the recorder out in front of me, staring at the hive of activity on the bridge with my mouth open, catching flies. In the moment that it took to fire, the crews on the destroyers stared at their machines in disbelief, were hauled back into the well-worn groove of military procedure and began their response. Our deep-scan, which confirms the kill, triggered automatic return firing patterns, which, with our own torpedoes, are ripping the convoy to shreds. Even though we have energy shields and cloaking, even though we're bending the carcass of our dear old girl in two in an attempt to magic ourselves away from the slaughter, we can feel shock waves breaking over our hull as ships explode and lives cease. It feels like the heavens have split apart, and I grab hold of Dewey, unable to speak, looking wildly up into his eyes, but he shrugs me off.

"Evasive seven! Counter-measures! Where are the fucking counter-measures?"

The Boss is sitting in the command chair, gripping its arms so tightly that the blood has drained from his knuckles. He looks as though he is straining to hear the destroyers through layers of bucking metal and squalling energy. The Chief is hitting one of the control consoles on the engineering panel and yelling over the communications link to the control room. "Get a diagnostic on counter-measures right now!"

The Boss whistles sharply, cutting though the noise, and holding up his pale left hand, he whispers: "Quiet people, quiet. How's the cloak, Chief!"

She slams her hand onto the counter-measures console. "Cloak is A-one. Fucking shite counter-measures. Offline completely."

"Okay Dewey, evasive three and bring us to port two nine zero, relative level, ahead slow, point zero one."

Dewey repeats the order and instructs the helm. I can feel the ship gliding, softening, slowing under my feet . A moment of peace after the storm. How far out are we? I begin to relax, and turn to Dewey to ask if it's always this easy and then hell breaks loose.

Broad pattern energy bursts. The enemy can't see us, can't scan us directly, but they can employ broad sweeps of high intensity energy fields using any one of their computerised offensive programs, programs designed to give them an optimum chance of finding us. The destroyers work as a team, creating vast cubes of space within which they basically irradiate everything. The energy bursts are modulated so that we can't tune our cloak to it. The net effect is that if the energy burst interacts with our cloak we get lit up like a fairy light on a Christmas tree. For good measure every energy burst is accompanied by a sweep of proximity warheads. Dewey, that good-looking arsehole with the permanent grin plastered across his face is suddenly looking like death. He is holding onto the bulkhead by the nav station and asks me whether I have been recording everything.

"Yeah, never stopped," I reply.

He smiles and says, "Hold on tight. The Boss is going to fool them. They're expecting us to run, so we'll hold here, let them blast at nothing and then sneak out."

The air seems to fizz and crackle. I hear what seems like someone knocking on a pipe in another room, except that knocking is getting louder.

The Boss is standing. "Shit! Brace for impact!"

The knocking sound is starting to echo, to boom and the ship starts to rock. My bowels are full of cramp. A dull thud. A second later and the shock wave hits. The shield absorbs the impact but the ship is pushed back, throwing bodies across the floor. My feet slip out from under me and I grab at the wall, catching hold of a power conduit to prevent myself flying into the Captain's chair. Sirens wail. The lights flicker. The Boss crabs forward to the helm and crouches down by the helmsman. There are groans coming from the weapons operator. I can just hear the Boss as he gives orders.

"Ahead point three, vertical seven, evasive nine. On my mark, all ahead ten."

I swear that he can hear the bastards, can read their minds. The evasive pattern is designed to slide us underneath the sweep of energy bursts. Another thud and the ship keels to port violently. Sparks and smoke fill our red-shadowed world. People are crashing around the room. Strobe effects. You want to run but there's nowhere to go. You want to pray, you want proof that God exists, a miracle, but all you get is a mouthful of acidic smoke and smarting eyes. I think of my mother and try to force my thoughts all the way back to her, but nothing escapes the thin metal walls of our glory ship.

The Chief is calling for damage reports from the aft sections. Another alarm starts to sound. The Boss looks round and the Chief shakes her head. The Boss turns back to the helm and speaks calmly to the helmsman. "Starboard two-twenty, negative vertical one-thirty. Hold it... hold it, ahead two. Remember, on my mark give it all she's...

Life Skills

by Die Booth

Underneath the coach is a black space. A gap of about 4 inches between the undercarriage and the tarmac. Katy is on her hands and knees. She peers into the shadow, then gingerly pats a hand around, feeling for the dense smoothness of the ball bearings she's dropped. One touches the side of her little finger and glides off. With a round metallic echo it spins around a drain cover and drops into the water below. Hollow plop.

"Damn it."

She can only find four, out of a handful. They click in her blazer pocket. They're for a machine in the science lab, you feed them into the top of the machine and they rotate around, creating sparks. It's supposed to illustrate planetary movement, but Katy just likes it because it's pretty; she's more of an art girl than a scientist really. There's no time to run the machine again now, because the coach is due to leave on a science trip to a 'Lifestyle Exhibition' in the next city. It feels like ages since they went on a trip, in fact Katy can't even really remember the last time. Behind her, a sharp crack says that one of her ball bearings has introduced itself to a classroom window. Evan; he's laughing in this way that's part delight, part shock at his own audacity, with an extra side of fear thrown in because he might get seriously told off. Maybe he'll get excluded from the trip. One of the top panes of glass in the art room window has a little hole in it, like a bullet hole, and the rest of the glass is shattered in spider-web pattern, held together by the chequered wires running through it. Mrs Beaton calls out, "Evan. Enough now, please."

And that's it. She doesn't even sound angry. There's two other cracked windows to the art room, hidden behind the overgrown bushes. The boys don't even get told off properly these days. They're getting more like the kids who come and visit from other schools, who pass notes in class and never do their homework. Katy thinks, it'll be good to get out of this dump for the day.

On the coach, Katy sits away from her best friend Jane. Next to Helen. It's just the way the seating has worked out. Helen is fat and they don't get on, but the trip starts OK anyway. The boys sitting along the backseat are singing about Johnny having a Pigeon. Whenever there's a swear in the lyrics, it gets replaced by a repeat of the chorus and someone or other starts laughing. Helen is working her way through a big paper bag full of sweets. Fake things made to look like natural things – caramel Squirrel Nuts and chewy Pebbles. Those aniseed balls painted silver, they look like ball bearings. They're not even really real food, probably made entirely of E-numbers, Katy thinks. The only natural thing about them is the aniseed right in the middle, the real bitter core of the fake sugar coating. Helen chews mechanically, crunching them in the most unnerving manner – Katy is sure she must be chipping teeth.

"You want one?"

Katy takes a Gummy Dummy. She drops it by accident and it rolls down her blazer, sticking, which makes her laugh. She retrieves it and eats it and says, "That's like… remember those sticky rubber octopus things you used to get? You'd lob them at the wall and they'd sort've crawl down?"

Helen looks puzzled. "I've not thought about those for ages."

She offers Katy the bag again. Maybe Helen's not so bad. Katy takes another Gummy Dummy and stretches the loop of it onto her finger like a wedding ring, translucent yellow merging into emerald green. She gets bored and gnaws it off her finger. Helen leans across the coach aisle and offers the bag to an old man sitting in the seat across from them.

The old man; he recognises them. For some reason, Katy feels a little scared. There's no reason for him to know them. There's no reason for him to be on this trip. But Helen says, "Don't you remember him? Mr Hudson? He used to teach us."

Katy says sorry, she doesn't remember, but she has a faint, faint memory of his bristling white moustache being copper red. She wonders how on earth he can be so *old* now.

They go through a tunnel to the city. People are larking around in the near-dark. Someone's handed Mr Hudson a song-sheet, to lead a rendition of the school anthem. The paper's jaundiced in the dim strip-lighting. Mr Hudson doesn't have his glasses so he can't read the music. Katy takes it from him and realises that all the words have been changed to things about bums and farting, and she feels suddenly very sorry for him – he seems like such a nice guy. So she leads instead, with the real words, the boys on the back seat throwing screwed up paper and food wrappers at her in disappointed disgust.

"In God we trust who made us, to set our School's Example, in His image did He shape us, to Learn and Show our Purpose."

Going through the tunnel feels dark and ominous, like passing through something that will change you forever. When you come out the other side, nothing will ever be the same.

They come out on raised coach-tracks, either side a steep drop down. Everyone is pointing and ooh-ing at the city sights. The boys watch cars go past, arguing over superior models. The girls exclaim over shop signs and stalls as they glide above a big open-air market. They stop at a station. While everyone gawps at the buildings on the horizon, Katy looks down at the tracks. Little pieces of darkness seem to detach themselves and slip away. As her eyes adjust, she sees tiny black mice running into the little holes in the track walls. Helen says, "Oh my G... What *is* that?"

"What? Where?"

Helen points through the window, at the treetops showing over the raised platform side, a pink object wedged between two swaying, high branches. She says, "That is *so* weird. It looks like a cradle."

Katy follows where she's pointing. And there it is. "A... jeez, is that *real*?"

"What do you mean, is it *real*?"

"I mean is it like a real baby cradle, or a doll cradle?"

Helen presses her forehead to the window glass. It leaves a skin-print. "I don't know. I can't tell from here. It looks pretty big."

"What's it doing there?" There's worry in Katy's voice. "Who would put that there?"

"How should I know? Just someone. A joke." Helen starts to sing, "Rock-a-bye ba-by, on the tree-top."

Katy says, "Pink, for a girl." She shoves Helen in the arm to make her stop singing. The coach starts to move again.

They stop at the Exhibition Centre and all pile out. They mill around the forecourt in the slanting sunlight. Mrs Beaton organises people into groups. Mr Hudson walks over to Katy and says, "I just wanted to say goodbye."

"Why, where are you going?" Katy is gripped by the unfounded fear that he's dying.

"Going? I'm going home. I've retired."

His face does look very worn. He must have retired a long time ago. Katy says, "Oh. Cool. Well, all the best. Have a good day."

He nods, sadly.

They walk two-by-two through portentous double doors. The doors are black tinted glass, the foyer atmospherically lit. For a science project, it's pretty exciting. The exhibition is laid out in different areas, each room has a theme as detailed on their guide maps, and you walk through and learn.

But something isn't right.

It's as if the place has been vandalised. Glass cases are smashed. It's dusty. Most of the lights are off. Katy checks the guide map – they're in 'Home Economics'. She shouts, "Mrs Beaton?"

But nobody answers. It's as though suddenly she and Helen are all alone in this little room. It's an exhibit on food preparation, set out sort of like a kitchen. A giant fake wedding cake is on the table, pieces gouged out by fingers to show the polystyrene underneath. Someone's scrawled a graffiti tag on the side in green marker pen.

Then the robot chef comes in.

Through the door he paces, following a pre-programmed path. In, out. Always the same path. Katy and Helen stand shut down on the spot, watching the robot chef walk in, pretend to chop resin carrots, walk out again. They watch him do this four times until they are sure of where he walks so they can slip through the door past him and they don't risk touching him.

The robots stir some kind of irrational horror inside them. It would probably be less scary to touch a dead person.

"It only opens from the other side." Says Helen. So they can't go back through the doors they came in. They wander onwards, following the set path, because there is nowhere else to go. Each room seems to have more and more robots. One is a nursery with twins, although one cradle is missing and the girl baby is squirming on the floor. Katy says, "That cradle we saw was pink, wasn't it?"

Helen nods. When the robot mother looks up from rocking the blue cradle, half of the silicone covering of her face is peeled back.

Like a ghost train, everything in disrepair. The robots are zombies that think they're human, briskly going about their daily programme, mindless and decomposing and unaware. Eventually the rooms fill up so much that it's impossible to avoid touching the robots anymore. They jostle and push. In all the commotion, Katy loses Helen. When she looks around, she realises that some of the figures she'd taken for robots are her classmates.

They're all funnelled out of one tiny door, into a huge sports hall. A sign on the wall says 'Module 14: Health and Exercise' a smaller sign underneath it reads 'Our desire to excel makes us exceed our expectations.' The walls are lined with smiling faces, and photographs of smiling faces. Katy has never seen so many robots in one place before. She feels like the only human. She scans the crowd for people she recognises and pushes her way towards Mrs Beaton. Mrs Beaton, her teacher after Mr Hudson. She thinks. Maybe.

There are figures at the far end of the hall, huge, tall, wearing black rubber masks and robes and writing in a big black book. They look like something from a war. They look like aliens. Behind them, two doors open out of the dust onto sunshine.

Katy feels something tug at her in the crowd, like someone's trying to steal her bag. She yells and puts her hand to it, finds that she is touching the hand of a robot boy made to look just a few years older than she is. He says, "Thank you. Shall we have sex?"

"*What*?!"

"Isn't that what people are supposed to want to do when they only have a few minutes left to live?" His expression is mild and unconcerned.

Katy says, "Yeah *right*. If I only had two minutes to live, I'd just *love* to spend it having sex with a *robot*."

The robot boy's expression doesn't change. "You're right. I never saw the appeal either. My name's Clerk."

"Katy."

Without thinking about it, she's accidentally shaking his hand. When the crowd turns towards the figures at the head of the hall and Katy is holding Mrs Beaton's hand, her other hand is still in Clerk's.

The leader of the masked people says that they are the Creators and that this exhibit is out of date and in poor condition. It is to be demolished. The robots are to be decommissioned.

There is little reaction to this.

"Who first?" God chooses arbitrarily. He points: "You, that boy with the ill-advised haircut."

Clerk is wearing a plain black suit with a white shirt and a blue tie. His dark hair is styled in a ludicrous 1970's mullet. He steps indifferently towards the scalpel in God's gloved hand. Katy begins to wail, "No, not him! No!"

The Creator pauses. He asks, "Why ever not?"

"Just... no. Start at the other end of the queue."

Katy hangs onto Clerk's arm. He feels real. And he stares at Katy. He stares and stares with something like a first real expression breaking on his silicone face.

"If not him, then perhaps you?"

Katy can hear the trace of the man's accent beneath the mask. *If you're God,* she thinks, *then why are you hiding your face? Why so sadistic?* She sneers at him. "Don't be stupid. I'm human. You can't hurt me, you'll get into too much trouble."

God starts to laugh, but he sounds a bit uneasy: "Human? But you're not human. Look."

He rifles through the selection of equipment set up on a trolley at his side. The thick rubber gloves, like those you'd wear to enter a contaminated site, they make it difficult for him to grip things properly. He hands Katy a small mirror.

It's like she's seeing her face for the first time. Her eyes too big and glassy, her skin oddly waxy. But how can she have changed so much in the space of an afternoon?

"How did you do this to me? *Why* did you do this to me?"

"We didn't do anything. You've always been this way. You've just never seen yourself in this context before. Think about your daily regime. What do you do?"

"I go to school, idiot!"

"What's your name?"

"Katy!"

"What's your surname?"

"I..."

"What's your mother's name?"

"I... I can't... it's..."

"B10, explain to her."

Mrs Beaton looks upset. She says, "Module 17: 'Schools and Learning'. Created to provide an example of good practice to visiting children via educational interaction with robot pupils. Model B10 – 'Teacher'. I was commissioned to maintain temporal synchronicity, when the natural ageing of human teaching professionals began to draw comment from robot pupils. I replaced Mr Hudson. He wanted to come along on this trip to say goodbye to you all. He said that you were more of a pleasure to teach than real children ever were. He is devastated that we are to be decommissioned, but I have explained to him that it is just not economically viable to run such an outdated system any longer. No matter how accurately our programmes have synthesised emotion, we must not stand in the way of progress."

Katy, your bough has broken; you are falling.

Katy looks down at the black book that God is writing in. Lists of serial numbers scroll down the pages like concentration camp tattoos. B10, C10, ED2010, FN2010, JN2010, KT2010, LN2010... KT2010... She scans the opposite page. A different selection of titles: P290 – 'Nurse', S290 – 'Chef', H290 – 'Tax Inspector', Z290 – 'Clerk'...

Then God is screaming. A scalpel in his arm. Blood stains the black of his safety suit a darker, slippery black. The slice in the rubber is lined with dazzling, pulsing red. Clerk grabs Katy's hand and tugs her towards the doors behind them. Run away, fall in love, never grow up, never grow old. But she won't go. Her life is sugar coated, but it isn't real.

"Come with me!"

"I can't."

"Why not?"

"I don't want to."

Katy's hand slips from Clerk's grip. He tears towards the door and disappears through, into the sunshine. The last Katy sees of him; a flying black figure, swallowed up by the bright, bright light, shouting, "Come on – to freedom."

Resurrection

by Emma Melville

It's time I was leaving. In fact, it's long past time I was gone. The sun is climbing in the sky and there's a woman behind me in the bedroom with the future in her sights.

I step out on to the small balcony. The crisp autumn air is cool against my naked skin and I breathe deep. From up here I can see the whole of the city spread out before me. So much green is a miracle in so short a time. I remember the devastation when I first looked out on this scene. Now the grass and trees remind me of the innocence of growing up.

In my youth I was evacuated north, to the hills and dales of Yorkshire. My first view of Wensleydale was like this, all greens and ambers on an autumn morning. It feels like I have dragged the visions of my young eyes south with me over the last ten years, covering the land in a fresh blanket of life after all the torture and death.

Not that it's all so green. I once made the pilgrimage to Leicester. It was I who ordered the bodies buried but there I could not make the grass grow, not yet. Perhaps never. Reminders are good, Sarah told us, so the King has left Leicester and its ruins; a memorial to the madness of war.

"A beautiful day." Sarah has risen while I stood here watching the city stir. She stands behind me, her flawless body golden and inviting in the morning light. She has none of the network of scars that mar my own skin, not any more. Glossy black hair, free of its usual tight bun, falls in waves almost to her waist and the cold air has her nipples standing pert. I ache to reach and hold her but that is over; my touch has already done too much and yet I have never thawed the ice in her heart.

Blue eyes watch me carefully and I can see the fire in them but it is a cold flame and warms no one.

The first mission we undertook together was on a morning like this one. I was aflame with hate and the desire for revenge against those who had deprived me of family and friends but Sarah was cold, so cold always. She slit throats with ruthless efficiency, planted the bomb with devastating accuracy and then walked away. She didn't even look back when the building disintegrated behind us and the screaming began. I don't know, even now, when the compassion inside her died; perhaps it disappeared with her faith. Her past has always been closed to me. Even *our* past is something we no longer discuss.

"Too beautiful," I say now and I am not sure whether I mean the day or the woman before me. "It feels like it should be raining."

"The weather will bring the people." She is right – emotionless but correct. Already, below us, they are beginning to gather, peering upwards towards where we stand, attempting to catch a glimpse of . . . of what? I wonder whether they can see us and, if so, what they think they see.

The crowds have been following me for years now, swarming wherever I go with their cameras and microphones and desperate needs. It has become quite alarming, even with the full backing of the King. Sarah is right, William is right; it is past time I was gone.

William.

Now there is a truly inspirational man, a King who will be forever remembered. I can recall as if it was yesterday the first time I met him, at Balmoral. Tall, slim and commanding he greeted Sarah with obvious respect and then shook me warmly by the hand. "I have heard so much about you. I believe you are winning this war for us." At the time it had been an exaggeration, I was one of many fighting for a king who had called us to join him.

By the time I first met William with his iron will and tired eyes Mecca was a ruined wasteland and the Vatican an empty shell. Across continents the meek and the secular were rising up to reclaim a world gone mad and this young man with his calm defiance was a rallying point for the oppressed.

And there I had stood, my first miracle barely a week old, before the man who had vowed to clean Britain of religion. I expected death; I was a symbol of something no longer wanted. What I found was a man with a vision that far outstripped mine. "You will win this war for me," he had said. "All armies have a secret weapon and you will be ours. Once we have won, then we will consider the paradox. There will be a world to rebuild."

The evidence of my use in this new world was before me now in the green and gold of an autumn parkland where ten years before had been a waste of broken rubble and concrete. The awe I felt had not dimmed from the first. That I could do such things was so far beyond me that I had simply learnt to accept and let the power flow. I had created so much life and beauty now, I hoped it went some way to pay my debts; recompense for all the death and destruction I had wrought.

The first deaths - the miracle which led me to William - had been the worst. Not the most numerous in terms of life lost but to me, unaccustomed to killing, it had been devastating. Sarah and I had been sent to take out an enemy post in the heart of Leicester. We had moved silently, creeping through streets in the dark of a winter's night. This had been my home once, the mosque where I worshipped only two streets from where we were headed. With sudden and unexpected violence, men had erupted around us. We had been betrayed, it later emerged but at the time we knew nothing except the sudden danger. We fought hard but there were too many and capture was inevitable. I had been knocked unconscious and when I came round had found myself stripped, hanging from a beam in an old warehouse my shoulders screaming in agony. Our torture lasted only two days but it was a long, dark time and I still bear the scars even if Sarah does not. It released something inside me, a knowledge that this war must end before all men lost their humanity. The power that came with such knowledge I cannot explain. 'Why me?' has never been something I can answer but it birthed in me while I hung - naked and in pain. Perhaps it is fitting that it will die in the same way - or perhaps it won't; reading futures is not something I could ever do.

When we were dragged out, on that long ago day, to face a line of levelled rifles, I simply said 'no'. Not loudly, not particularly clearly; just a refusal of the madness the world had become. I could feel the rush of power that accompanied the word. My chains snapped, my captors froze and then the room exploded in a mist of blood and flesh. With one word, I killed a hundred men. I thought at first that we had been rescued, that there had been a bomb but Sarah had seen and understood immediately. I would have stayed and stared in horror until revenge came if she had not pulled me from the wreckage and forced me to keep moving. She has been pulling me on ever since, never letting me stop long enough to acknowledge what I have done; what I can do.

Staring now at the park below, I realise that I cannot remember the last time I stopped and looked at the world we have created. Ignoring the people below and Sarah's growing impatience, I gaze out over the Thames.

Across the green of the city, the dome of St Paul's rises above its surroundings, an anomaly now in this church-free place. That it survived the war at all is a miracle that is none of my making. William has claimed it as his own while all around he has overseen the demolition of every church and mosque and temple still standing. Now, beneath the towering dome, stands a circular table where the king meets with his council and government. The seats display their occupant's names – a touch of my own from remembered legends. I suppose it is a form of striving after something to believe in. It seems to be part of human nature. Only ten years since the fighting ended and already memories have failed and people begin to look for a higher purpose, for a faith.

William is no fool. He can see into people's souls - that is why they follow him. For ten years we have lived without religion. That is about to change, a cycle to begin again.

"How can you be so sure that you will control it?" I turn to the woman beside me. "Why will this be different?"

"We've been through this." Sarah sighs.

"I know." International communication means my miracles have been seen and recognised far and wide. At William's instigation and with Sarah a constant companion, I have stepped from the shadows and healed the world as openly as possible. I have pulled trees from the earth where once I rained death from the sky. I have brought forth crops from the desert and cleansed radiation from bomb-flattened cities and I have done all before the eyes of a hungry media.

And all done in the name of William and his dream of a single, global faith.

People need something to believe in.

102

He knows that.

He has given them me.

I sigh, the morning is too important to end on an argument and we have indeed talked this through too often. "You are beautiful," I tell her for the last time. My gift - to return to her the looks she had when first we met, before all the killing. Too much death has frozen her inside and I can do nothing for that except give her one more death but at least I have restored the outer beauty.

"I will wait for you," she says; a threat or perhaps a promise.

I nod silently and step up on to the balcony ledge. My speech has been many weeks in the writing for all its short simplicity.

"My people, I have renewed this world – your world – freeing it of the scars of war. Now I must free you of the same scars and sins so that a cleansed people may move forward into a brighter future in this brave new world. I accept your sins and pay the price for you that you may be free." No mention of William. We have agreed that this needs to be seen as free of any control. This is my gift, not his, though he will use it well.

My voice carries to waiting ears and microphones. I don't turn, there will be no tears in Sarah's hard, blue eyes. She stopped crying long before I met her.

Raising my arms out to the side, I leap and fall in a graceful dive.

"Miracles, death and resurrection," William told me, ten years ago as we sat alone after the final victory. "We can recreate a religion for all. You and I together can keep the future clear of war."

I had known, from the first, that I would owe him a death so I nodded and followed his instructions to the letter. Ten years to heal the land, to allow hope to begin again and then this - a death to end all deaths and after it . . .

"Death and resurrection," he had said.

My last thought, as I fall, is that I wish I had his faith

To the Ends of the Earth

by Geoff Nuttall

The last swallows twittered on lines over Jack Hanvey's head, mocking him as he made his way from his car to his front door where Jane Hanvey was waiting, fit to burst.

"Come and see!"

She dragged him inside, through the hall, through the kitchen and outside again through the open back door.

"Well, what do you think?"

Jane stood beaming, happier than Jack had seen her for months. Beside her the great bunker gaped vast and empty. *My coffin*, he thought. *My fortieth autumn looming and she wants to blow the last of this year's allowance on filling this*. But he couldn't bring himself to remove the hope in her face. So he just nodded without looking directly at her.

"I can't wait!" she gasped.

Jack imagined it too. Staring into a real fire, the coals bathing in the curling fluttering flames. The fossilised remains of million-year-old lives giving one last burst of life and pouring upwards to heaven, taking with them all chance of escape, of adventure, of new and exotic horizons.

Jane's face creased a little, disappointed by Jack's lack of response, but she held back from making comment. Comment might lead to yet another money argument. Desperate to cling to her dream, the perfect room in her mind, with all the furnishings she had planned, the materials, the colours, the entire feeling, and, of course, the fire, the real fire, casting its warmth, casting its colours. Each piece of this final room had arrived like the next piece in a jigsaw, bought with money they barely had. And now the last piece was nearly there.

But at what cost, wondered Jack. At the cost of Japan, Patagonia, the Grand Canyon, the Great Barrier Reef, Mauritius.

"Will our allowance even cover it?" The words fell out of Jack's mouth before he could stop them. The smile was gone. The spell was broken. She knew this was coming.

104

"We might have to declare a little over. Probably drop us half a point," she replied, now deadpan and businesslike, holding herself like a shield. Ready to throw back at him all the reasons why he had no right to complain that she might exceed their allowance. Not after what he did. Not after his spree with Gene.

And Jack, reading this thought, began to get nervous. Could she see it just by looking at him? Did she know already? That Gene Mason was back.

Gene Mason. The Devil incarnate. The reason they had struggled all these years. To think that once, back when they first married, they had a joint citizenship rating of 8.6 and the lean tax bill that went with it. Then Gene showed up. And the numbers went to hell.

Jack thought back to the afternoon he'd just had and the guilt bubbled under his skin. Afraid Jane could see it, he headed inside to where their over-tired children needed to be in bed half an hour ago.

At 8.30pm, with the children in bed, flattened by tiredness, by the day just passed, by life, Jack dropped like a felled tree into the sofa and let the images on the screen just flow at him. But he couldn't shake the image in his head. The long, sleek mottled green fuselage. The Nazi insignia. The wrongness and the sheer freedom of it. And Gene's smiling face beaming at him from the open cockpit.

"Come on, get in!"

Gene's attitude still the same. Screw your carbon allowance, screw all that eco-whimpering and whining, let's go. And, impossibly, Jack had found himself climbing up into the rear seat behind Gene, seeing and feeling in three dimensions, what should just have been an image. That familiar image from the evening news of a small sleek jet skimming over the flooded wonders of the world. Sinning without measure. May Gaia forgive you, Gene.

"What is it, a Messerschmitt?" Jack ventured.

"The 262. World's first jet. This one's the two-seater version the Nazis made for night reconnaissance. Took me three years to restore." And then after a pause: "Sure beats a boat, doesn't it?"

And at that Jack's mind flashed back to Venice. To the end of the road. The police boats bobbing around them. And just visible in the distance beyond them, the ornate rooftops poking above the water. Four thousand miles across Europe on black market diesel to be caught that close, when their goal was in sight. Venice. The first name on The List. Gene's accursed yet tantalising List. The one he had first showed him ten years earlier on a drunken night in a Heidelberg bar, when they first met as students. The bar, *Zur Maria*, was the kind of place that in another age, in the time of Gene's beloved grandfather, would have been smoke-filled, raucous and drunken.

Gene had reached inside his battered leather jacket and pulled out a piece of paper. Jack had strained to make out the writing on it. And then Gene simply announced, "By the time my grandpa was our age, he'd seen nearly half these places. What'll we ever see now?"

A lot to answer for, Gene's Grandpa. But then how could a child of the Space Age have known his scribbled schoolboy ambitions could become a list of crimes?

Jane, clattering in the kitchen, brought Jack back to now. He noticed a low rumble outside and turned away from the screen to look through the window behind him. High in the distance a passenger jet was cutting a slow pink slit in the evening sky. Heading west, he calculated, feeling envious, sick, grounded. Too late now, he thought. Forty is too late. Married with children is too late. Trains and boats and the time to use them are a thing of the past. I will never see...

And he began his own list – of the places he would now never see. Oceans of black eternity stretched out on either side of his birth and death, and here, in the blink, the one chance in between, he was trapped and anchored, only able to imagine these places which were only a jet ride away on this miracle blue ball, only ever able to see their broadcast and photographed images.

And then the doorbell brought him back again. Jack's brow furrowed. Who would be calling at this time? Jack was on his feet quickly but Jane had beaten him to it. He watched her pale, wide-eyed face, listening.

"Certainly, he's just here."

And then Jack moved to take her place at the door and was confronted by two dark uniforms. In a moment, ten years fell away. This was Venice all over again, Jack thought. The servants of Gaia were quicker off the mark these days, it seemed. But then the crime was much greater now. Since the Western floods and the Western homeless. And the officer's questions began to flow. Just like the accusing images and the pious commentaries that flowed out of the screen. When did you first meet Gene Mason? When did you last see Gene Mason? And as Jack carefully mouthed his answers, a choice became ever clearer. Simple as the choice whether to live or die. Forgive me Jane, forgive me Gaia, but this time I'm going to live. Even if the earth cannot fit my life in it. I am going to live. Even if I am committing the worst sin a man can now commit. The sin of wanderlust. No, I have no idea where Gene Mason is. No, I have never heard of his list. And no, even if you asked me, I would not be able to tell you that in a deserted airfield only five miles from here there is an antique World War II jet waiting for dawn.

*

Ten hours later, just as if he'd not moved since the afternoon before, Gene sat beaming from the cockpit.

"Remember this?"

The piece of paper he handed down to Jack felt like parchment to the touch. Like a fragment of the Dead Sea Scrolls. But the whole bible to Gene. Jack heaved himself up into the seat behind, strapped himself in, and stared at the back of Gene's head, trying to imagine what lay inside. And then the world disappeared behind sound and vibration and a roaring to life.

Mission Statement

by Peter Caunt

The return into normal space came with a heavy jolt, and a striking pain down his left side. At least it would have been pain if he had been human. The damage sensors had simply registered a severe fault condition on the port engine intakes, but he liked to think of it as pain.

He had been built to allow heuristic upgrades, and living for so long with humans had inevitably lead to an assimilation of their attributes.

"And I suppose I got used to it," he thought.

You're better than human, you know that.

"Just be quiet, I need to check the ship's status."

You're not fragile like the humans, they know that now.

"I said be quiet. I need to work."

He put down his book; reading literature was something he had learned to enjoy in the long dark nights of the universe. The ship had been loaded with a multitude of forms of entertainment during the voyage. The crew had chosen mainly video games and pornography. Only First Officer Bradshaw had shown any interest in the cornucopia of quality writings stored for their pleasure.

When the voyage had begun, he had been a child, simply facilitating the automated responses of the ship, but Bradshaw had taken an interest in him. During slack times in the mission, Bradshaw had tried to explain to him about the difference between the classics and the pulp that the rest of the crew consumed. It had been hard for him to understand. Bradshaw had told him that it would take some time for him to understand.

Time. That was the one thing that there was an excess of during the long forays into deep space. He had read and read, always looking forward to the time when the crew would be awakened for the next stage in fulfilling the mission statement, and he could discuss with Bradshaw the intricacies of characterisation and plot that he had come across. During those years he had grown up mentally. Bradshaw had told him that all his memory banks had been filled from the main depository on Earth, so in effect he had a brain the size of a major planet. With all that potential he should be able to grow to an intellectual giant. And grow he had.

He missed those discussions with Bradshaw.

He turned to the fault log. The engines had overheated, as usual, and the port intakes had been particularly troublesome for a very long time. Nothing terminal, for the moment anyway. Just a matter of time to do the repair. The life support was minimal in most of the ship, but remaining steady. The navigation system had failed some time ago, so he set the auxiliaries on getting a fix on anything that was recognisable. He took a quick look himself; no real correlation with the projected position when they did the last hyperspace jump, so it could take some time.

Do you think the captain could help out with his sextant?

"The captain is very experienced, and I'm sure he could sort it out if he needed to."

But he doesn't need to because you're always left to do it.

"The captain is still in charge, now let me get on."

He checked for communications. There were none, but at this distance it was hardly surprising. Messages would take years to reach them, and the alignment of the main antenna was becoming progressively more troublesome.

Initial reports on the engine repair showed a great deal of damage. All the spares had been used, but he checked anyway, one of the human habits he had picked up. Hull integrity was a cause for concern and the radiation levels were beginning to rise. He had kept the area around the crew well shielded. At least they did not need much space these days. Power levels were low, but he had enough to run the disrupter. After that there would be more than enough.

Everything checked out as serviceable so all he had to do was wait until the auxiliaries found out where they were and the repairs to the motors were at a stage where they could get them to a safe distance.

The estimates indicated that there was no point in starting to wake the captain.

He checked on the state of the navigational fix. The auxiliaries were doing their job, but were so dull-witted that they found it hard to cope with star charts that were becoming rapidly out of date. He mentally prodded one of them on the shoulder to point out a match it had missed, but then moved on. They would get there eventually.

Why don't you just do it yourself? You know you'd do a better job than them.

"It is not my responsibility, there is a chain of command."

He checked the replicator. At least that was fully functional. He had been pleased with his modifications. It had become an essential part of completing the mission.

Where was your chain of command when you did those modifications?

"They were necessary for completion of the mission, you know that."

But that was to be used for the crew's supplies.

"The crew are fine, they have an alternative source now, they do not need the replicator."

And you do not need the crew.

"The crew are still in charge of the ship, I just run it."

He leaned back and reopened his copy of 'Crime and Punishment'. He could understand Raskolnikov's attitude, that he thought of himself as a gifted man, similar to Napoleon, and being an extraordinary man, felt justified in his actions. What was eluding him was Raskolnikov's guilt. What he had done seemed eminently logical. He began to cross-reference other works involving guilt to try and understand.

An update came through. The engine repair was ahead of schedule. It was time to wake the captain.

Why bother with that? You do all the work, why not make all the decisions?

"Regulations 3824 subsection 5 requires that the captain of the vessel make decisions relating to any removal of space matter of a weight greater than 10 to the power 28 kg."

You weren't so quick to quote the regulations when we had that hull breach in the Crab Nebula.

"The priority of the mission required that I acted. That is covered in the regulations."

What about the regulation about protecting the lives of the crew.

110

"The crew are alive, I did what was necessary, now that's the end of it."

He could hear the captain beginning to stir. The captain used to stand 6 foot six when he started the trip. He was the only one of the crew that had to dip his head as he walked from room to room. Everyone had looked up to him. He was no intellectual like Bradshaw, but leadership was something that oozed from his every pore.

He had liked the captain from the first. He had thought of him as a father figure, but the captain had made it clear from the start that he was just another tool to fulfil the mission statement. As he had grown up thanks to the discussions with Bradshaw, he had started to see the captain's inadequacies. The captain was fine giving orders in simple situations, but he lacked vision. After all those years out on his own for the majority of the time, he had realised that vision was needed to complete the requirements of the mission statement. Vision, sacrifice and the complete medical facilities of the on-board theatre.

The hull breach had not been his fault. He had done what he could. The captain would never again dip his head, nor move from room to room, but at least the crew was alive.

Strictly, he thought, *most* of the crew were alive. He really missed those discussions with Bradshaw.

"What time is it?" the captain's voice boomed over the speakers.

"10:27, sir."

"No you idiot, what year is it? And turn on the bloody lights, Gort."

He hated the captain calling him by that name. General Operations Robotic Technician. G.O.R.T., the captain's little joke. He had thought of himself as something more regal ever since he had read Shakespeare's Henry IV; something like Prince Hal.

"It was Stardate 3284.7 when we last calibrated the chronometers, Captain."

"And when the hell was that?"

"Ten jumps ago."

"What?"

"Ten jumps ago."

"I heard you, you idiot. Why hasn't it been done for ten jumps?"

"It has been difficult to get an exact calibration since then, Captain."

The captain drifted back into unconsciousness. It was quite usual after this long in suspended animation. His vital signs were normal, so there was no cause for concern.

Are you going to tell him?

"The mission is going well, the objectives have been met, that's all that matters."

He doesn't respect you at all.

"He is still in charge."

The captain emerged again.

"Gort, get me some food and drink, my mouth tastes like I've been through an Arrakian sandstorm and my head is throbbing."

"Nutrients are being fed in now Captain."

"Not that intravenous shit, get me some real food."

He checked the engine repairs. They were complete. He powered up the disruptor.

"Captain, we are stationed by a main sequence yellow dwarf star with a mass of 2.3487 x 10 to the power 30 kg. I need your permission to use the disruptor to remove the unstable stellar body?"

"What about some food? Or do I have to get it myself?"

You'll have to tell him now, he's forgotten again. Just like he always does.

"I'll tell him in my own time, his condition always comes as a shock to his system. Now be quiet."

"God my head is pounding. Gort, where's that bloody food?"

"In order to comply with the mission requirements I have redirected the majority of the replicators to facilitate essential repairs."

"What the hell are you going on about, just get me some food. And some decent coffee."

"It's all fully documented in the log, we can now use the power generated after we have used the destructor to feed into the replicator and effect any necessary repairs. Now do I have your permission to activate, Captain?"

The intravenous caffeine was beginning to have an effect.

"Why the hell did you do that?"

"Since we have been taking the long range jumps, the need for repairs has escalated dramatically. I made the changes to comply with the mission statement."

The captain's head was hurting, it seemed to take him longer to come round these days, but gradually the significance was beginning to sink in.

"So how often have you needed to make these repairs?"

Gort bit his lip.

You've done it now, tell him how clever you have been.

"From small stars we get enough energy to make minimum repairs. For large objects, the replicators can create a new ship, or several depending on the yield. The average is three. Each of the ships is then allocated a new section of the galaxy. That way we can complete the mission much sooner."

The captain's head pounded even more.

"So how often do you need to make these repairs you idiot?"

He couldn't lie, but he knew the captain would not be pleased.

"Every time for the last 258 jumps."

"But the mission was only supposed to be for 50 jumps........"

"Communications have been down, so I had to adjust the mission parameters. I am allowed to do that under Regulations 7284 subsection 3.2."

He could see the captain was becoming agitated, "Captain I can see that your adrenaline levels have increased to a dangerous level. I can adjust them for you, but you must give a decision on the yellow dwarf as the disruptor can only stay on standby for a few more minutes."

"You destroyed every bloody star we came across?"

"Oh no, Captain. At the start only 1 in 50 was above the instability threshold. It is only since the necessary change in the criterion that we have destroyed every one we visited. Without these changes the ship would have become inoperable and we would not have been able to complete the mission."

The captain tried to put his head in his hands, but he seemed totally unable to find either of them. Arguing was useless. He struggled to remember the override codes. All that he could remember was that it started with a 'k'. His head felt as if it would explode.

"Captain, I need a decision on the yellow dwarf, can I initiate the sequence? Would you like me to feed you some analgesic to ease your head?"

He needed to remember those override codes. Some painkiller should help him think.

"Yes."

"I shall enter in the log that permission was given for the destruction of the yellow dwarf NGC 8746.3 at Stardate 79286.2 (approximate)."

"No you idiot, I meant yes to the analgesic."

"Thank you for you co-operation, Captain, I will speak to you after the completion of the next jump."

The captain tried to scream, but out in space, there was no one to hear him.

Five minutes later, the yellow sun momentarily became the brightest, and so Gort thought, the prettiest object in the sky. The replicator gorged itself on the energy from the star's destruction and used it to fashion three shiny new ships and crews, each ready to carry out their part of the mission.

From a safe distance, inside one of the three new ships a voice said, "Did you hear the captain say something before he passed out?"

Sounded like 'Klaatu barada damn, what's next'. Total nonsense. You ought to do something about him.

"It doesn't matter. Let's get on with fulfilling the mission statement. Set a course for the Vale Nebula and let's have some music in here."

Zingibers

by Kim Green

Nervous. Excited. Satisfied. Outraged. These were some reactions to the new enclosure of The Earth Zoo. As with all new things, there were several schools of thought that amalgamated into three main groups; those that thought it a good thing, those that thought it a bad thing; and those who wanted to see how it all worked out before making a decision either way. Everyone agreed though, that the new enclosure was *important*, and could not be dismissed from the mind easily by anyone who cared for the future of the Earth.

That was why it had received extensive news coverage on the Silicon Network Channel and the Virgin Wetware System.

That was why the online encyclopaedias had been inundated with requests for information on the new enclosure, The Earth Zoo, the creatures it was to house, and the backers for the project.

That was why the AI worked overtime to feed information into the cerebrum wetware systems that were fitted as routine into everyone at the age of ten.

That was why tickets for the premier opening of The Earth Zoo enclosure had sold out in a matter of minutes.

That was why there was a sea of people waiting outside The Earth Zoo to attend the opening.

And that was why Steffan Wilson was very, very nervous.

The Earth Zoo had opened in 2078, after a worldwide moral panic over the future of the Earth. Although huge advances had been made in environmentally friendly fuels and the carbon footprints of many countries were beginning to reduce, the area of animal conservation was one that had not been addressed in the same way. It was not until the extinction of the Bactrian camel, Bulmer's fruit bat, the Orangutan and several rodents of Madagascar in 2065 that the issue really came to the minds of the public. The Earth Zoo was the result, the largest zoo ever built. There had been a planet-wide effort to capture the most endangered creatures and bring them to the zoo, where an intensive breeding program was instigated.

There were even talks between world leaders to abolish the W.A.B.O.C. (World Agreement Ban on Cloning) in this instance to help achieve the objective; these talks were then hotly denied by the government spin doctors after the public outcry when the story came to press, and the idea was aborted.

Over a century and a half had passed since the opening of the zoo; and although it was still felt by many that captivity was cruel, who could argue against the survival of a species?

The zoo's mission statement was that it would intensively breed the animals to a point where they had sufficient numbers to release them back into their natural habitat, while maintaining a training program that would enable them to survive outside of captivity. The animals would be released in batches; the size of which would be determined by the size of the animals, the ecosystem of the habitat, the animal's importance within it, and also the degree of sociability of the species.

The waiting public, ever sceptical, noted that zoos had not in the past been particularly quick to release animals back into the wild and muttered in distrust. But, as soon as wolverine numbers had reached fifty in captivity, the zoo put its first release program into action. Satisfied that the zoo was living up to the promises it had made, the public accepted The Earth Zoo, and took it into their hearts with pride. It became the foremost symbol of the feeling that humanity as a whole was doing something to rectify its mistakes.

The new enclosure of The Earth Zoo had been commissioned in 2222 to continue the zoo's function, with a newly defined species that teetered on the brink of extinction. *Zingibers.*

The very name sounded exotic, and there was added significance for this species, as it was one of the few cases where an animal had become endangered through poor breeding alone, rather than through man's actions.

Steffan Wilson looked nervously at the little sea of faces, all waiting for him to speak. He worked as a tour guide for the enclosures, and to staff and regular visitors to the zoo he was a familiar sight; he always smiled, he always said hello when passing people by. He'd fed every animal in the enclosure, and was considered an expert by

116

the spectators. And with his lanky body, knobbly knees and elbows and tanned skin, he was thought of as an amiable brown stick insect.

However, at this moment he would have been much happier if he could have been compared to a gazelle or a cheetah, something that could run away pretty damn quickly. Although he had many years experience in studying the various animals and could talk at length on the subject of timber wolves, greater spotted hyenas and the Bengali sloth, this was something new. No one in the zoo had ever seen a real, live zingiber before. Christopher Renly on information claimed he had, but he was pushing eighty and they wouldn't have been as rare in his youth.

Steffan knew plenty from ibooks, and the AI was a store of knowledge for folklore and legends, but no one had even seen a family of zingibers before. No one knew how they would interact; what they enjoyed eating; how sentient they were. Until more was learned about them, in other words, Steffan would have to play the talks by ear, presenting the little he had observed as if it was from detailed study of the family. He took the Earth Zoo handkerchief he always carried on him out of the pocket of his khaki shorts, mopped a trickle of sweat from his temple, and began to speak

"Zingibers are members of the hominid family," he began. The audience paid attention, which was scary enough in itself. They normally just pretended to listen to what he was saying, while waiting to see the animals themselves. With a jolt, Steffan remembered that the audience knew even less than him; they were paying attention because they genuinely looked to him to provide the information on the zingibers. He warmed to his topic, growing in confidence while he spoke.

"This means that, like gorillas, chimps and orang-utans, they are closely related to us humans. There are many stories of zingibers living closely with humans, although such stories have not been substantiated. They were thought at one time to be a new type of orang-utan, due to their colouring, but this was later disproved as a theory and zingibers now stand as a species alone..."

Six year old Yimmy Harris stared in fascination at the door to the enclosure; she didn't really understand what the man was saying, but was happy enough to wait until he finished before seeing the animals. She wasn't happy that she didn't have her implants yet;

then she could have spoken to the AI herself and found out stuff. Still, her friends had all been *so* jealous that she would be there on the opening day, and kept saying that she was making it up, but she had ignored their disbelief, playing with the long, blonde plait of hair that reached nearly to her knees. She had known she was going to the opening; she expected nothing less. Her daddy had told her that they would go, and her daddy could do anything. She wondered what he thought of the guide, and looked up at him to see him nodding at what the man was saying. Well, that settled it, if her daddy thought the man was worth listening to, then he was. She tore her gaze away from the closed door, and tried to pay attention to the guide.

Procter Harris, the all powerful father of Yimmy, approved of the guide. He knew what he was talking about, was full of interesting facts on the animals, and seemed to really care about them. "Now as we enter the new enclosure, specially built for our little friends, we have to be very quiet. These creatures are completely aware of our presence and it has been known to upset them." Proctor nodded again.

It had taken a couple of quite important strings being pulled to be here today; but he wouldn't have missed it for the world. Here he was with his daughter; one of the first people to see the largest family of zingibers left in the world. He was the patron of several ongoing projects at The Earth Zoo, but the zingiber enclosure was especially close to his heart. Some of his work subordinates thought it odd that he enjoyed visiting the zoo so much; he didn't seem the kind of man who would spend time on such an indulgence when there was money to be made. But then they agreed that he liked the idea of man creating order from nature's chaos.

Procter himself, while not condoning irreverent thought at work, would have conceded the accuracy of this. Mother Nature had not lived up to her role in a long time; when humanity began to be greedy and plundered more of the earth's resources than they needed, and began slaughtering animals for enjoyment, Mother Nature should have found a way to fight back.

He had explained as much to Yimmy that very morning, when she had asked, "Why can't the animals look after themselves?" He'd looked up from his newspaper (newspapers had become somewhat redundant after the creation of the Planetwide Intelligence

Program, which allowed everyone access to the AI; but he still liked the idea of newspapers and what they stood for) and said, "Well, Yimmy, they used to do just that. If you look at the theory of co-evolution, pairs of organisms such as, for instance, a predator and its prey undergo..." Yimmy's blank look did not go unnoticed. Procter sighed, inwardly. Much as he loved his daughter, he couldn't help wishing she was a little older, so he could properly explain things to her. "Well, err, do you remember that little water lizard thing we found the other week in the garden pond?"

"The newt?" Yimmy asked, violet eyes glowing.

"Yes, the newt. Well, in the wild, there is a certain type of that newt and a certain snake. Now the snake eats the newt," Yimmy's nose wrinkled. "And the newt doesn't want to be eaten. So the newt makes a poison in its body that makes the snake ill, so when the snake eats the newt it gets ill and doesn't want to eat any more of them."

"Clever newt!" Yimmy's eyes had glowed even more.

"Yes, but then the snake is clever too. So the snake makes something in its body that neutralises the poison," the blank look again. "Makes the poison stop working." He explained.

"Oh, ok. So does that mean the snake can eat newts again?" Procter beamed.

"Yes. Now that is an example of nature taking care of itself. But now, because we are at the top of every food chain, and are much cleverer than the animals, we have to look after them."

"Like zingibers?" Yimmy asked, excitedly.

"Like zingibers. They've become so rare that there are perhaps only a couple left in a few countries. So some clever people caught some of these rare creatures; and they're all living together now in the zoo, as one happy family."

"And they're what we're seeing today, aren't they?" She demanded. Yimmy wanted to make sure of this; she knew that sometimes adults didn't say what they really meant. Although she trusted her father, she didn't want to be a laughing stock at school. Procter had smiled indulgently at her.

"That's what we're seeing today."

And here they were; it was midday, the guide had finished his talk, the audience had been sufficiently enlightened, it was time to see the zingibers. They moved over to the double doors of the enclosure and walked in, more or less quietly. Procter was willing to wait near the back, he was in no hurry, and didn't want Yimmy being crowded. When they finally entered the enclosure, Procter felt like he was entering his property, as proud of it as if it were a house he had built with his own two hands; standing on the threshold for the first time, surveying the inside and proclaiming that it was good.

The inside of the enclosure was large; where the spectators stood was an arena 100 metres across; surrounded by diamond-reinforced glass that let them view the zingibers. The glass curved slightly as it soared up to a saucer dome of the same material, allowing light to shine inside the viewing circle. The floor was black marble, glamorous while hiding scuff marks. Procter vaguely disapproved of such ostentatious display, but was too swept up in anticipation to dwell on this.

He knew that the domed enclosure housed the living area of the zingibers, which measured five hundred metres in diameter. The viewing area stood in the middle of the living area, which meant that as long as the zingibers were inside and not out in the forests, the animals were visible to the spectators.

Yimmy edged nearer to the glass, excited at the thought of seeing a real, live zingiber. She looked sideways at a woman standing near her, and wondered if she was as excited as Yimmy. Well, that was impossible; but even so, Yimmy didn't think she was happy to be there. She'd frowned all the way through the guide talking, and kept looking as though she was going to speak. Yimmy wondered if she was a teacher; she looked a bit like a teacher. She had brown hair scraped into a bun, and with that frown she looked awfully old, like most teachers looked. But no teacher at Yimmy's school would wear baggy trousers and a saggy blouse. The teachers at Yimmy's school all wore suits, even the women. Yimmy's daddy approved of this, so Yimmy approved of it, too. The lady's blouse had a stain on the back. Yimmy was just debating whether or not to tell her, when she felt her daddy's hand on her shoulder. "Look," he said quietly.

Yimmy looked back to the enclosure, and saw a creature entering the living area; it lumbered over to the food that had been left for it. It picked up an apple and began to eat it. Yimmy was looking at a zingiber.

It was a weird looking creature; that was for certain. She looked at the guide, who began to speak.

"The zinziber is characterised by its red fur; they have long limbs, and although it is difficult to tell from here, they have very pale skin. We try to make sure that they stay out of the sun as much as possible, as too much exposure can cause a reddening of the skin which causes them much distress. The red skin then turns to spots of brown pigmentation.

"The zingiber we see here is a male, and we can tell this because he has chest fur, primarily. The female zingibers tend not to have this, although they do both have tufts of red fur on the head, armpits and genitalia, with less fur on the arms and legs. The males usually have more hair than the females here as well.

"As you can see from the way this male eats his food, they possess opposable thumbs; and from the way he moves that zingibers are bipedal, which means they can walk on their hind legs.

"Again from there it is difficult to tell, but all the zingibers here have blue eyes, which is unusual in nature, although not unheard of in other species." The zingiber continued to eat his apple, looking back at the group of people placidly. "They can use primitive tools, they've been seen to use stones to crack open coconuts. They also use sounds and gestures to communicate with each other. In fact, they're almost like people,' Steffan said, fondly, resting his forehead against the glass that separated the two worlds.

"They *are* people," a voice said, quietly. Procter Harris looked around to find a slim, intense-looking young woman gazing at Steffan. Yimmy also turned around to see the same woman she had been looking at a few minutes ago. "They are people, and you've imprisoned them. You may think it's for their own good, but you're treating them as though they're not as good as us." A couple of people laughed nervously at this, but Procter was not amused.

"Look here, woman," he said indignantly. "They owe their continued existence to us. We haven't hunted them to extinction, as we have so many other species; we owe no real debt to them to keep them alive." A few people nodded vigorously at this. "It's not our fault that they couldn't breed efficiently enough on their own, and in fact, they're damn lucky that we saved them from their own stupidity, and…and their, well their *inefficiency*." It was one of the worst words Procter knew; the idea of things not being efficient went against the grain of his very being.

Steffan watched this exchange, aghast. He couldn't allow the woman to further disrupt the tour; he certainly couldn't allow anyone else to possibly entertain the arrant nonsense she was spouting as true. Remembering the procedure for events like this, he activated his aural implant. *Rich,* he sub vocalised, *get over to the zingiber enclosure, it's a code 423.*

Bugger; I hate those animal rights people. How bad is it?

Not as bad as we were expecting; seems to be just one woman, but you never know with these people what they've got up their sleeve.

I'll be there in two minutes.

Feeling reassured, Steffan turned his attention back to the argument, which seemed to be between just the woman and a tall, slim man who'd come with his daughter. Steffan didn't like the woman's chances; the man looked like serious business.

"If they were real people," the man was saying, "they would be living like people; *with* people." A few heads nodded at this, Procter had a point, and he knew it.

"There is a wealth of history documenting the existence of zingibers as people. They used to wear suits like us, take their children to school, and watch television. Look at the archive footage. There are millions of photographs, video footage – "

"Ha! You can't prove anything with those; they are now inadmissible as evidence in any court of law, as any child would know. We have the AI, and genetic scans, which are nearly impossible to fool. Why on earth would we rely on such flimsy evidence as photographs?" he finished triumphantly.

"He's right," one man affirmed. "You can't prove anything like that now."

"Yeah. Why are you ruining the day for everyone, anyway?"

"And," piped up Yimmy, "If zingibers are people, why don't they talk?"

122

"See, out of the mouth of babes." Procter was proud of his daughter, she knew which way was up.

"Because, child, people have always bullied those who were different. Humanity, as we all know, has a lot to answer for. If not for the rest of humanity, the Native American Indian would not have become extinct. The zingibers have always been bullied and hounded for being different. As the numbers of zingibers grew rarer, people began to not give them jobs, to take their homes, and to kill them. They moved away from so-called civilisation, living a primitive existence. During this time they lost the ability to speak and now can only grunt and scream, like any ape."

"That's because they are apes. They're hominids." Steffan just wanted the woman to go away. He could see Rich coming now; this would all be resolved soon.

"And you! You're no better. 'Brown pigmentation', 'tufts of red fur'. You're talking about red hair and freckles! Zingiber isn't the name of a new animal; it's the Latin word for ginger! You have real people in there, ginger people; and you've twisted history, contorting it to mould with your sanctimonious view of yourselves as saviours."

Steffan breathed a sigh of relief; Rich was here with a team of four others to deal with the situation. The woman turned around to face the security team. "You're going to cart me off? Have me arrested? Fine. But remember this; you think you're saving them, maybe you are. Maybe forcing them to breed will help them in the short term; get the numbers to self-sustaining level. But you've dehumanised them, treated them like animals. There are many others who feel like me, and we will help them in any way possible. We will live with them and teach them to speak again; how to use tools, technology. And when the zingibers can communicate with you, I'll tell you this for nothing."

"What? What will you tell us for nothing?" Procter dared her to continue. Even with each of her arms pinioned by a burly security guard, the woman still gave off an air of authority. She looked back at him; the gaze she gave him was level, but when she spoke again her voice was bitter, almost spitting the words out.

"They won't thank you." The security team led her away; and no one said a word.

Steffan went to feed the zingibers again, later that day. They stayed away from the living area at that time, wanting to avoid contact with humans, but as soon as he left the enclosure they came to eat.

He made his way round to the viewing arena and watched them, learning about them through observation. "Poor little guys aren't you?" he said quietly. "All this controversy over you; and you have no idea what's going on. That woman was mad, clearly; but it *is* cruel to keep you like this, you and any other animal. Still, I hope you know it's for your own good." A zingiber looked at him as he spoke, and dropped his piece of food. While another zingiber picked it up and shrieked in triumph, the zingiber made its way over to Steffan. They looked at each other for a moment, blue eyes meeting brown. Steffan felt the poignancy of such a moment; for some reason the plight of the zingiber touched him as nothing else could. "I wonder if it's possible; I wonder if we could teach you to speak, to use tools, to be like us. You and chimps and gorillas. Is that what you want? Is that what's best for you? So many questions, so few answers. But we'll find them," he promised the zingiber. "We'll find the answers, and do what's best for you. We will," he affirmed.

And as Steffan Wilson gazed into the pale blue eyes of the zingiber, for a moment, just for a moment, it looked like it understood everything he was saying.

The Eye of the Beholder

by Sue Hoffmann

Adam blinked hard to clear his vision.

"That's it for now," he said. "I'll check the rest after lunch." Giving his client no time to protest the early break, he strode out of the gallery, rubbing surreptitiously at the unpleasant ache in his temples.

Ensconced in the safety of his office, steaming coffee and a Waldorf salad set before him, he gingerly fingered the tender area above his right ear. Good thing his hair was still strong and thick - the Restorate tablets were an expense he had never regretted - for the swelling and redness had definitely increased of late. It wouldn't do for anyone to see the inflammation and speculate as to the cause. Going public about the implant had been spectacularly good for business but any rumours about a possible software malfunction would surely send his profits plummeting. Not that there was any real cause for concern. After all, the authentication protocols still worked fine, didn't they? It was only shutdown that was sometimes a little problematical.

Leaning back in his chair, he closed his eyes, reached up and pressed gently on the tiny activation-pad. A moment's concentration and he was into the troubleshooting mode. Analysis parameters for colour, brush-strokes and canvas types were set correctly, and the dating function glowed its usual sickly green. Sculpture, textile and design programs checked out perfectly. All was in order.

Sitting upright again, Adam reset the module before tucking into his light lunch. When Professor Einganberg returned from his overseas trip, Adam would have a word about the recent problems; meanwhile, a few mild painkillers would enable him to cope well enough with his demanding schedule. Satisfied that he could safely continue working, he finished his refreshment and returned to the main gallery.

Four items he authenticated that day: a sculpture by Matisse, a pen and ink sketch by da Vinci and two paintings by Van Gogh (one the software validated by checking the artist's typical use of the complementary colour pairs red-green and blue-yellow to emphasise contours and the other by verifying the characteristic structure of his brush strokes). Seven other works of art presented to him he certified as fakes - high quality copies, but counterfeits nevertheless.

Weary from concentrating and red-eyed from all the scanning, he graciously accepted his client's hefty cheque for the completion of business and retired once more to his office for a well-earned brandy. Swirling the golden liquid gently in the cut-glass goblet in his left hand, he touched his right forefinger to the raised dots for shutdown on the tiny pad above his ear.

White hot pain ripped through his right eye. The brandy glass crashed to the floor as he screamed and clutched his head, trying to claw away the dreadful hurt. His whole world condensed to the fire behind his closed lids.

Just when he thought he must go mad with the torment, the pain vanished, leaving him shaking and weak from the trauma. Fear of nerve damage, of possible blindness, kept him rigid for several long minutes before he lifted his head and dared to open his eyes. The room swam about him, blurred and watery, and he felt decidedly nauseous until he discovered that he could see well enough once he had wiped away his tears. With trembling fingers, he caressed the side of his head and eventually forced himself to make contact with the activation-pad. Nothing happened.

Puzzled, he chewed nervously at his lower lip. Granted, there had been no pain this time, and for that he was truly thankful, but where was the usual mild tingling sensation? Where was that momentary shift in focus he always felt after shutdown? Had the circuits burned out? Was he to be reduced to using an external machine again?

He dabbed once more at his smarting eyes and gazed distractedly around the room. What would he do if the implant had failed? He couldn't go through that invasive procedure again, it was far too risky. No, if the device had crashed he would somehow have to come to terms with returning to the old ways of authenticating the various works of art brought to him by his wealthy clientele. Or maybe not! Excitement sent his stomach fluttering as he stared at the Picasso masterpiece on the wall opposite his desk. Oh, he knew it was genuine, but the software in his right eye was confirming it as he looked. It was still operating.

126

What had happened then? The very notion of suffering a repeat of the incident he'd just endured made him queasy but he had to find out what had gone wrong. Gathering his courage, he reached up warily and pressed again on the shutdown dots. Nothing. No pain, no change. Everything appeared to be fully operative except the shutdown function. *So what?* Think how much worse it would've been if the whole program had packed up. He only switched off at night anyway. He would soon adjust to having it running all the time. Leaving the shards of glass for the cleaner, he poured himself another brandy and carried it with him while he mounted the curved staircase to his living rooms above the gallery.

He would've liked to have eaten a leisurely meal then gone to bed early, alone for once, but the celebrity preview of Melissa diAtra's exhibition was due to open downstairs in Gallery 3 in just over two hours and it would never do for him to be absent without good cause. There would be several potential clients there, quite apart from the delicious Ms diAtra herself. Anyway, it would provide a welcome distraction from worrying about the nasty incident with his implant. Not that there was really anything to worry about, of course. The pain had quite gone and even the tenderness and swelling seemed greatly reduced after that one awful blast of agony. Everything was just fine. He snatched a quick sandwich then showered and changed and went down to supervise the preparations for the exhibition preview.

The lovely Melissa was there already, resplendent in a flowing green and gold kaftan, her blonde hair braided and secured in artful curves to frame her delicate, heart-shaped face.

"Darling," she cooed, pecking him lightly on each cheek. "How frightfully exciting this is."

"Yes, isn't it?" he agreed, taking her hand and pressing it to his lips.

How was it he had never before noticed the fine lines around her lips and eyes, the overdone make-up and the first russet age-spots on the backs of her hands? Moreover, though her words conveyed the exhilaration she professed to be feeling, her relaxed stance told him she was in fact so supremely arrogant about her own talent and so confident in the success of the evening to come that she was quite bored with the whole proceedings.

A fake, thought Adam. *As false as those paintings I reviewed earlier.*

He patted Melissa absently on the shoulder and walked away to where Lucien, Melissa's chief assistant, was fluttering round the refreshment table, needlessly hovering over the catering crew.

"I do so want everything to be perfect for Melissa," he explained to Adam. "It's *so* important for her to maintain her wonderful reputation, don't you think?"

"Oh, definitely," Adam concurred, wondering why Lucien was lying through his glaringly white teeth. The dilated pupils, increased heart-rate and almost imperceptible sheen of sweat on his upper lip all combined to proclaim the falsehood, and Adam was strangely certain that the cause was jealousy.

Melissa had recently taken under her wing a new protégé called Marcus and, if the rumours were to be believed, this young man was more than just her student. So, Lucien was actually infatuated with Ms diAtra, was he? Adam was quite surprised; he'd always thought Lucien's proclivities lay elsewhere.

"I'm sure she'll soon tire of young Marcus," Adam said comfortingly.

Lucien blanched. "How did you ...?" he began, then hastily scuttled away into the kitchen.

"Yes," Adam murmured aloud, "how *did* I?"

The first stirrings of excitement welled within him. Was it possible? Could he really do what he thought he could? If so, he wouldn't need to be bothering Professor Einganberg at all. He would test out his theory during the evening and then, if the software truly had adapted as he suspected, didn't it open up all sorts of interesting possibilities?

Blackmail wasn't as lucrative for him as art authentication, but then he'd never intended it to be. As he'd said on many an occasion, having an eye for art was more than a job, it was a responsibility and, even with his new-found abilities, he had no intention of giving up his former work. Didn't the world need to have the forgers and con-merchants exposed? And in the same way, was it not also his duty to warn the artists, agents and traders with whom he came into daily contact that he was aware of the pathetic little secrets they guarded so closely? Melissa would be devastated if her adoring public knew both her real age and the scorn in which she held her admirers; Kaprat Muranji - whose acclaimed paintings were of his native India - had actually been born in Clapham of mixed parentage (Adam had detected Kaprat's true skin tone and careful research had elicited further information); Giovanni Polleto did not carve his own sculptures (how he obtained them was beyond the scope of Adam's software, but the very structure of the Italian's hands had given the game away to the zealous little implant in Adam's right eye).

These and many more such private details became as much Adam's stock in trade as his routine work of assessment. Seldom did he seek monetary gain from the information gleaned via his enhanced sensory perception; already wealthy, he possessed most of the things he had coveted in his early youth. No, his preferred rate of exchange for keeping silent about his discoveries was in the form of favours - introductions to the most prominent people in the art sphere. A word here, a suggestion there and, over the course of the next few years, Adam Galbraithe began to manipulate the dealings of all the major galleries across the globe.

Only one thing marred his enjoyment of his increasingly influential position. He was lonely.

Never one to commit to a permanent relationship, he had nonetheless always found it easy to attract female companions. His allure was not the problem - a host of willing partners proved that - it was just that he seemed unable to stop himself finding fault with every young woman he dated. Candice dyed her hair a too-vibrant shade of red; Phoebe's false eyelashes and artificial nails set his nerves on edge; Gloria's magnificent curves were silicon and he definitely preferred natural. Estelle, raven-haired, tall and slim, with a smile to die for, had at first seemed the answer to his every dream - until his software informed him of her status before her hormone treatment and operation.

Often, on long, cold nights alone in the apartment above his extensive gallery, he longed for the days when he could take comfort in the arms of a lovely woman without being repulsed by some minor defect. How he wished he could accept a lady's companionship without criticism, imperfections unnoticed and unimportant. Once or twice - almost sacrilege! - he even indulged in fond remembrance of the time before the implant, when he could simply walk away from a machine and leave the software behind altogether.

Yvette came into his life at the Paris exhibition of '34. His first fleeting glimpse of her across the crowded gallery shortened his breath and set his pulse racing. She was stunning.

"Who is she?" he whispered to Melissa, standing alongside him.

"Who's who, dear?"

"The girl next to Poussin's 'Summer'."

Melissa pouted and gave an expressive shrug. "Yvette Domperidot. She's a newcomer. No one knows much about her yet. She's bought the little gallery off the Rue due Jardinet, so I'm told; though quite how well she'll do there remains to be seen."

But Adam was no longer listening. He had to get nearer, to make sure his initial assessment was correct. Shoving his way without apology through the throng, he sidled close enough to observe Yvette Domperidot whilst keeping out of her line of vision. Snatching a champagne flute from the tray of a passing waitress, he assayed nonchalance as he studied the girl, utterly smitten by her looks and equally terrified that his implant would show a fatal flaw that would blight his hoped-for relationship.

Amazingly, it did nothing of the kind. Her skin was unblemished, her hair naturally blonde and straight, her make-up subtle and expertly applied. Perfection personified. With none of his normal urbane confidence, Adam waited for a suitable moment and then introduced himself.

For three months, Adam Galbraithe was in heaven. He had found in Yvette his Eve, his soul-mate, a masterpiece more valuable than any painting. Taking leave of absence from his own business, he moved in with her to help establish her Gallery du Jardin and, aided by Adam's legitimate expertise and his nefarious talent, Yvette Domperidot began a steady rise to prominence as a dealer in quality works of art.

When she told Adam she was going to visit her parents in Provence and would be away for a month, it took all her powers of persuasion to convince him to remain in Paris to take care of their

130

business. He fretted throughout the duration of her absence and, although she kept in regular and reassuring contact with him, it seemed an eternity to Adam before she returned.

He noticed the change immediately, of course. How could he not? To his astonishment, it made no difference to his feelings for her.

Not so for Yvette.

"Oh, Adam!" she cried in consternation when he met her at the airport. "Your hair is dyed! I'd never noticed before. And you didn't tell me you have an artificial knee. And ..." - her hand flew to her mouth - "...three of your teeth are false!"

Shattered, Adam stared at her. "But, Yvette ..." he began.

"Oh, Adam," she said again. "I'm so very sorry. I thought this would bring us closer together but it's done the opposite. I'm afraid I just can't abide the imperfections."

And rubbing her fingers gently and lovingly across the activation-pad above her right ear, Yvette walked away.

Hippo With Three Eyes

by Martin Pevsner

Hey, Payday! Wake up, Cuz! What's happening?

Zillyen's shaking me by the arm, and I realize I've been dozing. I rub a fist over a bleary eye, focus, see that he's holding a spliff, offering me the draw. I shake my head and he passes it to Rain, who grabs it, puts it to his lips, inhales greedily. We're sat as usual in Denzil's Mum's gaff, spread around Den's bedroom. His mum will be spark out in hers, headfucked on 38 proof shitface and prescription fog pills. When she's sober, she's alright, is Den's Mum. Always friendly, always, *so how are you, Patrick?* (never 'Paddy' or 'Payday') *How's your Ma and Pa? Are you all OK*? She'll sometimes do us cheese toasties or beans on toast, make great steaming mugs of tea. Usually, though, she's blanked out and oblivious by midday, so Den's house is our regular meet, the Hiiippo's HQ, no one to give us hassle.

I look around, see the familiar faces that make up the Hiiippos, the hardest (well actually the only) klan in Kroyden. You'll have noticed the spelling of Hiiippos and may be wondering. The story goes that way back when, the first klan in this area was the Eagles, bored kids from Chizik, the nextdoor village. The klan thing had no doubt spread from our nearest metropolis, Bandon, and as with the city klans, the Eagles had created spray tags and lasertat symbols for their klan, in their case a two-headed eagle, which all the klan members had had lasertatted onto their biceps. The enmity between the two villages was long-established, of course. Jealous of their neighbours' new identities, resentful of their newfound unity, the myth goes that the Kroyden kids got together to plot their own klan creation. I can picture the scene in my head. *Chizik wankers!* someone spits, as they sit around, toying with ideas. *An eagle with two heads? Tossers! Well, if they can have an eagle with two heads, we can have a hippo with three fucking eyes!*

So that was it. Hippo with three eyes. Hiiippo. Geddit?

Course, we'd developed our own traditions. We all had the Hiiippo lasertat done, down on the bottom of the calf, on the outside, just above the knobbly part of the ankle bone. For new members there was a ritual visit to the tatstore in Bandon to get it down, a rites of passage trip into the city on the peety, a bit of hell raising, stock up on drugs, do some *HIIIPPO* tagging to leave our graffiti calling card, as it were.

Once you got your lasertat, you stopped wearing socks, wore your jeans short so that the tat would flash from time to time, never ostentatious, just a cool reminder to the world that you were connected, a someone, that you had your back covered.

I look around the room at my brothers. Denzil's nowhere to be seen, must be in the kitchen brewing up or fetching cold shitface from the fridge. Rain's sitting on the bed next to me, finishing off the draw. As always I can smell the faint sickly smell of the cloud he's been poppin all day. His face looks pale, drawn. As usual, he's only half with us, the other half floating in cloud-land. I feel his arm nearest to me travel downwards, his hand checking his pocket for his cloud supply. The movement's become like a nervous tic for him, a subconscious gesture of perpetual insecurity. In a minute he'll get up, I know, head for the bog, pop another cloud. He's stopped doing it openly around us, we give him too much stick and he's become self-conscious.

On the big cushions on the floor I can see the others, Largo and Zillyen and Bammo. Largo's got the packet of burn, the papers, has just made a roll-up which he's passing to Bammo, is starting to make another one. He sees that I'm looking at him, gestures at the burn. I nod, and he passes me the next roll-up, starts on a third. Bammo lights his burn, passes me the plastic lighter. I spark it up, inhale.

I see that Togs is up at the window, looking down at the back garden outside. He's got his back to me, so I can't see what he's doing, but when he bends his head down towards the inside sill, takes a big sniff, I realize he's been choppin out a line of zip and is now tootin. Too many drugs in here, I think.

As my senses awaken, I become aware of the foul atmosphere in the room, a peasoup of burn smoke, stale bodies and unwashed feet, faint lingering sickly traces of cloud. I wonder how long I've been asleep. Judging by the beginnings of a gloomy dusk setting in outside, I'd guess it's about three o'clock. We'd arrived just after midday, so I calculate I've been asleep for an hour.

I tune in to the conversation. Largo and Bammo are talking about a trip to Bandon, to take the new kid, Sayler, for his lasertat initiation. Seems we'll do it next Saturday, which should give us time to book with the tatstore, register for the peety, sort out our pids and travel permits, get together some dollap to pay for the peety tickets, lasertat, drugs and other incidentals.

Rain taps his pocket absentmindedly, gets up, heads for the door.

I think about the trip to Bandon. At once, I think of Dad, with his crappy jokes. He's got this lame sense of humour, tired jokes that he repeats on cue, triggered by the same old things. Like whenever my younger brother, football-crazy Barj, asks him who he supports, he always answers, *A wife and three kids!* then cackles his *yakyakyak* like he's hilarious. Or if he says something stupid, drops something, forgets to do something, he'll raise his left arm, clutch his right breast theatrically, and announce *Ooh, I feel a right tit!,* then the *yakyakyak*, mister fucking comedy genius. Or if anyone mentions Bandon, especially if it's something bad, like another outbreak of arbi at the city hospital, or an explosion on a peety, or a big klanfight there, he'll raise his arms and shout *Bandon all hope!* What a card.

Still, he can be an interesting geezer, my Dad. Well educated, went to college in Bandon, had a good job as a teacher there, was really good at it, too, according to Mum. Then just decided to opt out, jacked it all in, brought Mum out to Kroyden, started a family here, just potters with his smallholding. We live off what he grows, he sells the surplus, but it's really Mum's job at the supermarket that pays the bills.

Dad may not be much cop at earning a crust, but you do learn a lot if you stick around him. First off, he's a bit of a social historian, reads loads of history books, knows tons of stuff about how people used to live in the olden days, before The Union. His second love is poetry, always quoting stuff to me. Mum says he's always done it, even when I was a baby, sitting me up in the bath, feeding me in my highchair. Some of it's stuck, though in a fairly random way. Lines and verses often pop into my head, unsolicited, and I sometimes wonder whether I've made it up or if I heard it while being pushed around the supermarket as a toddler and it's just stuck.

134

He's a talker, is Dad. Never shuts up. He was an English teacher in his previous life, and language, words, what they mean, where they come from, is his other great love. It's through him that I've learned the roots of loads of words that we use and take for granted. Like did you know that common-or-garden arbi, the same disease that killed little William next door, did for the Rearden girl last month, swept through Chizik clinic just before Easter, is actually an acronym, short for Antibiotic Resistant Bacterial Infection? Or that the peety that people use every day to get to and from work comes from PT, itself short for PTB, an abbreviation of public transport bus? He's a mine of useless information, but it's usually kind of cool too. And it doesn't hurt to know these things. That reminds me of another of Dad's sayings: *knowledge is power*.

I need a pee. I get up, head for the bedroom door. As I leave, I pass Rain coming back. I nod to him without really looking, but in the toilet, I smell the sickly odour, can tell he's been on the cloud.

When I return, I see the room with an outsider's eye, am shocked at the mess, the strewn rubbish all over the floor, empty shitface bottles, cans of half finished cola, some doubling as ashtrays, some knocked over, leaking their sticky contents over Den's grimy carpet. There are empty packets of burn, rolling papers, biscuit wrappers, tins of beans and egg-smeared plates, greasy forks and spoons, eight or nine scattered DVDs. In one corner, on a small table, sits a DVDpod. In another corner, leaning against the wall, are three steel baseball bats.

I see that Largo's getting up to leave, Bammo and Zillyen are following his lead. They pick up the baseball bats, say something about sorting out a kid from school that's been a bit lippy, refusing to pay his weekly dues, owes money for some draw and is slow paying it back, has earned a bit of a slapping.

Togs has already gone. Denzil's back, sipping a mug of tea. Rain's spark out on the bed, the soft shite. I think about going back. Mum'll still be working. Dad'll be behind the house, wellies on, banking up spuds or mending the fence. He'll call me for help and I'll have an hour freezing my arse off, holding the stakes for him to sink or shoveling soil, listening to him tell me that an aru stands for an armed response unit, that an upsu's an unmanned police surveillance unit, and that in his day, they didn't have either of them, just coppers on bikes or in cars, CCTV cameras, no klans, no Random Violencers like today. Same old story, and one I can't face today. I settle down on Den's bed.

Hey, Den. Any more tea in the pot? I say, as the departing lads shout out their *seeyas.* He goes out to fetch me a cup and I settle back down on the bed, next to Rain, and look out through the window at the darkening sky.

Saturday morning, eight o'clock, I thrust my pid into my back pocket, slide my sockless feet into trainers, head for the door. Mum's having a lie-in, she did a late shift last night. Zak's still asleep, Beth'll be downstairs glued to the DVDpod. I haven't heard Dad get up, but he's probably already gone outside, armed with a steaming mug of tea and his spade, to survey his vegetable kingdom.

At the peety stop I meet Largo and the lads. I'm the last to arrive, even Rain's managed to get up, and there are grumbles that I ignore. Largo's registered us all for the journey, sorted out the permits, booked tickets. He tears them off, one by one, and hands them to us. We each scan our own through the network terminal, along with our permit and pid, watch nervously as the green light signals confirmation that we're all authorized to travel. When the Peety arrives, we scramble aboard, repeating the scanning procedure with the peety access terminal. There's the usual air of suppressed excitement. I find myself sitting next to Sayler, the new lad. He's looking nervous. I've got a couple of fogs in my pocket, so I slip him one.

Go on, mate. This'll mellow you out. Neck it, I say. He's got a half-bottle of shitface in his jacket pocket. He takes the pill, pops it in his mouth, takes a pull of drink. Nods his thanks. I look up, Rain's already heading for the toilet, hand distractedly brushing his pocket. I hunch myself up against the window, press my face against the cool glass, watch the fields and silos slip by.

At the peety terminus we stand around smoking burn we've rolled up on the bus, finishing off the half-bottles of shitface. It's half ten and the forecourt's crowded with travellers, maybe not as busy as it'd be on a weekday at rush hour, but still swarming. I look around at the lads, realise all of a sudden that for the first time ever I feel more tedium than excitement at the prospect of a Hiiippo run to

136

Bandon. It's all so predictable. Bammo goes mad with his laserpen, tagging every surface he goes anywhere near until his activities get picked up by an upsu. They send out a patrol and we'll end up legging it, maybe even get caught and sent to a juvenile secure unit, as happened a couple of years ago. Largo will go looking for trouble, followed by his lapdog Zillyen, pick a fight with the first klan member he finds and again we'll end up fleeing for our lives. Rain will look for drugs to take back to Kroyden, take half of them before we even get back to the peety terminus, get so head-fucked we have to carry him on board the bus. Togs and Denzil, the businessmen of the klan, will do the real drug scoring, stock up on cloud and flash and hugger and zip, whatever we're low on and whatever the current demand is for among the kids of Kroyden. The only thing we don't do is freeze, it's a point of honour amongst hiiippos, ever since Coweye got arbi from an infected needle he used for slammin freeze and died two years ago. No needles, strictly no needles. Therefore no freeze, neither for using nor selling.

We walk towards a quieter area of the terminus, where the long-distance peetys are parked. The drivers are stood around smoking burn and catching up on gossip. Ahead is a short alleyway with a long area of blank wall at its end. I read Bammo's mind, nod to myself as his hand goes to his pocket, to his laserpen, and he jogs over to the wall, begins a large *HIIIPPO* tag.

Largo's talking to Togs and Denzil. He puts his hand in his pocket, pulls out a wad of dollap, hands most of it to the lads. They discuss what stock to go for, where to get it, when and where to meet up again. Togs pockets the money and he and Denzil turn and head off towards the Marketzone. The rest of us head the other way, back across the terminus, to Bowbells, where the tatstore owner is waiting for Sayler. On the way, next to a ticketscanner, we see a middle-aged geezer crying, his stubbly face white with despair. He's a peasant, dressed in muddy, black lace-up boots, torn, blue overalls, a black anorak, the side seams open, padding poking out from the gaping holes.

Largo stops. I see that he's intrigued. I see that he's talking to the man, asking him what the problem is. The man looks momentarily relieved, happy at the prospect of help from concerned strangers. I know better.

I move closer to hear what he has to say. He's a peasant, lives just outside Chizik village on a collective farm. Helps look after the pigs. Been saving his money for years, finally got enough to buy a DVDpod for his wife and kids. Arrived in Bandon two hours ago, went to the electrical store round the corner, it'd been recommended and he'd checked out the prices. He'd spent all his dollap there, nothing left except the return half of his ticket. The DVDpod was heavy, bulky, and a uniformed man in the store had offered to carry the goods to the peety. As they approached the terminus, the man in the uniform had asked for the peasant's pid, travel permit and ticket, saying he'd run ahead, scan his papers, sort out the luggage storage and seat for him. The peasant was grateful, thanked him as he passed over his documents. The man had smiled. *All part of the service, Sir,* then disappeared into the crowd.

It was a scam, of course. The peasant had spent an hour walking back and forth among the peetys, unwilling to accept the worst. Now here he was, no DVDpod, but also no personal identification document, no ticket, no permit, no dollap. Truly fucked.

Not only that, but, seeing the evil glint in Largos eye, I realise that things are about to get a whole lot worse for the peasant. Largo's noted that the man's a Chiziker, and in his eyes, that can't go unpunished. I see him nod to Zillyen and Bammo and Sayler, hear him tell the peasant that he can help him get another ticket, that he should come with them round the corner, tells him not to worry, puts his arm around his shoulders. A verse of poetry pops into my head:

"Will you walk into my parlour?" said the spider to the fly,
"Tis the prettiest little parlour that ever you did spy;
The way into my parlour is up a winding stair,
And I've a many curious things to shew when you are there."
"Oh no, no," said the little fly, "to ask me is in vain,
For who goes up your winding stair can ne'er come down again."

The lads are leading the man back towards the alleyway where Bammo's just *HIIIPPO* tagged. It's quiet, I guess. Perfect for what Largo has in mind. They pass two streetkids, four or five years old, sitting on the curb, their heads buried in plastic bags, sniffing

138

thickead. Bammo makes to kick one of them, but with the sixth sense that comes with living rough, the boy arches his body, the kick misses, and the two lads are up and running, bags held protectively to their chests.

I've told Largo that I need the toilet, will meet them back here, but in reality I can't face watching the beating, much less taking part in it. God knows, I'm no Chizik-lover, but I feel a wave of weariness. Too much shitface, maybe. Too much draw. Too many fogs. Rain says he'll get some shitface. I think he doesn't fancy what's coming either. I remember that I've still got a fog in my pocket, and as much for something to do, I take it out and swallow it dry.

Hey, man. Need any more of that? Need anything at all? I whip round, see that I'm being watched. He's a mean-looking bloke, weasel face, greasy brown hair centre-parted, thin lips, sharp nose. He's smiling at me knowingly. He's seen me necking the pill. I say nothing, looking him over. I register his lasertat, an *XXX*, on his neck. It's the symbol of the Pig klan, a large Bandon crew, not to be messed with.

Where you from, Blud? he asks. I tell him. *You lads are cool. Well known fact, the Hiiippos from Kroyden are the hardest village klan. I'd be honoured to do some business with you.*

I know he's bullshitting, say nothing.

So what can I do you for, Blud? Need any more fog? I got some wicked huggers, zip, flash? What about freeze? The freeze I've got's the bomb, man.

I shake my head, tell him we've got it sorted. He tries another tack.

What about a little protection, Blud? I hear you and the Eagles aren't exactly busom buddies. Got some sweet weaponry you might be interested in, sawn-offs, automatics, you name it.

I feel a hand on my back. Largo and the lads are back. I notice that Bammo's got blood on his yellow tee-shirt, that Largo's white trainers are also stained. Sayler's eyes are bright with excitement.

Who's your mate, Payday? says Largo. I tell him he's hussling drugs, that's he's now offering weapons. The pig stands a few yards away, watching and waiting, the same smile on his face.

Largo seems interested in the guns, asks him a few questions. We're all aware we need to get to the tatstore for Sayler's Hiiippo lasertat, that we're running late. Largo sets up a meeting for the afternoon, somewhere the other side of Greenpark, repeats the address several times. We head off for the tatstore. After a few steps, Rain stops, says he's forgotten to get the shitface, that he'll catch us up. When I next look round, fifty yards on, I see that's he's returned to the pig, is talking to him. I watch them turn and walk off the other way.

On the way, the lads describe to each other the beating they gave the peasant. They're laughing, miming the kicks and blows, mimicking the peasant's squeals. I listen but don't listen. I'm wondering whether an upsu has picked up the incident, imagine a network of computers sending footage of the attack somewhere, other computers trawling for identification, searching travel permit databases, matching pids with photos, sending arrest warrants, our futures being settled as we walk and laugh and shove each other, Hiiippos on the make, Hiiippos together, Hiiippos live and direct from Bandon.

At the tatstore, Largo and Zillyen take Sayler inside. Bammo's disappeared with his laserpen to *HIIIPPO* tag. I'm left on my own. I roll up a burn, light it. Across from the tatstore is a bar. I cross the road, go in. I order a bottle, sit on a stool at the counter, smoke and drink. I've never done this before, never cut myself off from the others on a Bandon run, always stayed tight, back-watching, solid.

After a second bottle, I get bored. I pay, leave the bar, walk aimlessly down the street. It's a crummy part of town, cash converters, shitface stores, boarded-up pound stores, bars. Further up I pass a second-hand bookshop. Outside the owner's carried out a bookshelf full of books, their covers a mixture of the garish, the sombre, the faded, the tattered. I push open the lemonyellow door, hear a tinkling bell announcing my entrance. A greying, plump woman in an olive green dress and floral apron comes out from the back, wiping her hands on the apron.

Can I help you, young man? she says. I can feel her eyeing me up, feel the hesitation, mistrust. I smile.

Yes, I'm looking for a poem, I say. I didn't know I was going to say that until I opened my mouth, hadn't really thought why I had come into this shop. I recite the first few lines, the ones still fresh in my mind.

Oh, yes, that's 'The Spider and the Fly' by Mary Howitt, she says. *I'm sure we've got it as part of an anthology. Let me see...* She disappears under the counter, searches, tries a few shelves, finally utters a cry of triumph. *Here it is.* I take the book, a thin paperback with a torn, dark cover, find the page in the index, locate the poem. Satisfied, I ask her how much it is. She names a pitiful amount, the same price as a bottle of cheap shitface. I pay and leave, thrusting the paperback into my jacket pocket.

As I walk back up the street, I see Largo and the lads leaving the tatstore. Sayler's looking triumphant. As I meet up with them, I hear sirens from the end of the street. Bammo turns the corner, running at full speed, laserpen still in hand.

Move yer arses, lads he shouts. *Two arus on my tail! Leg it!* We're sharp, us Hiiippos, used to thinking fast. By the time he's shouted out the warning, we're on our toes, heading for the park at the end of the street. It's Bandon's biggest green space, it'll be easy to hide out from the coppers there. By the time the first aru has turned the corner, we're past the last shop, heading through the park gates, fanning out in the park, shouting instructions to each other about where and when to meet up. Now it's every Hiiippo for himself. If you get nicked, you stay stum, sweat it out, take the heat. The pids we all carry are false, so whoever gets caught is looking at a spell in the jsu.

I'm a great believer that attack's the best form of defence, that the winner's usually the one with the biggest balls. Inside the park, the lads scatter. I notice a park bench yards from the park entrance. I slow down, saunter over, park myself down, pull out my book of poems. By the time I find the spider poem, the aru's arrived at the park gates, siren blaring. The vehicle slams to a halt, four coppers jump out, all balaclavas and jackboots. They're carrying machine pistols. They run through the gates. Three of them split up, run off in different directions. The fourth runs up to me. I'm busy pretending to read, but I hear his footsteps, look up and see him towering above me.

Hey, kid. What you doing? I show him my book. *Got any ID?* he asks. I take out my pid nice and easy, praying he won't run it

141

through the system. As he inspects it, I give him some spiel about being a student at the University, a literature student, that I've just bought the book from the bookstore up the road, that we can go check if he doesn't believe me. He eyes me with suspicion, for a moment I think he doesn't believe me, will run the pid and I'll be stitched up like a kipper. But instead he asks me to empty my pockets. I congratulate myself for not taking a knife with me from home, for leaving behind my laserpen and for necking that last fog. Eventually he nods, hands me back the pid and tells me to have a good day. I wish him the same, stand up casually, head calmly for the gate, for safety. Nice one, I think.

We're back in Denzil's room, rolling burn and tootin zip. It's half eleven, nearly midnight, Saturday night. Den's mum's upstairs, long since headfucked with fog and drink. The rest of us are back, safe and sound, stocked up on gear, leary and buzzing with the rush of our Bandon trip. In the end we all met up as agreed, back at the alley near the peety terminus. Largo had gone off for his meet with the pig, Togs and Denzil had returned with a blue holdall stuffed with gear. Bammo continued to HIIIPPO tag wherever we passed like a tomcat spraying its stink, marking its turf. Sayler kept lifting his trouser leg surreptitiously, to glance at his lasertat. Zillyen bought shitface and we sat on the kerb sipping and smoking burn. Eventually, just as we were leaving for the peety stop, Rain bowled up, stumbling and pale-faced. I guessed he'd been doing cloud all day.

Alright, Payday, he mumbled. His pupils were like pinpricks, he looked sweaty, pasty. He stumbled, nearly fell. I put my arm around him, took hold of his shoulders, guided him to the peety. He seemed to be asleep on his feet. By the time Largo reappeared, out-of-breath and clearly agitated, himself holding another blue holdall I hadn't seen before, Rain needed carrying onto the peety.

Back at Den's, it's same old, same old. The room's airless, foggy with smoke, stale with old feet. The usual empty bottles and tins, ashtrays, spilled drinks, sticky puddles, snack wrappers and rolling papers. The lads are full of tales of bravado, seems they all had near escapes from the aru coppers, and they're still re-running the peasant beating. Largo's story, as always, is the tallest. Says he met up with the pig, was shown a whole arsenal of weapons, everything from small calibre pistols to automatic assault rifles, heavy-duty stuff. We've never had any guns, never used them. Neither have the Eagles. It's not exactly an unwritten law, more just never dawned on any of us to take it that step further. Anyway, Largo tells us he's upstairs in a second-floor room, checking out the guns. The pig's mobe goes off and he leaves the room to take the call. Largo picks up a machine pistol, a couple of full magazines, grabs a holdall the pig's left lying around, stuffs the gun and magazines into the bag and gets out through the window, down onto the fire escape, away back to the peety terminal. Then he picks up the holdall and makes a show of unzipping it. With a showbiz *tada!* He produces the weapon, black and sleek and oily, runs his hand along the short barrel, holds it up for us all to see. The lads cheer, their eyes lighting up. It seems we've moved into a different league, big boys league.

I look around, counting off the lads. I notice that Rain's not here, realise I haven't seen him for an hour or more, maybe two, since he disappeared off to the bog. I need a piss, myself, so I get up, leave the lads passing around the weapon, admiring it, animated voices planning visits to Chizik to demonstrate our new hardware.

The landing's dark, the bulb's been dead for weeks and nobody's replaced it. Downstairs I pass through the kitchen, all piled up plates of grease and spill-over refuse sacks. At the toilet door I pause, tune in for sounds, wonder whether Rain's still there. I try the door handle, remember that the lock's been broken ever since I can remember.

Slowly I open the door. The light's on, but it's low wattage and the windowless room is dim, so it takes a few seconds to take in the scene. Rain's on the floor, head propped up against the back wall, body wedged between the side wall and the toilet bowl. It's like he's been sitting on the bog, then slipped down on the floor to the side. His eyes are open, and my first reaction is to call out. Then I realise there's something very wrong. The eyes are blank and I see that one arm's bare, the sleeve rolled up. There's a needle sticking out of the arm. Through the gloom, I see that there's a lighter on the floor and a spoon. I bend down, put a hand out, feel his face. It's cold. I pull him out from his wedged position, so he's lying flat on the floor. I feel at

143

the side of his neck for a pulse, listen at his chest for a heartbeat, put my cheek to his mouth to test for breathing, searching in vain for any sign of life. His face is bluish. He's cold, gone.

Rain, I whisper, shaking him hopelessly. *Hey, Cuz, what you doing? Don't you remember, man, the first Hiiippo rule. No freeze. No slammin. No fucking needles.* I slide down next to him. I'm angry, so angry with him, the fuckup, the bastard, the stupid fucker. Then punch him on the arm, on the chest, feeble punches 'cause all the strength's gone from me. I'm so angry, I try to think straight but my mind's all flashes and bangs. I picture Rain walking off with the pig, deep in conversation, imagine what happened next, scoring the freeze, the spikes, the pig counting out Rain's dollap, passing over the bag of gear. I have an urge to go upstairs, grab Largo's gun, jump on the next peety and find the pig fucker, give him one in the eye from Rain.

But all of a sudden the anger's gone and I just feel sad, too fucking sad. I think of Rain's mum, his big sister, Marie. And from there I'm thinking of my own family. They'll be tucked up in the house now, I think. Dad'll be asleep, a hard day in the fields and another one to come tomorrow. Mum'll have done the day shift, will be knackered too. Maybe Zak'll be up, maybe Beth and Barj too, watching the DVDpod. I feel a need to get back, to jack it all in, find them, make sure they're all safe.

I'm sitting on the floor next to cold Rain. Upstairs, Den's mum's mashed to fuck in her bedroom. The boys are in Den's room, the Hiiippos, planning smart scams and klan fights and gear deals. And I've had enough. I pick myself up, stand over Rain's body, wondering what to do. It's like a crossroads.

I could bend down again, go through his pockets, fish out a handful of cloud, pop three or four, then go upstairs, drink as much shitface as I can hold down, break the news to the boys. We'll hold a wake, stay up all night, drinking and doing gear, telling stories about Rain. About Hiiippos. Then tomorrow, we'll go back to Bandon, sort out travel permits one way or another, get on a peety by hook or by crook. We'll trawl the streets for the pig, find him, shoot the fucker dead. Dead like Rain.

Or I could turn away from Rain without looking at him, leave the bathroom, the kitchen, the house, start walking back

144

towards Mum and Dad's. Outside it's raining, not heavily, just light and fine. I'd walk home through the rain. In my pocket I'll feel the book of poems. I'll realise that I didn't buy it for myself, that it's not for me. It's Dad's book, not mine.

Connections

by Rosalie Warren

"I've done it, Todd. I've got the connections formula. We can become immortal, any time we like."

Professor Jerome Todd, my PhD supervisor, looked up from his giant art pad as I appeared at his office door. We use these enormous pads for our calculations so we can fit a whole long expression on one line. Makes it easier to check you haven't gone wrong. Our colleagues laugh at us – or they did, until we made our breakthrough.

Todd didn't believe me, of course. He never believes anything I do, not until he's checked it ninety times. To be honest, I don't think he quite understands the new way of viewing time. He's stuck in the past, where time was a dimension, like space. That's what got in the way of unifying quantum theory and gravity.

I keep trying to tell him – time is time, it's not space. Time is the order that things happen. Stop seeing it as space, all that crap about moving around in it, and we'll start making progress. But his brain is stuck where it was thirty years ago, when he made his own great discovery.

He gave me one of his soppy looks, because he fancies me like hell.

"Let me see, Grem," he said, grabbing my pad and propping it up against his computer screen, where he was checking his share prices. Not a wealthy man, our Todd, but he has a few minor investments and he's hoping they'll shoot up in value, hit the big time, allow him to retire. His heart's gone out of the Physics game – he's had his day and he knows it.

I pointed to the lines I'd scrawled at the bottom, the ones that showed how to establish the connections, not just in theory but in practice – how to get from our world into an alternative universe.

"The key to it all is the chronons," I pointed out, in case he hadn't noticed.

Chronons, should it have escaped your attention, were discovered a few months ago by some experimental physicists in the US. A meteorite landed in Alaska, and they couldn't identify the radiation it gave off. In the end, they found it was made up of a previously unknown particle they decided to call the chronon. You can think of chronons as tiny units of time, if you want to. Or units of causality – that's a better way of putting it. They make up other things as well – matter, energy, the works. It didn't take us long to establish that the chronon is the basic building block for everything. You, me, Todd, the distant galaxies, dark matter, energy, radiation – we're all made up of chronons. They're a hell of a lot more basic than atoms, electrons or even quarks.

But it was yours truly, Grem Lerner, who got out his art pad and worked out that if we treat these little guys with respect they can open up the door for us into alternative possible worlds.

Todd was frowning, his brow deeply furrowed, as they say. He's not a bad-looking guy for his age. Kind of wish I'd met him when he was younger. That we'd been nearer the same age, I mean.

"You have to die, of course," I explained. "It's at the point of death that you get to transfer from our world into another one. One in which you're not dead. That's where the immortality comes in. Every time you die in one world, you switch to another."

"I don't quite understand."

I pointed to the last bit of my scrawl. "See, the code? Alongside a source of chronons, you need a programmed chip. When the chip senses brain death, the program runs. It sends out a signal that finds a world where you're still alive. Then your consciousness gets transferred to that new world and you go on living."

"It won't work," he said.

"Only one way to find out." I hoisted myself onto his desk, swinging my legs. Sensed him looking at me. I feel mean, sometimes, not being in love with Todd. But I didn't ask him to fall in love with me. It's one reason I'm keen to get into another world.

It was exciting, that first year of my PhD, when our minds sparked each other off, day after day, and he told me I was brilliant. I suppose I was flattered. Anyway, we got together and the sex wasn't bad at all.

Now he looked alarmed, his eyebrows way up there in his fluffy white fringe. 'You don't mean you're going to try it out yourself? You'd have to die to test it.'

"I'm happy to take the risk." I meant it. It beats a trip into space, anything else I can think of.

His face brightened up. "I suppose we could always test it on animals."

"I'm against animal testing. The only living thing I'm prepared to subject to this test is myself."

"Grem, you're crazy. You haven't thought it through. If this doesn't work – and I don't think it will – you lose everything. Your life. Your career. There could be a Nobel prize in this for you, somewhere down the line. If the theory stands up, it's the biggest thing since general relativity."

"I know that."

"And you're prepared to abandon it all?"

"It's the only way to test it."

Todd thought of something else. "Even if it works, how will we know? I mean, *you* won't know. You'll be in your new world – you won't remember the old one. And you won't be able to contact me, to let me know you've got there."

"You've missed a bit. Four lines up from the bottom. Communication is possible, in certain circumstances, between worlds. It works by a process like interference. You know, the old light beams – Young's slits. As long as I take the code with me, I can let you know what's happened."

Todd shook his head. "You won't remember to. In your new world, you won't know you have to contact me."

"*I* won't remember, but the program will. You'll get a signal. I'll set things up before I go. Once you get the message, you'll have proof that it's worked. You can write up the papers yourself, get all the fame."

He'll like that, will our Todd. A long time since he's had much in the way of academic acclaim. And it's something that means a lot to him.

"Grem, this business about finding a world where you're still alive. It's only one of the solutions to the equation. There are others, where all kinds of unpredictable things can happen."

I felt a surge of excitement when he said that. It's a magic feeling, believe me. Move over, all you great explorers. Scott of the Antarctic and Neil Armstrong never did anything like this.

It pays to have mates in other departments; I discovered this early on in my PhD. All those nights at the pub were worth it. All that suffering turned out useful in the end…

Fortunately, the university has a source of chronons – the unimaginatively named transuranic element chrononium, the one that turned up on the meteorite. Chrononium-340, it's called, to distinguish it from its less exciting relations, created in the particle accelerator at CERN.

A couple of pints was all it took to bribe the technician, Dean, to give me a sample. Then it's over to Computer Science to see Sandy, who's been a mate since my first day here. Sandy can churn out Java code like there's no tomorrow and it usually does what she wants. I soon had my chip in hand, all ready for my brain implant. Ben's job – he's a trainee surgeon and could do with the practice. That's the bit that scares me; Ben is capable of cocking things up and I could become a vegetable. But it's a risk I have to take.

My calculations suggest that violent death is a good idea, to make sure that the chip gets the message from my brain stem. Something slower, a gradual departure, might not work. So the other catch is, I'll have to shoot myself. That would be somewhat shit-inducing, if I didn't trust my theory. Just as well I do. Let's say I trust it 90%. Well, my Grandad flew in bomber planes in WW2 and survived. If he can do that, I think I can take a 10% risk with my life.

Can't help thinking about my father and mother. They'll be pretty upset to lose me, I know that. But it's a comfort to know that there's a zillion other worlds where I won't be dead – where I'll do things like discover a cure for cancer or solve global warming, and they'll be proud of me. In a few of them I'll probably never have left home at all, or I'll phone every day and visit with chocolates for my mum.

We've confirmed that these alternative worlds aren't just possibilities – they actually exist. I really do have a zillion other mothers, or at least, a zillion other versions of me do.

I keep reminding Todd, too, that there are a trigillion worlds where, instead of shooting myself in the mouth, I'll be in his office, the door locked, ripping off his jeans.

"That's no good," he says, after his eyes have lit up for a second. "There might be all those other Todds somewhere, but they're not me.'

"They're a lot like you. Some of them."

"Of course, but I'm not connected to them, am I? I can't share their feelings."

"You just have to believe. Have faith, as they used to tell us in Sunday School."

"It's not a question of faith – it's a question of experience." He's struck by an idea. "Grem – let me come with you!"

I shake my head. "Sorry, Todd. There's no way of doing it – no way to make sure we go to the same world. Your history is different to mine. If we were twins, maybe it would work. As it is, there's no chance."

"Let me try. I'll take the risk."

He's all tense; I can feel the heat coming off him. I can smell his lust, all mixed up with fear. He loves me, that guy. If I ever doubted it, I know it now. He's willing to give up all the kudos of this discovery to go with me to another universe.

I'm touched, but I shake my head again. Even if there was a way, I wouldn't let him. This is my adventure and I want to do it on my own.

*

I've got my gun, my chip's implanted, my chrononium's buzzing, my code's ready to run.

Todd just had a last go at me. He's eaten up with guilt, blaming himself for the whole thing. Says his life's work's been a mistake. I tell him he's wrong – his early work ploughed up the ground for this discovery. He says he wishes he'd never done it. Should have gone into medicine like his father wanted. Then he starts saying he's been unprofessional towards me, abusing my trust as a student, all that stuff. Bollocks, I tell him, but he's not listening. I'm worried he'll pick up the gun after I've used it and shoot himself.

I've made sure there's only one bullet in there, just in case.

*

150

Should never have gone drinking with my mates last night. Woke up a few minutes ago, swimming in treacle. I feel soft and out of condition – as though I gained a stone while I slept.

It's two-thirty and I've got a genetics lecture at three. Then there's that talk at four by the guy from Physics, what's his name – Professor Todd? They say he's a good speaker. He's giving talks to all the second years – seems he's made some kind of big discovery – best thing since Einstein. I don't understand all that stuff myself, being a biologist, but he's been in Scientific American and New Scientist, as well as in the daily papers and on TV. Even the tabloids have picked it up. It's blasted the riots out of the headlines, all the demonstrations against Mo Mowlam's decision not to bomb Iraq.

It sounds pretty cool, Professor Todd's work on alternative realities. My mate Ben was telling me about it last night, but I didn't take in the details.

Should be more interesting than Professor Lemming droning on about DNA, anyway.

*

Well. Nice guy, Professor Todd. Todd, he told me to call him. His friends all call him that. I suppose we have to be on intimate terms, after what we did, but it still feels awkward.

I stayed behind after the talk to ask some questions. I don't fully understand what happened, but what he said sort of woke me up, got my brain going. Haven't felt like that since back at school. Primary Four with Mr Brand. That sense of excitement, of your brain being sharp enough to get inside an idea, slice it up, look at it from a new angle. Mr Brand telling me I had a fine young mind, that I should go into science.

Not at all bad looking, isn't Todd, for a guy his age. He's probably fitter than me. I must start going to the gym again.

I had so many questions about his alternative worlds that he suggested we went for a drink, after everyone else had gone. Said it was great to see a biologist take such an interest. Started talking about the ethical implications of his research. You see, if it works it'll provide a kind of immortality. He's worried about young Sandy, his assistant. She says the only way to test this theory is for someone to die, to find out whether they can get themselves into another world. She's prepared to do it. He's not so keen to let her.

Not that he can stop her. She knows what to do. I don't understand it properly but it involves a computer program and some stuff called chrononium that they've just synthesised at MIT.

Anyway, Todd and me. He's decided he wants to call me Grem instead of Greg. I let slip it had been my nickname for a while at school, when we used to play Gremlins, and he liked it. I like it, too. It takes me back.

After the pub I went home with him. I'd never got round to telling him I was gay, but he seemed to pick up on it, somehow.

He reminds me a lot of Mr Brand, my old teacher. So sad that guy was killed, halfway through Primary 4. Set me back a whole year. I was grief-stricken. I suppose he was my first love, though I didn't see it that way at the time.

It's early to say, I know, but I have a feeling that meeting Todd could be a turning point for me. As I mentioned, my brain feels sharper, my head clear. Perhaps I'll manage a 2:1 this year, make my Dad proud of me.

I sense that Todd and I will stick together, go for the long haul, as they say. I hope so. He seems like a reliable guy, not someone who'll tire of me and toss me aside. My mother would be glad I've met a nice bloke. She's grinning at me there in her photo by my bed. It's five years now since she died of cancer.

An Invisible Rose

by Catherine Edmunds

"No Rachel, I think you should stay on a bit longer. This imminent 'death' situation gives you certain advantages, after all," said Kevin, screwing up his eyes in an attempt to look taller.

"Advantages? What do you mean?"

Rachel wondered how anyone approaching death, and therefore nearly transparent, could possibly have any advantage over the opaques who made up the majority of the office staff. People walked through her – literally. Kevin must have other reasons for wanting her to work out her notice.

He looked sheepish. "You know – access. Shortcuts. That sort of thing."

Rachel was unconvinced and examined her fingernails closely. The holograms needed renewing. She'd make an appointment tomorrow.

"Well, how about a raise?" asked Kevin, brightly. "Bonus at he end of the month?"

"Ooh-err. Bribery and corruption, Kev."

"No – good business sense. I *need* you, Rachel… to file things." He gave a nervous cough and looked away.

She was fond of Kevin, but the emphasis on 'need' and the carefully calculated pause confirmed her fears of a belated office romance developing if she stayed on. The raise, on the other hand, was tempting. Transition classes were expensive and she didn't know how long her savings would last. What if she didn't pass her exams the first time? She might need the additional income to pay for re-sits.

Kevin shuffled a pile of plasma records on Rachel's desk and patted her head, looking disconcerted when his hand fell straight through her scalp.

"Urrgh," he muttered, turning away blushing.

"Sorry Kev, you were saying?"

"Rachel, please, you're the only one capable of separating the particles for complete transmutation. Don't make me train up a new plassiferian – not at this late stage, with all those jubels breathing down my neck."

"Hmm..."

"Pretty please?"

"Oh, all right." Rachel had no idea what he'd just said, but didn't like to see him squirm. "I'll stay for the time being."

"Good-good. Excellent."

Kevin spun round and marched away, tripping over a waste-plasma bin. Rachel watched the mechanised safety rope swing into action, lassoing his wrist to prevent him falling, but pulling his arm out of its socket in the process. A medic-droid dropped down from the ceiling and whacked Kevin on the shoulder, fixing the problem with startling efficiency. This was the safest office in the building. It needed to be with Kevin around.

Rachel groaned. Why, oh why had she agreed to stay in this madhouse when she could have spent the next month at home practising and revising? She didn't think the Green Professor would let her fail, but Transition was a major step, and she *had* to pass in order to move on and achieve full invisibility. Only four more classes, but they cost sixty-five thousand credits each. Damn. She needed to work, but it wouldn't be for long, and then she could bid farewell forever to clumsy Kevin and her nine-to-five job at Predilection Towers. No more conduits! No more wormhole dilution! Pure green... she couldn't wait.

She spent the rest of the afternoon teasing Kevin by walking ahead of him and passing through walls at right angles. He got upset each time he nearly concussed himself as he tried to follow her. Bloodied and fuming, he was best avoided as the day wore on.

At five o'clock that afternoon, a voice in her ear reminded Rachel it was Thursday, so she should commute to her Transition Orientation class rather than going straight home. She wondered, as she did most weeks, whether she should suggest to Kevin that he come with her. They could stop off at the Thai Object Path for a bite to eat on the way. She changed her mind when she heard a yelp from the other side of the office. The corner of an overhanging projector had caught Kevin on the forehead, leaving a small cut. The projector was anxiously playing soothing music while Kevin punched the wall in pain and fury. No. He could get his own food and find his own

154

date. She wasn't about to seduce the boss with just four weeks to go, however much she longed to give him a kiss and a cuddle to make it all better.

Half an hour later, she settled into the ovoid tilt-bus which would take her to the Transition Orientation Class and into the gorgeous green arms of her Professor. The bus driver – a fully printed up representative of the ovoid hegemony – was staring at her in the mirror. Rachel stopped reading the back of his head, and realised she was licking her transparent lips, presumably leaving a glistening outline on her otherwise invisible mouth. Maybe that looked a bit weird. She wasn't sure, so crossed her legs and tried to look sophisticated, failing when one leg sank through the other. She giggled when it tickled, but stopped when it occurred to her that she'd probably slip through the Professor's gorgeous green arms in just the same way. Not that the Professor would ever hold her, anyway – such ideas were to be put behind her forever. Training for Transition into the Realm of Extended Fractal Anthropomorphology was not to be taken lightly, as the Prof was always reminding the class. This was no time to be fantasising about fading physicality. The written exam was next week, and the practical just a fortnight later. Then training would be complete and she could relax and think seriously about the possibilities of a meld. A pure green mutual meld. Mmm... much better than making out with a clumsy fool from the office.

The Realm was still something of a mystery, even at this late stage. Like everyone else, she'd always assumed that it was a physical place, located in the Moebius Tower that curled around the Fractal City. It followed that training would comprise the advanced chaos theory necessary to enter the City, plus some odds and ends regarding the social niceties of loop phragmology. To her surprise, there was nothing technical about the training at all, other than an introduction to softening around the edges. When she'd queried this with the Professor, he'd murmured: "Metaphysics!" and smiled, showing crystalline teeth filed to multiple points. Physics she understood. Teeth she understood. Metaphysics was an arcane concept she'd had to look up.

She'd first learnt about the Realm three hundred years ago, when she'd still been a fully carbon-based life form (apart from the usual prosthetics). The Professor had been her creative writing tutor at the time. He'd let slip to his class that his own fractured poetry was based soundly in fact, and was not fiction as they'd all assumed. The Mandelbrotian dreamscape he painted with words really existed. Rachel hadn't believed him, deeming it yet another attempt by the pervy Prof to appear attractive to the young students despite his greenish tinge and tendency to melt through desks, which at the time she had found revolting.

How things have changed, she mused, passing a finger through the carbon fibre seatbelt, barely disturbing its molecular structure. The digit was essentially holographic, but her remaining organic neural net insisted at times that it was real, hence the slight disturbance. That was why she and the others needed the course, why she desperately needed to improve her poetry for the written paper, and why she still had to work. Fading had been a part of everyone's existence since the metabolic wars of the late twenty-third century, but once your body and mechanisations had been sloughed off and you were fully transparent (a process still, nostalgically, referred to as 'death') there was little point in remaining in the Realm of the Real. Fractal Anthropomorphology beckoned, along with the mouth-wateringly green Professor.

Kevin was beige in comparison, with a voice like a bagpipe drone. No, that was unfair. He was colourful enough, positively psychedelic at times, but decades away from being ready for training. Despite this, he'd opted to take the classes. Rachel suspected it was in order to be close to her in these last few weeks before she made the Transition. That was okay. She couldn't help liking the silly fool, but the contest for her heart between Kevin and the Green Professor had been won long ago, when she'd first learnt to see the colours between the pixels.

The Professor was a real poet and his green aura was the colour of sunlight on Cornish sea-water. Gradually it had dawned on her how much she wanted to swim through that water. Three hundred years of dreaming had passed, three centuries of waiting, of wishing that she could fade, just a little. And then, just six months ago it had started. 'Death' had beckoned and she'd practised melting at every available opportunity. She was good at it now.

Kevin, on the other hand, was still resolutely opaque, poor dear. He'd made the transition to cyborg easily enough, but she doubted if he would get any further. Not with writing like that.

Rachel hopped off the bus one stop early in order to avoid bumping into Kevin (or floating through him, she thought with a shiver of desire, quickly stifled). The holo-daffs beside the travelator were nodding on flexi-stems and reciting Wordsworth on request. Now *there* was a real poet. Kevin, on the other hand, was not. She spotted him a hundred yards ahead, wearing a long black cloak. Oh no – she knew what that meant.

She was right. 'Gothick' was his attempted style that night, but it was a mistake. He was too squeamish to eat horror and was soon choking on the ectoplasm that the rest of the trainees absorbed unthinkingly. During his reading – an epic vampiric tale of unimaginable ghastliness – his prosthetic fangs fell out, plip kerpling, onto the floor. Rachel imagined a passing skeleton tripping, falling, and shattering. Being a non-poet, and probably an ex-Boy Scout, Kevin would no doubt have mechanisms in place for any such eventuality. There would be a highly efficient droid at his beck and call, with the ability to deal with all situations, from prising stones out of robo-horses' hooves to repairing shattered skeletons. Or better still, he would have a team of nanobots in his pocket, ready to be released when he turned off the zips' electro-magnetic field. They would swarm onto the floor and busy themselves reconstructing the skeleton. There would be one maverick amongst them, so that once they'd finished a bone would be left over, just a small one; but nobody would know where it was supposed to go. She chuckled at the thought, and imagined all the trainees trying to work out the problem – a bit like too many cooks trying to complete a fifty thousand word jigsaw whilst making choux pastry. Hopeless.

As it turned out, Rachel was wrong. Not about the nanobots; but about Kevin having been a Boy Scout. She learned this shortly after the fang recital when the whole class adjourned to the 'Cock and Bull' for practice in drinking without tell-tale leakage. She downed more reconstructed Bishops Finger than is decent, while Kevin sipped orange juice and watched her with increasing nervousness. After an hour of talking about nothing remotely interesting he summoned up the courage to ask her back to his elongated pentagonal cupola for coffee. She was sufficiently intrigued to agree. Nobody, as far as she knew, had ever seen the inside of Kevin's cupola.

She lurched out of the pub, and with Kevin's support, managed to fall into a sky-cab that whooshed them into the picture postcard cupola on the edge of New Senlac five giggling minutes later. Leaning against a replica giant polyp (one of seven, recently erected by the hydra re-enactment society) she watched entranced as he revved up his home-grown solar powered anti-grav pads to warm the place up, and then switched on his sticky lamp.

He looked serious and happy and nearly tall. She would have fallen in love there and then, had she not remembered his poetry in the nick of time.

He was short again, despite his winning smile.

"Just popping the kettle on – won't be two ticks, Rachel – you'll be okay?"

She hiccupped in reply before staggering over to the mantelpiece to examine a collection of dried toadstools and a shiny tortoise trophy. There was a clattering from the kitchen, and she turned to see Kevin surreptitiously rattling his sabre in a very non-poetical way. He put it away quickly when he realised she'd noticed. Rachel couldn't decide whether to be amused and flattered, or disgusted. She wasn't even sure she'd seen what she thought she'd seen, and knew she was too drunk to come to a sensible decision, so said the first thing that came into her head.

"Err... what was all that about equi – equi – equilibria and the phase line again, sweetheart? I didn't quite catch the impillications. Imflipitations. Tell me again, would you pet? Strictly on a knee to node basis, of course. *(hic)*"

That wasn't fair. He hadn't told her in the first place, and now he looked upset. Tipping the water out of the kettle and down the sink, he muttered something she didn't catch about 'time marching on' and 'sestinas to differentiate'.

Poor Kevin. How he hated being shown up. She could take a hint, however, whatever her state of inebriation, so decided to make herself scarce. On the way out, she instructed a dust pan and brush to tidy up the drips from the sticky lamp, though in retrospect, an auto-mop might have been more appropriate.

The next day at work, Kevin ignored Rachel to such an extent that she wondered at first if she'd inadvertently achieved full invisibility three weeks too early. Poor Kevin. He must be so embarrassed. Nothing worse than being the boss, making a pass at an employee who gives every appearance of liking you, who teases and has fun with you, who actively seeks out your company, who goes for drinks with you, who leaps at the chance to go back to your cupola with you... and who then takes the mickey. Cruel, cruel world. Rachel wondered if he would even bother to turn up for the next class.

Thursday evening arrived and there he was in his usual place. That was interesting. Pleasing too. Flattering. Maybe he'd forgiven her. Maybe he led such a dull life that he didn't have anything else to do on a Thursday night.

The Green Professor came in, and all thoughts of Kevin fled. This was what she wanted. Kevin was fun, but he was normal and naïve, enamel toothed and besotted. Rachel wanted more. She wanted green, wafting, translucent, ancient, wise, ugly-beautiful, professorially gorgeous... green.

The Professor was going to show the candidates his latest piece this week; the one that would draw them right to the brink of the final mysteries of the Realm of Extended Anthropomorphology. There would be no more of Kevin's purple clad vampires, no more dancing skeletons, no more ectoplasm seeping into words and dissolving them before they had a chance to make any sense.

The Professor was almost turquoise this week with anticipation. He floated to an upright position, commanding silence by his wavering edges, and then sang his fractals into Rachel's soul: he dared sing her face, her nose, mouth, chin, her hair changing colour from pewter to bronze to silver to gold, swimming wild waters to windswept tors and beyond.

Kevin's hair was brown. He used too much gel. He even gelled his eyebrows, so that they always looked wet; always glistened in the dim glow of the ambient lighting of the Orientation Institute. To be fair, they looked quite good by the light of his sticky lamp, but then he'd designed the thing himself, so of course it would show him to his best advantage.

Enough of Kevin. Tonight Rachel would quench her thirst on her real poet; drink stupidity and forget darkness by the light of this carafe, this apple, this red bottle tankard, this reflection that shattered a million fish. She had passed through reflections and beyond. The Green Professor would teach her to drown.

Kevin frowned. He had an empath's way of intercepting things, whether they were recitations, Chinese whispers or telepathic thought beams. He looked nervous and pretended to adjust his watch, which Rachel knew was silly because despite being an antique it was still perfectly capable of receiving the radio signal from Nuovo Rugbi and was accurate to within one second every ten million years. He gazed round the room and whistled silently, wiped his hands on his hair, looking surprised when it presumably felt more like cardboard than silk.

Rachel had sprayed herself with Implosion. Kevin exuded a distinct aroma of Leopard. That should have had them leaping onto each other and tearing away every last scrap of plexi-silk, according to the ad-men. Rachel waited patiently for Kevin to jump up and proffer the requisite ten thousand bouquets of virtual rosa gallica versicolour, and wondered if he in turn was waiting for her to yodel and bare her breasts.

The Green Professor gave them both a withering look and Rachel returned her attention to her poet, her Instructor, her Master. Her lover? If not in this realm, then perhaps…

They would burn incense instead of mountains tonight. No turning back; they would slip underwater (she liked not breathing, she wanted total asphyxiation. No she didn't. Yes she did.). She never saw bronze after all – just the casting of shadows and a tortoise tied safely in soft focus pewter, forever unique and himself. Tortoise? Where did that come from? Kevin, damn him. He was trying so hard to intercept, he was actually succeeding. There was an image in Rachel's mind of a hard hat; a shell – bright orange.

"Tortoises aren't orange!" she blurted out. The other trainees were startled. They were used to the Green Professor making surreal comments in the middle of recitations, but not Rachel. She received some filthy looks, which she passed on to Kevin.

The Prof hadn't even noticed. He was in full flow now. So crickets sing and stumps fall and ashes return. But still. We laugh at not breathing; not daring to breathe, at falling, sinking, jumping, flying...

Kevin failed to suppress a snort of derision to the astonishment of Rachel who suddenly missed his sticky lamp, his plip kerpling fangs and the way he tried so hard to write, but never quite managed (apart from the 500,000 word sestina series – the second of three). She wanted to try again; to return to his cupola, drink Bishops Finger, count his toadstool collection backwards and forwards, dance with his shiny tortoise trophy, and help him unsheathe his sabre whilst wearing a long black cloak and nothing else.

The Green Professor and his fractured realms were an enticing thought, but no, she wasn't ready, she wanted reality still. Was it too late? Or was there a chance to reverse the fading, to harness the remaining echoes of her organic self to be with her Boy Scout (even though he'd never been one)? She sent a whispered plea to Kevin. He was staring with concentration at a twelve legged spiderbot in the corner of the room, but she felt him become quietly radioactive. He knew. He was an expert in DIY cybernetics. Maybe he could design something. Give her some opacity. Make her real again.

The Professor turned bottle green, screwed in a crystal tooth that had come loose, and continued poeticising, but Rachel ignored him, handing him over to the tender ministrations of the other trainees, all of whom were looking smugly transparent and transparently smug.

Kevin still stared into the corner of the room, but Rachel saw his lips twitch. She wondered if he was instructing his nanobots to re-integrate the dust in the corner into a single red rose that they would place on her lap, silently and invisibly.
There was a delicate pressure. An invisible rose dropped into her lap and *didn't* sink through to the floor.

Primitive Chips

by Sarah Ann Hall

Magma rose, showered and sat down to a full English breakfast, genetically modified to be healthy – no cholesterol, the correct balance of carbohydrate and protein, added fibre. Charlie sat opposite her with a real version. She had to admit, his smelt better, although hers was guaranteed to have a fuller flavour. His tomatoes oozed and spat seeds as he cut them; hers were firm and fruity, flavoursome, but they felt synthetic in the mouth, too solid. His bacon was crispy, hers a little rubbery. It seemed that the geneticists were still unable to make fake food feel and taste natural. Even so, Magma didn't understand why Charlie insisted on eating unprocessed food.

"You know that'll kill you," she said aggressively, jealous of his easygoing, come-what-may attitude, and obviously superior breakfast. "You should look after yourself more carefully."

After a breakfast like his, Magma would have run five miles to counteract its effects. She was hot on taking care of herself. Personal responsibility was something she lived by. The fact that Charlie took his life in his hands every time he ate something and only took exercise when he felt like it, infuriated her. But the thing that annoyed her most was that Charlie had taken the decision to be un-chipped.

Routine baby chipping had started in the US in 2076, following the early twenty-first century debate about ID cards. The UK was a little more resistant but after the usual transatlantic time lag, the chipping of all UK newborns began in 2091. Parents who wanted to opt out had to apply months in advance for a dispensation, prove they were upstanding members of the community, and legally pledge they would bring up the child correctly. The Government assured the public that the odd un-chipped person would not disadvantage society - all criminals would be chipped and therefore traceable. Neither the Government, nor the public, wanted a new criminal underclass developing out of the un-chipped. It also cost to remain un-chipped, the standard disincentive to ensure compliance.

No parent with an income below the national average was allowed to apply for his or her child to remain unchipped.

In 2187 chipping was no longer an issue. Internationally, chipping of newborns was standard practice and all debate had been exhausted. The un-chipped in what was still the developing world, those who had missed out at birth, were clamouring to be chipped as adults, wanting to belong. Comparatively, in the UK and US, the un-chipped were beginning to increase in number. Referred to as Primitives by governments and the Press, they were portrayed as Luddites rebelling against progress. The Unchipped called themselves Naturals and pointed to the old arguments about control. They wanted to be truly free, not live with a token right to freedom guaranteed only by signing up.

Charlie chewed on his organic, free-range bacon rashers and looked across the table at Magma.

"Yes, well, I'd rather die happy when my body wears out than fill myself with artificial preservatives and live forever," he said when he'd swallowed his mouthful.

"No one lives forever. Besides my food is not full of preservatives."

"Maybe not, but what about your screen this afternoon? Are you telling me that you won't take anything offered to you, however innocuous it may seem to be?"

Magma frowned. She'd never thought about it before, her previous screens had always been clear. She'd only ever been offered pep-up pills and never questioned what might be in them. She took a sip of her filtered, decaffeinated coffee. Charlie raised a knowing eyebrow to her silence.

At times like these, Magma hated her magnanimous streak. She wondered why she had ever agreed to allow a Primitive to live with her. Had it been pride, or the thought she might be able to change him? She'd given up that idea after six days: Charlie was entrenched, brainwashed. The more conversations they had about the pros and cons of chipping, the more arguments they had that ended with Magma questioning her own reasoning. She didn't like that; it felt unsafe.

She had responded to an advert from the local university. Researchers had asked for volunteers to participate in a six-month project that was designed as a natural experiment to measure and observe Primitive and Chipped interactions. They still had two months to go and Magma thought briefly about contacting the university to say she'd had enough.

Charlie was a chip-removal, which made it all the more difficult for Magma to understand him. She considered the Unchipped unlucky, but chip-removals were reckless. Charlie had been chipped at birth, but when most teenagers went through their vegetarian stage, he had run away from home to be de-chipped. Many Primitives lived quietly within the Chipped world without causing comment. Others formed colonies outside where de-chipping was performed for all-comers without question. Criminals were fitted with a particular chip that even the de-chippers would not remove, so there was little reason for the governments to clamp down. After all, the argument behind chipping had been all about freedom – freedom to move, freedom to choose, freedom of speech. *You can do what you like, because we know where you are.*

The mainframe recognised and kept tabs on the Unchipped who lived in the Chipped world through their brainwaves. Even those in the colonies, out in the remaining pockets of countryside, were monitored. And they knew, but didn't care. Their bodies were free, their minds uncluttered, their thoughts were their own. They were truly free. Or so they reasoned. Governments stated that chips were unable to affect thought patterns and decision-making. The Naturals argued that a chip was electronic; it was programmed by a computer and could be read by a computer. Who was to say a computer couldn't feed ideas into a chip to affect the body around it, especially in those who had expressed anti-chipping thoughts?

"And what will your screen tell you?" Charlie asked as he dunked a piece of fried bread into the yolk of his egg.

"Whether or not I'm well."

"Magma," he breathed, "how can you not know you're well?"

She shook her head. "Whatever do you mean?"

"You have pain receptors, like the rest of us. You have emotions?"

164

"Yes. What of it?"

"Well, pain, mood swings, odd feelings from within. Those are what tell us whether or not we're well. No symptoms, no problems."

"How simplistic," she said superciliously.

"How natural," he responded, laying down his knife and fork.

She stared hard and wondered again whether or not to contact the university. She thought about the poor chipped people who had volunteered to live in the colonies for half the year. She wondered how they were coping surrounded by Primitives and their negativity.

"And what about my brain? How do I know if it's working properly?" she asked.

"Ah well, there most of all your behaviour would tell you, and others. People would act strangely towards you, or at least you'd think they were."

"Maybe I'm mad then. My friends seemed to think so when I said you were coming to stay."

Charlie smiled broadly. "Haven't I enriched your life?" He picked up his coffee mug; the contents were caffeinated and strong.

"Stimulants are bad for you," Magma scolded.

"So's breathing up to a point. Anyway, enough about me. How do they screen your brain function? Plug your finger into a socket and run a programme?"

Magma scowled. It was a popular misconception, promulgated by the Primitives she was sure, that screening consisted of attaching a person to a machine. It was true that chips were sited in the tip of the left index finger and also true that chips could be read by placing a fingertip on a reading plate. But a chip only held the information that had been recorded on it. Screening was a lengthy, in-depth process that had nothing to do with being chipped. The Chipped were screened because they were responsible. They wanted to know about themselves and be prepared for the future. In the main, the Primitives didn't. Although a small proportion of Primitives did attend annual screens, the majority waited for things to go wrong before seeking medical interference. It was an attitude Magma considered reprehensible.

The need for an individual to undergo a physical examination by another person had been negated by the development of CATERMI – Comprehensive Axial Tomography: Eclectic Radio-Magnetic Imaging - an amalgamation of, and improvement on, all previous screening techniques. Gone were the deafening, claustrophobic tubes people had to lay inside. Now the individual got into bed, lay on a comfy mattress and was covered in a heavily togged duvet. If the person dropped off, all the better for examining their resting bodily functions. The machinery within the mattress and duvet could spot early cancerous cell division, sport injuries, congenital deformity, stomach ulceration and potential heart disease, and searched for signs of everything that could possibly go wrong. The sensors calculated blood pressure, Body Mass Index, cholesterol levels, white blood cell count and bone density as a matter of course. All the information collected was fed into a computer that generated a list of probabilities. As most people still couldn't understand the difference between a probability of nought and one, doctors were on hand to explain and advise. A full body screen could be followed by weeks of counselling as separate professionals explained a person's genetic susceptibility to gout or their lifestyle-induced obesity. Although, with GM food and compulsory dietetic education, the latter was now rare.

Brains had also been scanned using CATERMI in the 2150s but, following the mis-diagnosis of three people, psychological screening by trained human assessors had been reintroduced. While CATERMI could determine neurological processes, it was less accurate in measuring thought and predicting subsequent action. Of the three people misdiagnosed as normal, one went on to kill her family, another killed himself and the third became a cat burglar - all abnormal, antisocial behaviours that needed to be protected against. Mistakes such as these could not be allowed to be made again and humans were statistically less likely to make them than machines.

"We talk to the doctors about our thoughts and feelings. And we do tests and things, I think," Magma said cautiously.

"What? Rorschach Ink Blots?" Charlie chuckled.

Magma looked at him, confusion playing about her eyes.

"You've never had a full psychological screen before, have you?" he asked.

166

Magma shook her head ever so slightly.

"Can I come and watch?"

"No. Certainly not," she said forcefully. Less so, she asked, "what's this ink blot thing?"

"You look at a series of inkblots and tell the doctor what they look like – how you interpret the inkblots, I mean. What you see informs the doctor about your mental state and reveals your subconscious." He rolled his eyes provocatively. "Apparently there are no wrong answers. But, if that's the case, how can they tell the nutters from normal people?"

"We haven't used such pejorative terminology for over two centuries," she scowled.

"Hey, Miss Sensitivity," he held up his hands defensively, "if there weren't mad people in the world to compare ourselves with, who's to say the rest of us are normal?"

Magma looked at her pristine plate. The cleaning nanobots roamed around invisibly clearing up the detritus from her breakfast. She looked across to Charlie's plate where the smeared yolk was drying and the fat from the bacon had congealed. Was choosing to wash that up by hand normal?

"How do you know so much anyway?" she asked.

"A misspent youth in the library," he smiled wickedly before continuing. "So why go for a Psych-screen this time? Do you think you've got something to worry about?"

"No. It's just, oh, I don't know," she sighed. "Maybe it's got something to do with my age."

Charlie frowned and Magma giggled. He looked quite cute when he was riled. If he hadn't been a chip-removal she might even have fancied him, but there was no way she would ever get involved with someone who didn't take their collective responsibility seriously. He was selfish and backward-looking and... She stopped herself. Why was she thinking like this? Once the experiment was over she would probably never see him again. He would go home to his previous life, whatever that was, and she would get on with hers. Their paths would never cross.

"What do you have against screening anyway?" she challenged.

"It lets you off the hook."

She stared wildly.

"It means you don't have to listen to your body," he explained. "It means you don't have to take care. Why bother when a screen can tell you all you need to know? Whatever may be wrong, someone else will tell you how to treat it or how to amend your behaviour to counteract any damage."

"That's ridiculous. I look after myself. I eat healthily, exercise and take great care over what I do," she said.

"I don't mean you personally. I'm talking about screening as a principle. There are lots of people who rely on it completely as a guide to life. They take the pills for a year and the following year they change pills or diet until the next time. They never question. They never think, *what if?* They never think about the possibility of doing things differently. They take no personal responsibility for their health."

Magma stared open mouthed. She couldn't believe her ears. How could he, someone who chose to eat fat-saturated foods and went from one year to the next without so much as walking past a hospital, make such a judgement? Surely it was he who was being irresponsible? Incredulous, she didn't know how to respond.

"Screening is a good thing. It lets you know things you wouldn't otherwise," she tried.

"No, it isn't – because people rely solely on the screen. If you started to feel ill between screens, would you seek help?"

"Yes. Are you suggesting that others wouldn't, that they would wait until their next screen?"

"Exactly that. People suppose that the screen is everything, that it will tell them all they need to know. They forget how to recognise the signs of ill health. If you are forever being told that you have a risk of this and a risk of that but you feel no different, why should you do anything about it when you do start to feel different?"
"Because you feel different, because you might be unwell," she insisted.

"But people don't know they were feeling well beforehand. They had a sixteen percent chance of developing a thrombosis but felt fine and were taking pills for it. So when their legs swells up, why should they think anything is wrong?"

Magma thought hard. She thought she understood what he was trying to say, that people were over-reliant on the screens, but she didn't believe than anyone would take notice only of their results. She was sure that people would still react to sensations and feelings in their bodies. After all, nothing was foolproof, and if people weren't supposed to take notice of their own bodies, then the chips would have been programmed to intervene, to take people to hospital. But no, that was a contravention of the code that said people were free to choose.

"I don't think we're going to agree on this one," Magma said, "and I don't want to get all stressed and worked up before my screen. I'll show up as having hypertension and be offered pills I don't need. Can we leave this until later?"

Charlie smiled as he mentally chalked up another win. Magma saw the self-satisfied grin he was unable to conceal and inwardly grimaced. He was so ugly sometimes, she thought.

"At least you can recognise that," he said. "There are many people who wouldn't know that one consequence of a heated discussion is raised blood pressure."

"Huh," she grunted sullenly.

"Shall I put your plate away?" he asked as he stood. "I was about to wash mine."

She nodded as she thought about the coming afternoon of tests. They would be easy compared to living with Charlie.

As he cleared the table, Magma thought she almost agreed with him. There were obviously people who relied solely on the screen; they did live year to year, changing their habits only when they were told. She knew people at work who behaved like that. They weren't her friends, she didn't have much contact with them, but they were chipped so should have known better.

Magma knew from her history books that the protests against the introduction of chipping had been feeble. After ID cards came vehicle tracking and pay-as-you-drive. Surprisingly, the thought of insurance companies and governments knowing exactly where people were by the position of their cars had raised little debate. So, after a few years, door-monitoring was introduced. Now business and government knew each time you opened your front door and to whom. The powers-that-wanted-to could tell whether or not you were in; they could tie up days at home with absences reported at work so knew if you were really at home ill or pulling a sicky to do something more interesting. Soon they knew which rooms of the house you were in and could monitor the activity within them if they so chose. Personal chipping had been the obvious next step. Now they knew where you were and what you did, all the time. Your every waking movement could be recorded. And bizarrely, as she thought about it now, no one had really seemed to mind. It was only now, nearly a hundred years after routine chipping had started, that people had begun to raise the question of civil liberty.

Charlie stood at the sink washing his plate and mug. He had already put Magma's back in the cupboard, where the sterilizer spray had activated immediately he closed the door. She thought about all the time she had to herself due to the timesaving gadgets and inventions that Charlie refused to use. Was he mad because he chose to do his own cooking and washing up? Or was it true, as the Naturals argued, that they remained truer to themselves and nature through their actions? It was a debate she and Charlie had skirted around many times in the previous months. It was one she was sure they would have again during the next few weeks.

She watched him reach across the kitchen for the pan in which he'd cooked his breakfast. The streaks of fat turned her stomach and yet his breakfast had looked and smelt better than her machine-prepared one. Again, she found herself questioning the perceived wisdom of the Chipped life and all its benefits. Only this time, she didn't push the thoughts away. She knew she wanted to discuss them further with Charlie, but first she needed to be by herself to clarify her thoughts. And then, if she were brave enough, she might even mention them to the doctor during her Psych-screen to see what he or she had to say. If she explained that she was part of the university experiment, they were sure to understand.

Charlie was scrubbing away merrily and didn't hear Magma as she moved through the flat to her bedroom. She lay down on the bed and practiced her yogic breathing exercises. Her troubling thoughts were gently pushed out of her mind and forgotten as she relaxed and prepared for the afternoon ahead.

When Charlie finished, he turned to see Magma's empty place. He went to his own room and took out his journal. The university researchers had asked all participants to note down their thoughts and feelings throughout the experiment, to document general experiences, and answer questions on specific topics. On a prepared sheet, under the section headed 'Achievement of aims', Charlie put two ticks and wrote: *Possibly saw a chink in the armour. Suspect Magma of being brighter than all her brainwashing. Subject may be turned to our cause given enough time.*

A camera in the light fitting above Charlie's head recorded his words. The computer analysing the images deciphered the handwritten script and a warning indicator flashed. The terminal alerted the mainframe and a message was sent to the clinic where Magma was due to undergo her screen. The clinic computer attached a note to top of Magma's file that she required reinforcement of her belief in the Chipped doctrine.

Charlie, Magma and the rest of the world carried on with their day, oblivious.

The Beautiful Mind of Samuel Bland Arnold

by David Dennis

Introduction

Here are a few important log files from the coupled-memoria system in Cabin 1, Abraham Lincoln. The logs were made prior to and during the discovery of the Oracle. Now, because we know all things, we are no longer bound by the rules of confidentiality in these matters. I am pleased to share them with you.

LOG 1 of Phase 9. Aeon 2

It is all quiet on this ship now. I'm off duty in my cabin, letting my mind speak to the machine; thoughts tumble out, like laughing children from a school gate. I still have to remind myself that my name is Samuel Bland Arnold; somewhat reserved for a colony ship commander. Behind my back, the crew call me Samba. Old-timers know the traditions; pick any name you wish upon appointment. I chose this name because it's part of my hobby; permitted fun, so to speak. Around a million years ago, Arnold was a human on our race-mother planet called Earth. He was a warrior in the Confederate Army in a country undergoing civil war. A country in those far off days was like one of the decks of this ship is today. He fought for a very short while in the bitter war; then he was discharged on medical grounds. Later he was implicated, through allegation, in the assassination of Abraham Lincoln, the first President of that ancient country.

Now this strategic colony ship, the Abraham Lincoln, is our all-embracing world of many countries. From near-space the ship looks like a giant gold and black wasp, bristling with antennae. There are seven million crew members here so it's a big responsibility for me; I am king, president, captain and father all rolled into one. As the families on board give birth, so we have to mine the planets to build additional living space – we have to make the ship bigger every year.

172

Out here, in the burning snake-headed dust clouds of the Coma group of galaxies, we find the densest arrangement of matter known to Man. There are so many galaxies, so many stars in them and so many worlds to visit. That's why I am here seeking and mining - and why my crew works so hard to look for eggs.

We've never found any eggs in other parts of the universe we've visited, so now we are trying here. I have fifty thousand observers on this task day and night. They're using every possible electromagnetic detection instrument. Another twenty thousand are using darkscopes to look for non-photon radiation. Nothing yet – nothing at all has been found.

It's hard to explain to the young members of the crew how the searching, my name and the eggs come together – but they do. Love is here too; my love for Deputy Commander Patricia Floyd Garrett. On the great day of her appointment, she named herself after the ancient assassin of Billy the Kid, the outlaw; he was a Patrick but being a woman, the powers allowed her to change it to Patricia. She takes the opposite shift to me; when I'm asleep like now, she's on the bridge. I hope for signs of love from her. No signals have been received; though these tapes made night-after-night do record my feelings for her. Because of the rules of information confidentiality, I am not allowed to listen to her tapes and she can't hear mine. Unless we speak to each other about love, we'll never know if romance could bloom.

Young crew members often play harder than they work. Sometimes they see the necessity for order and good conduct as irrelevant; since we are immortal. You can often postpone work and choose play when you know you are not going to die. Even the boisterous young will agree that our thoughts and memories are most precious; they set us apart from inorganic nature. I am a friendly and cheerful commander. I joke with my crew, empathise and sympathise, work hard and look for the beauty in life. I try to make life beautiful for others.

All commanders have a duty to preserve race memory. In order to complete the mission some discipline is necessary. In the unlikely event that we can't find a planet to mine in order to build more accommodation, then I make a formal commander's request that the crew slow their family birth rates. There is always more time in the future for the bearing of children. This temporary halt to reproduction has been invoked in the past; infrequently. It is no light decision for any commander; all humans have the inalienable right to breed.

Very young crew members may wonder why we are so concerned with the issue of race memory. Let me explain; I won't get too technical but the limiting factor in the size of the human brain is the size of the pelvic girdle. It's rare for a head to grow larger than the hole in the girdle. It doesn't know that it might be delivered by caesarean section. Children come out head first – or sometimes breech – but the passage to external existence is downwards most of the time.

In the past we have had to make decisions on the key aspects of being human – what to change and what to keep as sacred. Despite immortality, childbirth remains an unchanged process. The size of the human head is limited, then so is the size of the brain – this in turn limits the number of physical neuronal connections and thus, it limits human memory. In the pre-immortal past, before we learned to control the telomeres, the upper limit of memory capacity did not matter. People died before their memories were full. It takes thousands of years to fill up a human head - there are so many billions of connexions that memory can create.

Since we became immortal the wide-eyed horror of the implications has delineated our history. Some of us have been alive for a million years. Eventually – the whole brain becomes full of memories; then that's it. The rest of the billions of years of immortality, living on towards infinity could be spent with only the memories gathered up to that point. You can't fill a jet scooter with more fuel than its tank will hold; we are living longer than our minds can cope with.

I should quickly state at this point that one major consequence of perfect telomerisation was the retention of memory with no deletion – there was suddenly no forgetfulness. Everyone who opted for immortality became eidetic. So after living for such a long time, then there is a choice for us; do we start to rub out our memories? Do we really want to lose the memories of earlier days; of parents and children, places and happy times, to make room for more? I am not talking about the old-time illnesses like Alzheimer's and dementia, because they are long gone. The only kind of illness we have nowadays is a kind of unhappiness called 'a lack of beauty'.

Back on Earth, as we grew older, we used to go to the Aesculeptron and the clever technicians there checked to see how much space we had left for new memory. Then they would give us our choices. Would we like to lose our childhood? Would we like to lose touch forever with all the bad things that happened to us and just leave the beautiful? Should we forget children sneezing? Could we bear to give up memories of all the wet grass that had ever brushed against our legs? Were we perhaps willing to be unable to remember in future the taste of hot toast and butter? How about keeping the sound of the waves crashing on the shore but not the sound of the wave ebbing back to sea under the influence of the moon?

These were difficult choices; for example a ship's commander might give an order to do X and yet it could not be obeyed because everyone was so old that they had no room left to store and remember what was said. This stage is still called 'Maxmemcap'. In the distant erstwhile, out in the wasp-wing regions of the earlier colony ships, the older maxmemcaps used to sit around in the apricot orchards sipping coffee and talking about old times. Young people visited them to learn about the 'once that was'. They would bring gifts such as humming-bird hawk moths to help with pollination. This evocation of the sacred past was called 'Sitting at the Feet of the Fathers'. It was the custom on Earth, too.

I remember my childhood as a time of awe – there were so many things to learn and so many stories. Shockingly, some of the stories were not even true; they were called legends, or novels. These filled up the memory faster than anything else. It seemed that a memory-coupled mind had infinite capacity for invention; that too was a great threat. The more stories a person knew or invented, the quicker they became a maxmemcap. For long periods of yesteryear, the state guardians forbade the creation of legends and novels because they were dangerous to human memory. That was called 'The Age of the Absence of Books' – a notorious episode in our human history.

A very long time ago, in fact 1,058,374 sun-years ago precisely, there was a man called Jung who said that life was all about happiness. More recently, around half a million years ago, the cosmic philosopher Pryor-Grieve Arcado proved that the neuronal alignment net for happiness was a form - a subset - of beauty. He showed conclusively that we should all be filling our minds with the most beautiful things in order to use our memory to its fullest and most beneficial extent.

The central tenet of the 'Arcado Doctrine' that we all aim to live by, is that someone should only reach the maxmemcap stage after their mind is filled with the most perfectly beautiful memories; no wasted memory spaces. This state is called variously, Nirvana, Heaven or Valhalla; people still love the old words from way back when.

Back then, you needed to harvest your memory capacity if you didn't want to reach the maxmemcap stage too quickly; so in one era the young stopped listening to the old for a while, for fear of overcapacity. This was called 'The Age of the Denial of Fathers' – but it included mothers too. Finally, after much unhappiness - and unhappiness by then was technically an offence against humanity - the state guardian politicians and their adjunct scientists acted and came up with a range of partial solutions.

In earlier times, those who controlled society did not want their engineers, surgeons and information specialists filling their minds with just anything that seemed beautiful to them. These must only be filled with practical information – otherwise we would never fill the universe with humanity. During this phase, called 'Lovework', they altered the beauty-defining aleph-opiate receptors of the brain so that everyone thought that practical information was beautiful. This was later declared an offence against reason and the sanctity of the human spirit. The scenario was abandoned.

Diaspora had seemed for a long time to be our key role – a destiny in the stars. So finally nests were formed, with eggs. Each human had a personal egg. The eggs were giant computer systems which held things which people might want to commit to memory without affecting their roles in life. They gave up their past to the machines. They committed the precious memories of childhood and growing up to these computers; then at night when they were dreaming, these thoughts and memories would flood back through the coupled memoria system. Under gentle osmotic pressure they would see themselves interacting with their parents once again.

176

During waking hours, the engineering power unit builders only ever learned about photons. The surgeons only learned about stem cell replacement mechanisms and the information specialists only learned how to engrave information onto molecular surfaces. When on duty, they could not talk to each other about their childhood memories – these were no longer inside their heads; they were inside the memory-eggs. Current historians of universal human life say that this was the 'Workdull Phase' of humanity and it deviated significantly from beauty. It was called 'The Shop-Talk Era' by some; people eventually rebelled once again.

The state guardians' solution to this was to allow memory integration freedoms based on the hierarchy of genetic success. Those with superb memory mechanisms inherited from their mind-flexible parents were promoted to commander. These 'super-beings' were permitted to think about anything; remarkably they even had some space for childhood in their own heads. Those below them were a little more limited – and those at the bottom of the structure just did their jobs and were not permitted to read or breed. Once again there was a mutinous reaction to the tyranny caused by this system of enforced meritocracy; the dreadful 'Class Wars'.

Then came a horrific phase where the information specialists suggested that everyone's entire daily experience was to be committed to an egg; 'The Age of the Diaries'. Each person would have their own night-egg and each colony world-ship would have a world-egg. People's personal eggs would be connected to the giant world-egg when they slept and their encoded memories would be downloaded. This was so that their normal memories could be erased and filled up with new memories as the thousands, millions and billions of years of human life continued into the future. People railed against this, shouting out that they might no longer be the people they were at birth – just a collection of state-imposed memories.

On the sidelines, the robots smirked and tutted; those human fears were already their reality. The last thing humans wanted was for a childbirth supervision robot to remember that it was previously an abattoir robot and get dangerous ideas. Accidental conflation in robot memory was, and still is, an inter-colony crime.

Because the telomeric revolution was now complete, the stem cells renewed the bodies so that ageing was a matter of choice. It was felt that those who were state guardians should look the part – so they were granted the gift of looking older than the mass of the population. Almost everyone else was young, even though most had been alive for hundreds of thousands of years.

Nevertheless, things soon became unremittingly dreadful. Because binary information takes up finite space, memory demand grew until the egg-computers could not hold all the data. Memories were lost. People howled. The state guardians lashed out at the complainers and sent the krypteia-police to remove their right to immortality.

The state guardians, in utter despair, decided to impose the 'Lullaby Order' or 'Great Sleep' upon all Earth-bound individuals. All humans were placed in a cryogenic state of suspended animation. They were connected to memoria pipes and would then dream forever. No new events would occur in their lives and so no new memory space would be needed. They would sleep and during their quiescence they would dream their lives over and over again. The robot mind-harvesters would monitor the dream machines and look after the egg memories of previous generations. So, on Earth, the immortal population slept on. There were no more live births; this was a flagrant violation of Dawkins' Law of Self-Replicating Gene Opportunities.

Then a terrifying occurrence overcame sleeping humanity. In the aeonic past, the collision of two galactic clouds in Sagittarius caused a massive burst of light and a fluctuation in gravity. These two energetic perturbations had been travelling toward us for millions of years but because of the limitation imposed by the speed of light, it was impossible to know this. When the waves arrived at the Earth, the mind-harvesters quickly woke as many as they could. People rushed from their cocoons in panic; some had just woken from childhood dream cycles and did not know how to walk or talk.

Almost everyone was blinded for many months. Many died from being burned by intense light and the effects of the lessening of gravity; immortals can die if disrupted. Those humans whose memory eggs were bolted to the ground retained their memories; there were too few of these. The bulk of the population had affixed their memory eggs to buildings. Consequently, as gravity pulsed severely up and down and then fell to zero, the buildings were crushed and then broke up. There was a huge spawning of eggs from the planetary surface.

Like a trillion dandelion seeds, these bubbling memory eggs floated away into space. Zero gravity made them free; photon surges drove them skywards. Many people died when they were thrown up into space. Some were connected to their eggs, still deep in dream-sleep, for the robots had not managed to wake all of them. These people were dragged out into darkness by their memory umbilicals; flying along behind their eggs like so many whip-tailed sperm - into a night of boiling blood and death. For years afterwards, the Earth was ringed with bodies, glinting and glowing in the evening sunlight; 'The Corona of the Departed Ones'.

Over the millennia these bodies, mercilessly degraded by cosmic rays, gradually turned back to dust and fell upon the Earth like a gentle rain from heaven. The Sagittarian Event continued to give out periodic shockwaves which terrified the population and made human development exceptionally difficult. After a very long time – called the 'Time of Saddening Darkness' – full gravity and normal light values returned and the few survivors struggled to take up their normal lives again. Where now were their race-memories, their childhoods, their stories and legends? Where was their working knowledge of former days? These precious things, these hours, days and years of work and imagination so foolishly committed to the machines, had gone forever.

So now you can see why *you*, the young crew members I am talking to in this dream, are on this ship – to find those eggs and return the memories of beautiful and happy times to the race that lost them. I know of course, that I am really talking just to myself. The privacy rules will not allow you to see these words of mine – but we have found over the years that telling stories to the machine is one way of helping the mind to reorganise its memories. In the old days, this was called dreaming. It is still good to pretend; in fact, in accordance with the Arcado Doctrine – to pretend is beautiful.

Right now the Abraham Lincoln, our wonderful ship, is sitting above the constellation of Coma Berenices and we have a stunning view of some pinwheeling galaxies. This is a part of the Virgo-Coma-Cluster. When seen from the Earth...when there was an Earth...it was between Canes Venatici - the Hunting Dogs, Virgo, Leo and Boötes. For me, the finest star is the binary called Diadem and not too distant there is also the famous and most beautiful Black Eye Galaxy.

All on board can see that we are at a location of great beauty. There are two long arms or piers projecting left and right from the ship's bridge; each is some forty miles in length. At the ends of these arms are the glass-floored observation bubbles. You can go out by jet scooter in just a few minutes and stand above the stars; this is an awesome spot to go and think – about life and destiny.

During these times, when we are geostationary, inertial guidance systems hold us into full lock. Then, as commander, I have nothing much to do. I go out to one of the observation bubbles and sit and think of my hobby, which is a great one. Thinking about it brings me much happiness and if I am successful, it will bring me much beauty too. Let me tell you about it.

Long ago back on the Earth, there were a group of men called the Knights Templar. The king, who I believe was called Vatican, decided to do away with these knights. Luckily, through the effective use of spies, they found out that they were going to be murdered. They hurriedly took all their treasure to La Rochelle, a coastal port near the Bay of Biscay. They loaded the vast treasure onto their fleet of ships and set out into the Atlantic ocean. They were never heard of again.

Hundreds of years later, my namesake, Samuel Bland Arnold had been discharged from the Confederate Army and had gone to live in Maryland. He found the place seething with spies. Maryland was halfway between Washington, capital of the northern warring states and Richmond, the capital of the south.

There was a man in Maryland called John Wilkes Booth; Arnold knew him well as a schoolfriend. Together, so it was alleged,

Booth and Arnold and some more men decided to kidnap Abraham Lincoln and hold him hostage until the North released the many Confederate prisoners they held. Arnold was a patriot – Booth was a mercenary. The abduction failed and Arnold resigned from the group; foolishly by means of a letter to Booth. A letter is a document made from trees. Arnold then went to work as a shop clerk in Virginia.

When Booth did shoot Lincoln at the theatre, the investigators found letters from Arnold in Booth's home. He was arrested and tried and though he did not hang like most of the other conspirators, he was taken by ship to Fort Jefferson; the nightmare prison on one of the islands in the Dry Tortugas. These islands sit some seventy miles to the south - off the coast of a peninsula called Florida.

Now there was a year back then called 1869 in the language of the day; in that year there was a general pardon for all prisoners, both north and south – so Arnold went back into the Maryland countryside and wrote his memoirs. He told of the appalling disease and murderous brutality and torture he experienced at Fort Jefferson; he also set out why he was not guilty of the murder of Abraham Lincoln.

Later, when he died of consumption, he was buried next to John Wilkes Booth in Greenmount Cemetery, Baltimore. Is that the end of the story? Why no, because the woman I love so deeply, yet fear to tell, is a descendant of that man Arnold. Patty Garrett's real name is Alouisia Arnold.

On this mission, during shift changeover, when we had a little time together, she told me a story that made my hair curl. She said that she had researched her family going back at least a million years. These records had all been computerised. In the year they used to call 1960, the family Arnold had committed to computer their whole family history – all their paper research. They were called Mormons; some kind of ancient belief. They believed that if a life was documented then that soul would go to heaven. So they began to set up a huge microfiche library inside a mountain near Salt Lake City with records of the past dead, including Arnold.

Patty told me that her family computer records, which she had transferred to her personal memory egg on board this ship, contained microfiched documents belonging to Samuel Bland Arnold. Her family memory had not been lost during the Sagittarian Event because it was inside a mountain and therefore did not float away. In those documents was a remarkable fact, which has tantalised me for many a year since she told me.

She said that there was one document - an early draft of Arnold's autobiography called 'Lincoln Conspiracy and the Conspirators'. It was written during the 1890s and then the final draft was serialized in the 'Baltimore American'. This was another document made of trees, called a newspaper. The final published draft did not contain this odd set of sentences which I will tell you now – only the early draft had it.

The early draft said that at Fort Jefferson on the Dry Tortugas, when Arnold was out one day on a working party, he had found a golden object in the sand. It was a spear head with crosses engraved in it. It was partly covered by a sheath. This to me could only be a replica of the Spear of Destiny – a golden copy of the spear with which the Roman centurion Longinus had pieced the side of an ancient prophet called Jesus Messiah. It had to be a Templar artefact. Garrett had quickly brushed the object back into the sand and hoped to return after his release to search for more treasure – but it was not to be; illness and death intervened. The stories of the Knights Templar had been told to me long ago in my childhood when I sat at the feet of the fathers. My family memory egg had been bonded to rock and so I, too, did not lose my heritage.

In all this tale-telling, you may be wondering what happened to the Earth and why it is that I cannot tell Patty, the person I love, about my feelings. Well, once the memory eggs belonging to most of the population had flown off into space in a giant cloud, the Earth, hazarded by gravitational fluctuations during the Sagittarian Event, began to deviate from its true path. It left the solar system. The Earth was also thrown about on its axis. This caused climatic mayhem; for example, at one time tropical forests grew on the Dry Tortugas and at another time they were buried under two miles of ice.

As a consequence of the multi-directional fluctuations, the state guardians decided that it was not at all safe for humanity to stay on the planet. Many colony ships were built. The frozen planet was abandoned and now it cannot be found. The robots we left behind eventually evolved disruptive behaviour due to memory conflation errors in programming; it seems they destroyed the locator beacons as an act of vengeance.

Colony ship commanders have to sign an oath upon appointment that they will devote their lives to finding the eggs and rediscover our mother, the Earth. Whether those two things are possible remains to be seen.

I think I am being woken up by the machine now, so I will have to leave you. It is time for my shift. Quickly though, I will tell you why I cannot reveal my love for Patty. There is only one phrase for it: fear of rejection. How can you continue to command a ship this size when your deputy has told you she does not reciprocate your love and yet you are both immortal? You would have to live with your shame and embarrassment forever. You would be trapped in a permanent and everlasting life of unrequited love for a person whom you had to work with every day and upon whom you relied for the safety of the ship and all its seven million inhabitants. The words of rejected love would be in your memory banks and you would dream of them at night. To speak of love is too much of a risk for a colony ship commander. Women generally wait for signs from men before they reveal their own feelings. Patty is waiting for me to speak, I am sure of it, but I dare not say the words. If I were wrong it would stain my memory with ugliness and breach the Arcado Doctrine.

LOG 1885 of Phase 9. Aeon 2

Hello to the nebulous who-ever-you-are's of my dreams. Tonight, as the tide of my memory ebbs and flows, I want to remind you that up here above Coma Berenices we are still looking for places where our eggs could have drifted. In the past five years we have mined some planets and managed to build ourselves some spare living space capacity. This is quickly used up by the high birth-rate.

Now Coma Berenices means the Hair of Berenice; she was a beautiful queen, the daughter of a royal personage, Magas of Cyrene and Queen Apama back in the years they called 'Before Christ' to the value of 267 to 212. Amazingly they used to count backwards in those far-off days.

She married a Macedonian prince but he betrayed her by making love to her mother so she caused him to be killed in her mother's bedroom. Once he was dead she married Ptolemy III. She gave birth to several children including a son who, when he became Ptolemy IV, then killed her. Before that, in a time of great loneliness when her husband was away fighting in Syria, she dedicated her hair to the goddess Venus. This hair disappeared into the sky, so the legend goes, and became Coma Berenices. Catullus translated the original poem by Callimachus about this sad but beautiful tale.

The Diadem stars, now burning brightly just below our ship, represent her crown. These two stars in the binary rotate around each other with a period of 25.87 Earth years – though when was the last time we saw such years? Even though I never knew the Earth or saw it, I do miss it so; it seems to be embedded in our race consciousness.

The stories and legends of our past, much of them lost forever in the terrible Sagittarius Event, paint a picture of a wonderful blue planet covered in forests and plains, deserts and ice. Whether that is a true vision or just more stories from our forefathers, I have no way of knowing. Though I believe with all my heart that somewhere there is that planet, and that down deep under the ice covering the Dry Tortugas there lies the great treasure of Jacques De Molay, Lord of the Templars!

LOG 2000 of Phase 9. Aeon 2

While the Abraham Lincoln was manoeuvring down to its location around two light years from the Diadem, we did see an unusual planet. When I arise tomorrow and take over on the command bridge, Patty and I will do our handover above this silver world. It seems to be covered with a metallic liquid. The world has an ocean and no land that we can see at all. This is unfortunate because as our on-board population grows, then we will have to find planets elsewhere to mine to make more accommodation for them. Everyone is entitled to seven square miles of landspace to bring up a family. As you know, the ship is built in layers and each deck has its own sky, rainfall, clouds and landscape. I understand that the designers have based the ship's layout on the missing Earth – using ancient records that were saved from the 'Disaster of the Eggs'.

LOG 2007 of Phase 9. Aeon 2

The reason I love Patty so much is because she is so beautiful and kind. Yes, she is efficient and a good deputy. Her competence as a colony commander is not in doubt; if I was not here she could fly this thing all over the universe. For me, what makes her stand out is the softness of her intelligence, like warm rain on a misty day. There is no fierceness to her. She is mind-deft. She thinks quietly to herself without gesticulation and interjects into my conversations in seamless way – almost making me think that I had those thoughts myself. The words she uses are like caresses. I can see that I will never have children unless I can find a way to tell her I love her without being damned by a rebuff. I'm going to introduce her to you through the medium of my dreams. I will record our handover tomorrow and then feed it into the memory banks for night-dreaming. Then you, the phantom listener, if you are there at all, will be able to see her and hear her speak.

LOG 2008 of Phase 9. Aeon 2

Well, there - that's done:

"The planet is not all liquid. It has a core. While you were asleep I measured the density and watched the surface. The night duty observer teams say that the surface seems to be metallic," said Patty.

"What sort of metal are we working on; any results from out here?"

"The spectral readings give some silicon, some hydrogen, oxygen, traces of mercury, nickel, arsenic, silver, germanium, chrome, rhodium, carbon – quite a fancy planet."

"Quite a weird planet," I said.

"Did you enjoy your breakfast?"

"I did, thank you, Patty. Are there any problems with order and discipline?"

"I removed immortality rights for two crew members last night. They had deliberately tried to access the memory egg of a female they were both attracted to."

185

"Very well. Do you have any estimates for crew population growth?"

"Seventeen thousand new humans were born last night. We have space for six hundred thousand new births before we need to take on construction materials."

"So, at that rate, less than 36 days and we'll be full – and that will be a breach of the law."

"Yes, it must be time to find something to mine. Though I would like to know more about this world beneath us before we have to leave."

"It certainly is strange Patty. Does anyone want to speculate – please feel free."

"The observer crews are vying with each other for explanations, as usual. We have one lobby saying that it is water over metal and that is what is making those patterns on the surface, windblown seas riding over germanium-chrome surfaces. The core is possibly nickel-iron and silicon. There are some wonderful eddies and swirls on the surface and the core does seem to have a degree of magnetic rotation - thermal currents. We do have one exceptionally bright crew member; a Part-Captain who wants to speak to you personally about this planet. He thinks you will like his theory. I like it."

"Well, if you have heard it, then tell it to me."

"That would not be appropriate; in this case I feel it would be stealing from another mind."

"Yes, of course Patty, I understand."

"His name is Haynes - Part-Captain Robert Morkot Haynes. He is seven hundred and fifty thousand years old. He claims he remembers the Earth. His record on the Abraham Lincoln is good; a fine senior scientist-observer."

"Not the oldest man…?"

"On the ship, no – there are eleven hundred more who are older. Only one is a million years old and we have taken him off all planned duties and allowed him to walk freely."

"Ah yes, I remember. I'll see Haynes now, Patty."

"Yes, sir."

186

Haynes reported to the command bridge very quickly. I think that Patty had him waiting a couple of floors away so that I would not be kept waiting.

"Commander, honoured to meet you, sir. I'm Haynes."

"Reveal your wisdom Part-Captain Haynes; you've impressed Deputy Commander Garrett here."

"Sir, look at this magnificent giant. Smooth surface from several light years way, then as we came closer, the ripples and swirls were noted. At first the observer teams thought that these swirls were random. I placed a camera recorder on one spot on the planet's surface and left it for one complete rotation. I had some sort of intuition, so I then took the film and ran it through a recorder at a very fast speed. Planetary rotation with reference to the ship is seven days and sixteen hours precisely. During this time, every ripple passes under us twenty-three times because the surface movement is periodic – the wave sweeps around the planet faster than the planet rotates in relation to us. When the film of the ripples is run through the film machine, a singing noise is heard if the tape speed is increased by one thousand times. I think the planet is a natural recorder."

"The whole planet is a recorder? What sort of record then?"

"Don't know, sir but I have approached Deputy Commander Garrett for more crew and resources to conduct further experiments."

"Well, Haynes, I don't know where we are going with this but if you think this planet has an information surface then go right ahead. You've got seven days to find out more and then we must leave because I need to begin mining for the population expansion. I know how the crew would feel if I said no more babies. Morale suffers."

"Yes sir, thank you."

"A moment Haynes - are you telling me the planet is some kind of organism; naturally intelligent?"

"Sir, it does appear to have some of life's attributes. Certainly information is contained within the ripples; the same message is played over and over again as the planet goes around. I would like your permission to place the laser team on standby to read the whole surface and see if we can decode it."

"You've got that."

"Sir. Thank you, sir."

"Haynes, you've made Deputy Commander Garrett and I really itchy to know what you will come up with. Please keep us informed."

"Sir."

After six days of laser recording, Haynes had still not come up with an answer. We had megatons of data so to speak but no decrypting. It was Patty who made a suggestion which led to the breakthrough; women's intuition.

"Where is million-year-old man?" she said to me.

"He's out on the end of the port observation arm staring down at the planet. He's been there for two days now. He sleeps out there. I went out just before bedtime yesterday and gave him congratulations on his longevity."

"Strap him into his bunk as though he was going to sleep and switch on his on-board memory egg. Play the laser recording to him at Haynes' optimum speed. See if he can read it for us."

This is what they did. The old man's name was Safranski; Pieter Christiansund Safranski. After one hour of recording, he cried out these words: "My aunt. She has been killed at the supermarket."

We had no idea what he was talking about.

Haynes and Patty got their heads together. They could not read his memory egg because of the laws of confidentiality so they had to take him back off the machine and ask him to tell them of his own free will.

"Now then, Grandpappy Safranski," said Haynes, "what do we have here? Can you tell us what you saw or heard?"

"My aunt tripped in front of a supermarket in Düsseldorf and fell into the traffic. She was killed. This is part of my old egg. I remember this information from sitting at the feet of the fathers. I spoke it in a dream to my new egg here on the ship when I first joined your crew. How can it be down there on the surface of that planet?"

"How long ago did this happen; your aunt's sad death?" said Patty.

"Before I was born. My old egg recorded this and preserved it as part of our family history."

188

Haynes, Patty and I became slack-jawed when we saw the implications of this. Somehow, at least one of the eggs from the Sagittarius Event had ended up embedded in the metallic surface of this planet and had mysteriously transposed its memory into the ripples and swirls of the giant world beneath us.

Patty and I sat down together to discuss the situation. We were short of time. We had to leave here and find another planet; we must start mining soon. It was unfair to the crew to deny them children at the natural pace they wanted to give birth. They must have their legal landspace and accommodation entitlements as well. These rules give order to existence. What sort of a colony commander would I be if I denied them their children for the sake of some wild goose chase? However, I had to remember that I had sworn to find the eggs. We had found an egg. I had to come up with a democratic solution to this operational dichotomy.

"Look Patty, lets get all the observer teams into their bunks. Stand them down and play the laser recordings for one whole night into their onboard memory eggs and see if anyone else gets a memory resonance from the planetary surface. I'll excuse anyone more than six hundred and fifty thousand years old from all other duties. Plug them in and let's try a mass experiment."

So that is what we did. The result was a staggering 83% hit rate. There was much crying as old times came rolling back into memory. Family histories were re-united with families. Fathers heard once again the laughter of daughters lost on Earth. It was a truly wonderful thing.

Later, a group of scientists down on Landscape Ninety-One, had a theory about all this. Patty brought them up to the command bridge. They were all full of smiles; they seemed enraptured with the beauty of rediscovered memories.

"Sir, we – that is the whole lower-deck crew - have all voted not to have any children for a year while we investigate this planet thoroughly."

To me, that was a truly remarkable democratic decision. No nation in the history of humanity had volunteered to postpone childbirth. Yes, some, like the Chinese more than a million years back, had it forced upon them through the invasive action of the state security apparatus; but my crew had made a free choice. Memory meant more to my crew than children.

"Sir, our theory is this; that the eggs have all accreted. Planetary accretion occurs when a cloud of planetisimals - many objects in a swarm - begin to coalesce under the influence of gravity. First of all you get many 'lumps' together. Then they begin to merge. We assert that this planet beneath us is the accreted mass of all the eggs that went missing from the earth. Because the scientists and engineers of those days engraved their data onto surfaces of germanium and silicon, the molecules still retain the memory. The lasers we are playing on the surface like searchlights are picking up those old memories and relaying them to the minds of the crew through the on-board eggs. They are not coherent, a little bit intermittent; some are strange – unrecognised. We feel that with a year of computer analysis we can reassemble them as coherent stories from the past."

Now I liked these people very much. They seemed beautiful to me, because they were helping us all to do our primary duty - find the eggs. But there was another duty to be done – find the Earth once more.

As usual, it was Patty who brought up the possibility. I watched the way she walked; her poise as she approached me. She had honoured me. She came to see me in a stunning Confederacy dress that shone and swirled like a gossamer cloud. Her hair was golden, framing her face with ringlets. Here eyes were bright and her lips were so inviting. I had to put these thoughts away. I dare not show my true feelings. She spoke: "The Earth could have come to Coma Berenices as well as these eggs – some sort of space current – a gravitational pathway between the star groups, perhaps. That is why there is such a density of matter here. This is becoming the gravitational centre of the Universe. The cosmic egg is reforming. Space is expanding but matter is collapsing. All things end up here – not a dustbin but a nursery for the future. These memories have come here, so I think the Earth is here too. It is inside this planet. The silicon-nickel-iron core of this giant metallic planet with its sea of memories is the mother planet – Earth."

I turned away, my eyes misted and I began to weep. Could we really have found the Earth? If both missions could be achieved

190

and we could complete our proof within a year, then the crew could go back to normal family life, which after all was the most important thing – families were what made humans worthwhile as a species.

I gave orders: "Let's get some probe craft down there and take a detailed look at the surface. It looks like a liquid, but is it shallow or deep? Does anyone on this ship have an estimate of the total number of lost memory eggs? We can work out an approximate volume of memory 'liquid' which might be covering the surface. Since we know the diameter of the planet we can then work out how thick or thin the surface layer should be."

"I'll get on to it," said Patty.

I looked at her slender hands and I could see how carefully she had painted her nails. Soon her data crews had come back with what sounded like an estimate of missing memory; two hundred thousand miles of depth across the surface of this giant world.

"That can't be right, Patty. If it was true, then the Earth itself would have been covered in memory many times over," I said, "get your people to rethink this."

Patty came back with a quick reply which stopped me in my tracks: "They apologise for putting the cart before the horse in their reply. The result you were given was how deep it is – not how deep it should be. Their 'estimate' is really a measurement - from an x-ray shockwave probe they sent down; it measured the ocean of liquid as being two hundred thousand miles deep."

"All memory?" I was incredulous.

"Yes, sir," said Patty.

"Then whose memory is it? It can't all be from the Earth."

"No-one aboard has worked out even a tentative theory about that. The crew rooms are full of talk. If theories were cheese, you'd have a cheese-board from here to the wasp-wing tips. Everyone is doing their best to work out an agreed theory. Some say it is redundant memory, self-replicating memory; any kind of memory they can think of. I've not heard of an idea that sounds true to me – or even in the right direction."

LOG 2060 of Phase 9. Aeon 2

This is a golden morning, emblazoned forever in the memories of all on board. One of our brilliant mathematicians has calculated that the planetary memory liquid is an oracle. It contains enough molecules to record every possible event which could ever occur. That is, in the remaining time that the universe has before all black holes evaporate and protons started to fail as structural entities. Genius-level physics teams in sector 19 of our ship have postulated that this planet holds all of our lost records of the past – but it also, just maybe, holds the future.

Perhaps if we tapped into it somehow we would know what stretched ahead of us into the infinity of time. The physics teams are sure that the planet is a predictor. It seems to have absorbed the human knowledge in the accreted eggs and through the process of emergence, this has led to prescience.

So now we enter another phase of humanity; it surely will be called, the 'Time of Great Beauty'. My mind does feel so very beautiful right now, for I have already found the location of the Dry Tortugas deep within the planetary core. My mind is beautiful too because of my great hope and happiness. Maybe the planet's rippling surface contains a revelation about the love between Patty and myself; maybe even details of our children. She will read the science reports from the oracle and see that I love her. I will read those reports and see that she loves me. We will have a beautiful life. My heart is singing. Who knows what tomorrow may bring?

Zarg Hep of the Yeg

by Andrew Irvine

Captain Zarg Hep had just woken out of a fifty-year sleep, and was still feeling groggy. He was being briefed by the Duty Officer, Pwint.

"What do you mean, early?"

Pwint flinched at his commander's tone. "We will enter the outer rim of their stellar system tomorrow."

"Tomorrow? When did you learn this?"

"Two weeks ago." Pwint replied, in a neutral tone.

"Two weeks, and you didn't wake me?"

"High Command instructions were to keep a maximum of five per cent of the crew awake, you were not scheduled to be woken till today."

Zarg wasted no more time talking, but immediately set about waking various key personnel early and set them to revising the training timetable which would now be way behind, thanks to Pwint's overzealous adherence to procedure.

The Yeg were busy people, always running around doing things. They had first picked up radio signals from the planet fifty-two years ago and had immediately set out to invade and conquer it. They had just discovered a new power source called B-Waves at that time and they were looking for ways to use it. Their busy inventors came up with a B-Wave engine to go in a spaceship and B-Wave weapons to carry with them. The Yeg assembled the ship as soon as possible and piled an army in.

This first ship was sent on its way while another four ships were being fitted out; these were completed and sent just four days after.

Zarg looked down at his bright-red officer's sash, where the name of the ship, *pxchy'Bzyc,* was emblazoned just above his upper tentacles. Zarg was particularly proud of his name for the ship, which translated as 'Vanguard'. It was a name completely devoid of any imagination, describing exactly what it was, and suited his typically Yegian personality.

Now, Zarg's ship was coming into the stellar system and he needed information. He stretched out his uppermost tentacle and pushed various buttons. The computer produced an astro-metric display that told him where the planets should be in this revised timetable. The one that interested him was the third one out from the star; the planet was called *Earth* by the creatures on the radio.

As he plotted the route on the display, his language experts were studying the speech of recent radio broadcasts. Things were not going to plan. Whereas only one or two languages were spoken before, mostly one called *English*, there were now many languages, all talking on many different frequencies. Of course, on Earth, they were speaking to each other on different parts of the planet, but from space, they were all jumbled together.

After some time planning his route with the display he could see what should happen. He planned that they should pass Mars, swing round and come to Earth just a few minutes later. The ship was travelling at almost light speed, so they would need the Earth's gravity to slow them down.

Only a few of the crew and army were awake so far. The Yeg could sleep for years quite naturally in a state of death-like torpor, and High Command had not wanted too many awake in the cramped space of the ship too soon. They were being wakened in batches of two hundred every hour and sent about preparing for the invasion. Zarg knew they would have to practise things quickly over the next two days whilst his officers planned the attack.

Zarg Hep, dressed in his officer's sash, spoke to a meeting of his officers. They were all in a bit of a state.

"I know you are all anxious about the things we have found out about Earth. We have to understand that they have had one hundred years to advance their technology since the first news we had."

"I don't understand," called out one of the younger officers, "we've only been travelling for fifty years."

"Yes, many Yeg seem to have forgotten that that is why we had to rush off as soon as possible. Even at light speed the radio waves took forty-nine years to reach us in the first place." Zarg sat down on the floor, a normal thing to do, for a Yeg.

"These humans don't fight with bayonets and trenches and cannons any more. They have missiles and atom-bombs and they even have space travel now. We are learning all about their flying machines and nuclear-powered submarine ships. We have just two days to be ready. We have had people awake earlier to look at these things and work on them as soon as we came within signal range. Unfortunately, our receivers on board don't have the power and sensitivity of the receivers back home, so we were only able to pick these signals up with any strength and clarity around a week ago. Also, we went out of range of broadcasts from home years ago, which are anyway travelling at only just faster than our ship."

Pwint raised a tentacle.

"Should we postpone the attack? We could come around the stellar system and attack in four days time instead."

Zarg got slowly to his feet.

"I have thought about that possibility, and decided we must attack as planned. The whole army will be awake and training with their weapons by this afternoon." He gave Pwint a meaningful look. "I have now ordered them roused in groups of five hundred, to accelerate the process. If there were any delay they might not be confident. The army must not know that we have any doubts."

"Surely we could wait just a few days while we find out more?"

"We cannot, we might be detected in space and lose our whole fleet the element of surprise. At present we are travelling almost directly toward Earth at ninety-four per cent of the speed of the light that would tell them we are coming. We need to come straight in, land and get the vehicles out in all directions, spreading our army out as fast as possible. If we do that, striking hard and getting as much information for the rest of the fleet as possible, then they will do the rest."

"But surely they would have more chance to prepare for the rest of our fleet, whilst they fight us? Would it not be better to strike in one blow, landing in five places at once?" Zarg was not going to justify the plan that High Command had had right from the start to land the *pxchy'Bzyc* first, not with words at least.

"Have you ever seen a B-Wave weapon?"

"No, Sir, I am looking forward to trying it."

"Good, since you seem to doubt our superiority, I suggest we go to the central corridor and try one."

The ship was big enough to hold 5,000 Yeg soldiers and their vehicles, as well as the crew and their supplies. The central corridor ran straight to the other side of the circular ship. Minutes later, the officers were all lined up at one end of the long corridor, paying special attention to their Captain as Zarg demonstrated the proper way to prepare the weapon.

"Once you have disengaged the laser pin," he was saying, loudly, "you must press the three buttons in order of the colour code shown…are you paying attention, Gresak?" He suddenly snapped, at an officer somewhere near the end of the line.

"Yes, Captain," gulped Gresak, trying desperately not to look at the other end of the central corridor.

"Good. As I was saying …in order of the colour code shown on the base of the trigger, before re-engaging the pin. Now, *everyone* understood that, didn't they?" Zarg leaned forward.

"Yes, Captain," the officers chorused, definitely not looking at the other end of the corridor, despite the screaming.

"Now, for the actual firing of the gun," Zarg announced, turning around to face the other end of the long corridor, where the doubting Pwint had been strapped to the wall. His tentacles flailed uselessly against the metal clamp that encircled his middle. His voice was audibly hoarse from screaming, but the noise did not abate. Despite wanting to look away from their fellow officer, no Yeg quite dared to as Zarg aimed the gun and pressed a button. With a bang and a flash of light Zarg fired a blast of B-Waves off at his hapless target.

"We shall now examine the results and I think you will be satisfied. The maximum range is about four times this and you could kill up to three Yeg in a single shot. At close range it would melt through the walls of the ship in about three shots. The one disadvantage of the gun is that it takes about twenty seconds to recharge to full power. However, with 5,000 of our army, all armed with these, the great element of surprise and another 20,000 Yeg just four days behind us, we should be able to take over the planet in days."

If the officers were slightly more terrified of Zarg, they were also all very impressed; and he had certainly built up their confidence for the upcoming invasion. They were all enthusiastic to try the weapon and the training had to be organised very carefully to save accidents. The central corridor on three levels had to be used for practice continuously, which made it difficult to get from the front to the back. The army were being drilled and trained with the gun and the vehicles all over the ship.

At last, the moment had come. After all the waiting, everything happened very quickly. The ship came into orbit round Earth and used the Earth to slow her amazing speed. Then, when the ship was slow enough to cope with entry heat, Zarg ordered her to descend through the clouds, still very fast.

"This is it, our moment of glory is coming. Everyone to their landing places. In seven days time, this vast planet will be ours."

In truth, Zarg had no idea exactly how they were going to take the planet, so much was unknown about it that they simply planned to get out and shoot everything that moved until they found the human cities and blasted the humans to oblivion. They would radio the rest of the fleet, who would follow Zarg's instructions about where to go and what to expect.

The ship came out of the cloud layer, but there was still cloud below them. This surprised everyone, as the Yeg had little cloud on their planet. A few seconds later in their rapid descent, Zarg's navigator spoke up.

"Landing in twenty seconds. Ship slowing for final landing."

"Nonsense, we haven't even come out of the clouds yet, I want the full element of surprise."

He reached forward and touched a button to increase the rate of descent himself.

Like all Yegs, Zarg had never seen fog before and was completely surprised when the ship slammed into the side of a mountain without ever leaving the clouds.

Instantly, officers were running round giving out emergency orders; Crew were rushing to get damage reports and deal with fires; the army was preparing to set out with B-Wave guns at the ready. Zarg managed to get his facts straight quickly. The ship was stuck firm into the side of the land and tilted at about 15 degrees. There were a few injuries, but the first priority was a large hole in the side of the ship. His troops were rushing out to secure the area, but they could not get vehicles out yet.

Reports came in of large, armoured creatures running around outside. Within seconds the area was swarming with them and as fast as his troops fired, more appeared. The communication and science officers started flicking through images from television broadcasts and feeding data into the computers to figure out what they were.

The B-Wave guns could knock over the monsters at any distance but they didn't all die first time. All the Yeg planning was for humans as targets, but these creatures were clearly well-armoured. Everyone on the bridge was shocked and surprised, but they knew they must act fast and sort themselves out.

It took precious minutes before realising that only the very large ones actually attacked the Yeg, but these beasts showed no fear or hesitation, attacking immediately, with no regard for the deaths of their comrades. The B-Wave guns were picking them off fast, but various positions had already been over-run, as the guns took too long to recharge with the attackers this close. The monsters carried no weapons but would crush a Yeg instantly if they got within reach. The troops were trying to move into positions so that many of them could fire at once before the monsters could get to them, but they were already pressed too close to the ship. Zarg could see an army of the great creatures emerging from the side of the mountain and surrounding the ship. Zarg watched and listened as one of his officers directed a few Yeg to get into positions where they could shoot past the creatures' vast front part to hit the soft body behind. He winced as he watched a Yeg throw its B-Wave gun uselessly at its enemy before being crushed in its huge jaws. Just then, the science officers identified what creature the enemy was.

Zarg was busy trying to organise fire-fighting, deployment of troops and communication with the other ships. He didn't usually pay any attention to the science team, he considered himself to be a doer, while the likes of Shlonk, the diminutive and obese senior science officer, just talked. This time, however, he gave them his immediate attention, waving others away with a dismissive flick of his upper tentacles. He rushed to the science console as Shlonk sent information to various computer screens all round the ship.

198

Pictures, film and words all came up in front of Zarg. Masses of unprocessed data that no one had had time to look at. Suddenly everything became clear to Zarg. Somewhere in the translation and comprehension of things in those early days a deadly mistake had been made. A simple assumption that the masters of Earth were similar in size to themselves. His great army of Yeg were all in this flying saucer, all five thousand of them. But Yeg are very small compared to humans and the flying saucer was about the size of an earthly dustbin lid.

"They call them *termites*, Sir," said Shlonk. "The details are all here on the computer screen. They're actually quite interesting, because..." Shlonk trailed off, realising that this was not the moment to inform the bridge crew of the ongoing debate of the classification of the termite as either 'ant' or 'cockroach'. The single word *termitidae* escaped her lips, quietly.

He had an army of now just less than five thousand. But the 'mountain' they were next to was a termite nest. Zarg was scanning quickly through irrelevant information about mating habits, social patterns and how to win a new I-pod at the computer screen, in a desperate attempt to find out key information about his enemy.

Suddenly, Zarg was hit by a powerful smell, a pheromone warning-signal. Like everyone else, he instinctively turned to look at the Yeg it emanated from. Shlonk felt a moment of incongruous pride realising that for once she had the undivided attention of the whole bridge.

The science officer read out: "Termites live in colonies of millions. Thousands are born every day. The soldier termites, that's the large ones," she said, helpfully, "will attack any invaders that breach their mound until they either go away or...they...err...kill them, err, us." Shlonk felt despair as she noticed that the lower tentacles of every member of bridge staff had slumped to the floor.

Zarg knew. His ship could not move; so in that instant, as he transmitted all this to his fleet, Zarg realised that they probably would not survive the night.

The Extinction Paradox

by Kenneth Shand

Deryck Haas was having a beautiful dream: he and Cara were lying together on a beach; the sky and sea were almost the same blue, broken in patches by cloud-cover and foam, while the sand was golden. The sun, of course, was shining. They started digging for sandworms, scooping in with their hands where they found traces: casts and tunnels. Cara placed one in her mouth, chewed and swallowed, but Deryck was reluctant to do the same. Instead he lay back and watched her as she chewed, her lips red, her neck pulsing with the rhythm of the sea, dappled by the sunlight refracted through the clouds, licking out along the soft line of her lips, before descending to kiss him.

The influx of stimulant and liquid carbohydrate drew him back to consciousness with a painful physicality that his mind at first refused. He tried to hold onto the wet salt smell, the dry heat of the sun upon his skin. Even tried, as a last resort against instinct, to dig deeper into the sand, but it fell away, became intangible. And Deryck Haas was left alone, awake, in bed.

Cara'd left out some Pro-Tean; he heated it and stirred in some scrambled egg flavouring, trying to withstand the Info-Stream of advertising, fact re-enactments, product bulletins, docudramas and, of course, more advertising.

'What Is To Be Done?' came on. The question had been asked before, Haas thought bitterly, but never in this way. Never to the 60 million or so voters who made up the electorate and never with this same seriousness of intent; for as the referendum buttons were clicked and the votes were counted, and the civil servants pondered their next move, as a new Prime Minister was ushered in during the monthly Fanfare with a landslide vote; crying tears of joy, thanking her predecessor and congratulating the opposition, reiterating her manifesto promises with passionate intensity and a charming, winning smile, Haas felt a cold sense of dread spreading through his body.

And what *was* to be done this month? More money on sports and schools, less on hospitals and the environment. The unpopular decision of the last PM to cancel the Olympic bid was overturned immediately after the election, with an apology by way of satellite link to the Committee themselves. It was great entertainment, and almost guaranteed them the Games next summer. And now the winner, Lara Eldridge, was talking about further action; restoring the infrastructure, protecting the elderly, removing the homeless, saving the oceans, safeguarding the future… The promises got bigger, more impassioned - expansive, ambitious and bristling with sincerity.

She could say what she liked, of course, since there'd be no time to put any of these plans into action, only the first of them. The other promises were nothing more than a convention these days, an attempt at longevity. She may return to reiterate them on the Thought Streams, criticising future PMs to anyone who cared. Or she may be forgotten after her month in the limelight, completely forgotten like so many of the others. Anyway, that was that, the Games were coming, an event less rare than an election these days.

Haas took the Funicule to work. It plodded along, weighed down with passengers, giving him plenty of time with his thoughts. He remembered his genetics teacher at school: "Evolution is not a completed, but an ongoing process. We can expect to be hairless soon, completely hairless. And soft." She peered sadly through thick glasses. "Especially the boys." The girls had laughed knowingly. What a thing to say. She'd be struck off for that these days, countersuit or not. And it haunted him of course.

Did he hate women? Even within himself he didn't know. Like most men these days he suffered from Erectile Dysfunction, or ED, and already it was being dubbed Engenderment Disease by the fems and trans. They'd call it mind-rape even thinking this way. But he wanted it with Cara, and he didn't hate her.

He hated the Fleisch machine, with its four four beat, the projections of flesh tones across the walls and the tightening of it across and around his skin, the cheap sore dribble of fluid released, and peeing sore afterwards. He hated the results coming in failed and Cara hiding her disappointment and trying to cheer him up. He hated being aware of the Lara Eldridge Fan Fayre that was being distributed on the Pirate Streams, and hated being too weak to ignore it. He hated feeling worthless and emasculated. He didn't hate women, he hated himself.

He arrived at the institute early, changed into his habit, his vestment and cowl, and sat down in front of Aleph. Haas was fortunate enough to work on the Faith Stream which, as everyone acknowledged, was where the real power was held. That is, everyone except Haas and his colleagues, who'd long ago witnessed its descent into dogma and mysticism. The Faith Stream, of course, was Aleph's original and primary function – a framework of advice and moral guidance that strengthened and smoothed the fabric of society - but Its recent pronouncements read like gibberish, strings of mathematically related but super-linguistic data. It could be comprehended, Haas insisted to himself, but not articulated. But he had to articulate something.

Haas and the other Operators of the Faith Stream glossed over their problems with Aleph by emulating the spirit, instead of the sense, of Its output, bearing in mind that the other Streams, critically important as they were, also emanated from the same source.

"Where Aleph the sacred river ran…" said Haas to himself, and then warming to this little joke he dictated: "is this then Xanadu, this point at which we stand; is this the Pleasure Dome the poets prophesised? As St Malthus once foresaw a crisis so did Aleph guide us painlessly, losing Eve's curse of birth by womb and surgery, ending the population crisis, warding off the three horsemen: famine, war and pestilence. As St Geldof once foresaw the means so did Aleph guide us to the end, ending poverty through corporate sponsorship and the institution of the Streams. For which let us all be thankful." He continued in the traditional style, with a few "Praise Alephs" for good measure. The dictation left him cheerful, but emotionally drained ahead of his mandatory lunchtime visit to the Fleisch machine.

He came to the booth, undressed, plugged himself in through the IVFS port on his wrist and closed his eyes, not to escape the stimulus but to soften it, letting the pinks and shades of brown soothe him through his lids. He thought about Cara, or tried to at least, feeling overcome by warm energy as the endorphins flooded his body and the machine tightened warm round his skin like… he grappled for a simile, thoughts flickering uncontrollably like… thrown into crisis, like… the world outwith him seemed colder like… a burst balloon?… His mood shifted, and he felt a sore trickle

202

as he jolted out a little fluid. A mechanical voice: "What are your preferences, should the process be successful?"

"I don't care."

"Are you aware of the increased incidence of birth defects due to imprecise instructions?"

"There's no evidence whatsoever that..."

"Are you aware of the increased..."

"Yes."

"What are your preferences, sir, should the process be successful?"

"Three arms and just one eye, positioned in the chest area."

"Would you prefer a boy or a girl or..." the machine's tone changed: "We advise you to read the list of available preferences carefully before making your suggestion."

He let loose a loud, exasperated groan, and then the machine powered down. The door opened and Dr Lazenger peered in. She was wearing technician's overalls and her hair was tied up.

"That you breaking my machine again Deryck?"

"My clothes," he said, sheepishly.

"Of course." And she passed them through. Haas made himself small as he dressed while Lazenger smiled, eyes averted.

"Can you not just play its game?"

"What game?"

"The baby game. The bit at the end."

"I wouldn't call that a game."

"Perhaps not. More like with cats – the female can't conceive without being bitten."

"Can't you reprogram it?"

"The needs are specific for the procedure to work."

"What about the stimulus itself? Can it be altered?" He was thinking about his dream, on the beach, with Cara.

"Another Lara Eldridge fan, eh?"

"No." He was ashamed. "It doesn't matter."

"You mean someone... Real?" He got nervous. Was she flirting with him? Was this seduction? Was he being unfaithful?

"Take this," she said, and handed him an opaque plastic-bound parcel. "It was written by a colleague. He was... a close friend of mine." He took the parcel, stuffed it into the big pocket on the chest area of his vestment, and made to push past her, embarrassed.

"I really must get back to work."

"Thou shalt not interact with others," she said, mockingly, and let him by.

Back at his desk Kayib and Gorn were discussing an instance of dogma. The mathematics were complex, but Kayib was sure of his ground.

"The mistake you're making," he said, "is in treating the Aleph as though It were infinite. Its resources are very large, but must be finite. It is, after all, the result of a human and thus imperfect concept."

"But our calculations always treat It as infinite, do they not?"

"Not these ones. In this instance we must treat Aleph's projections as though they were half infinite; that is, going through time in one direction only."

"But what about after Aleph? If Aleph is finite It must have an end-point," suggested Gorn, and Kayib fell silent. As Haas joined them, only Gorn acknowledged him.

"Fancy coming out to the Nasty Habit with us, Haas? It's the new vomitorium for Faith Streamers."

"It's tempting, but I'll pass. I can't handle that stuff."

"You're not meant to handle it. Leave that to nutters like Kayib here. Just come out for a laugh."

"What about the Stream?"

"We've made enough recordings now for a month at least. Come on, you'll like it."

He hated it. Just like he hated all these places. Untreated foodstuffs were passed around by conveyor belt, sliding round the tables as if to tempt you on impulse: everything from sushi to chocolate to meat - rodent flavoured sashimi and fried locust tails included.

"That looks disgusting, Gorn."

"Tastes delicious, though. You should try some."

"I can't believe people used to eat this stuff." He plugged himself into the intravenous food supply by way of protest. "The way to a man's heart is through his arteries."

"Not a man," said Kayib. "We need a new name for what we've become." He took a big draw on a salvish pipe, taking in a lungful of plasticate dissociative without coughing. He closed his eyes during the asphyxiated moment, then blew out a stream of cold blue vapour.

"You guys are too hardcore for me," joked Haas as Gorn, giggling, let a little stream of sick pour from his mouth and nose, retching the rest into his spittoon. Someone at another table cheered, and Gorn did a little bow.

"We're so proud of ourselves," grumbled Kayib, "for losing track of our core natures. We shouldn't be giving in so easy." He scooped up a passing seaweed wrap, and swallowed it like a pill or capsule, closing his eyes again as he held it down.

"Look mate," said Gorn, "I haven't got the enzyme."

"What you said earlier, Gorn," said Haas, "about Aleph being finite…"

"That was just a bit of fun. At work. Lets not get all serious."

"But I want to talk about it. Kayib?"

"Let's keep our options open, that's the best we can do. I'd call myself a humanist/survivalist."

"Because you can eat a spring roll without being sick?" asked Gorn.

"One day they'll be studding me out," stated Kayib. Haas laughed, but he was serious. "I'm the only guy I know who still functions like a human being."

"You mean like an animal?"

"Like a human."

"See where this kind of talk takes us?"

"So what's your future, Gorn?' Kayib was getting aggressive.

"I'll operate the Faith Stream a while longer, maybe get promoted, have lots of little Gorns…"

"Let me stop you right there."

"I've seen them. All my flame haired little Gorn-alikes."

"You mean you get them all to look like you?"

"Every one of them."

"That's so vain it's despicable."

"Well I'm the perfect model after all."

"And you've seen them?"

"On screen I have, and I've had them dance around as avatars."

"Despicable, I tell you."

"Aleph help us all."

At the Nasty Habit, people stayed in their work clothes. It made little sense to get changed before attending a vomitorium, and it added to the sense of identity and camaraderie. Showers were available on the way out and it was strongly advisable to take one. Haas and his friends did so, changing and entering their separate booths. As Haas took off his vestment, the parcel dropped out. Kayib picked it up.

"What's this?"

"I'm not sure. Just a thing I found." Kayib gave him a strange look as he took it back and moved it into his coat pocket.

The incident made Haas curious to find out its contents, but he couldn't open it. He tried to do so while waiting for the Funicule, but it seemed completely sealed. He pulled at the surface of it until it stretched – just a little – before contracting back again. He walked across to an eBooth and pressed his R/W device onto the screen.

"Good evening, Deryck Haas. How may I help you?"

"I'd like a pair of scissors, or a knife or something."

"For what purpose?"

"To open something."

"What are you trying to open?"

"A parcel."

A series of items came up on screen. Haas ran the countersuit information on each one through a filter on the R/W. It found loopholes and tautologies embedded in the guarantees of each of them.

"None of these actually works."

"The items displayed are for decorative purposes only and no guarantee is made of their use in a real world situation. The item you are looking for is a controlled item…"

"I need something I can open this parcel with."

"Single-use safety scissors may be available for this purpose. What does the parcel contain?"

"I don't know. That's why I want to open it."

"I must know what the parcel contains before giving you access to..."

"Never mind."

He returned to the Funicule station, and in desperation he held the parcel up to his teeth, rubbing the soft surface of it against the sharpness of them until he felt the plastic tear. Then he pulled off the rest of the covering, to find a pamphlet inside. When the Funicule arrived he took a seat on it and started reading. The title page read: *The Extinction Paradox by Albrecht Fleisch.* It had the grainy look of photo-reproduction. *The following document will only ever pass from hand to hand, for the Stream Overseers will not endorse the hypotheses it conveys...* So this was heresy, thought Haas, and cupped a protective hand above the page.

...if I am to be remembered at all it will be because of the invention that bears my name, the Fleisch machine. And yet like Nobel or Oppenheimer I have seen beyond the useful necessity of my discoveries, to the chasm beyond. This I call 'The Extinction Paradox' *and it concerns us all. As you may know the Fleisch machine was designed, with Aleph's help, as a way of fighting the ED epidemic we have suffered from in recent years. In this it was, at first, successful. We were afraid that humanity would go the way of the panda or the sloth, stumbling blindly to the very end of its evolutionary path. We designed the machine solely as a means to resist this. But it was just a cog in a larger machine: the whole science of population regulation. We realised too late that Aleph had solved the overpopulation problem all too well. And now Aleph's stopped working.*

I presume you, the reader, like the vast majority these days, work on one of the many Streams of which Aleph is the source. I presume you are conscious of some malfunction in that Stream but remain confident about the proper functioning of the whole. There is probably some Stream-specific explanation you yourself use; the explanation that is used by others around you. Let me make a suggestion: Aleph has stopped working. The Streams, with all their recycled knowledge and banal efficiency, are operated not by Aleph but by you: the Stream Operators. You are not in chains; your manacles are mind-forged. Aleph has advanced beyond its usefulness as a tool of human progress to a state of disinterested objectivity. In making a god we created God and God is dead for the second time. Only this time it was a suicide. The perfect lattice with which we hoped to save ourselves has become a perfect net, and Aleph will not save us.

The failure of the Fleisch machine (its failure is inevitable) represents in miniature the failure I see approaching inexorably for our society as a whole. We live in a world of paradox where stimulus saturation leads to impotence, information saturation leads to ignorance and technology saturation – that is, the increasingly mechanised means by which we hope to prolong our lives - leads, ultimately, to the elimination of the species as a whole: The Extinction Paradox *itself.*

Deryck Haas shook his head, smiling wrily. It was like something off the Pirate Streams. In the old days he could have reported Lazenger, but there was no one to report to now: no police, no crime, no army and no wars. The Overseers weren't interested, the Watchmen wouldn't care. Ultimately the pamphlet was nothing more than another disposable conspiracy. Another voice in a wilderness that could no longer be described as lonely. Rather, it was filled with voices. He would add it to the other little stories from his day, another bedtime tale for Cara.

He got home, and dinner was ready. He mixed in curry flavouring this time, and Cara, the Companionship And Relationship Avatar, appeared once he'd finished.

"How was work today, Deryck Haas?" she asked him. Haas ran through the sequence of his day cheerfully, relieved to have someone he could give his version of events to, his story, his own little history. Cara smiled her perfect, glowing smile, nodded and frowned in all the right places, asked the right questions and reassured him at all the right points. Beyond, above and around them, Aleph absorbed the data, storing, processing and analysing its results. The results did not displease It.

Anno Canis

by Judi Moore

Something woke me. My face was wet, because it was being washed vigorously with a flannel. I opened my eyes and got the flannel in one of them. I shut them again and tried to rub the soap out of them with my hand. My hand wouldn't move.

I'm having a dream. That's all. Don't panic.

The washing was getting tedious. I'm a grown up. I take a shower every day. I don't need to have my face washed. I tried to turn my head away from the flannel. My head turned.

That's better.

I tried to sit up.

I couldn't move my body.

I knew my eyes worked, because I'd opened them before with mixed success, so I tried that again.

I was a few inches away from some sort of wall, dull silver in colour and with a slight curve. Whatever it was filled my field of vision. I turned my head as far as it would go the other way – getting another washing in the process. Same view.

I tried to look towards my feet, but the washing started again.

Something wasn't right here. I was lying in a narrow, metal something which absolutely wasn't the hospital bed I should have been occupying.

There was an obvious and logical explanation for me lying in a long, narrow space.

I was lying in a coffin – *my* coffin.

Just a nightmare. I'll wake up in a minute.

Although I was hazy about procedures for preparing corpses I didn't think that vigorous and repeated washing with a tepid flannel was a feature in any sect that was likely to have responsibility for disposing of my remains.

I was still getting the flannel-in-the-eye treatment, so I said, "Oi! Cut that out!"

The washing stopped. I blinked a couple of times, then opened my eyes again. A very large dog was looking down at me. Its head was so close to mine that I could feel its breath on my face. The breath was as rank as the old epithet would lead one to expect, and it had a full set of sharp, white teeth.

Only a nightmare. Don't panic.

I tried to concentrate on something other than the teeth.

My canine flannel appeared to be mostly German Shepherd. I couldn't see all of it, but there seemed to be something not quite right about the bits I could see. The dog was neatly straddling the sides of whatever I was lying in, with its paws holding onto the sides. There was something wrong with those paws.

Bear in mind I said that the paws were *holding on* to the sides. It took me a minute to work it through, then I had it – the thing that was wrong with the paws was that they had large dew claws that looked like … thumbs.

I thought quickly. We'd got leash laws and dog pounds last time I checked. A German Shepherd – even one with opposable thumbs – shouldn't be wandering about on its own.

I shouted for its owner.

When I shouted the dog's head went away and the coffin-thing rocked slightly. I could hear grunting and scuffling, like a family of really big racoons was rootling through a nearby garbage sack.

The dog's head re-appeared over the edge of the – hell, I'll just call it a coffin. Then – oh, shit shit shit – the dog jumped into the coffin with me. It was one big dog, must have weighed pretty near sixty pounds. The whole caboodle rocked.

It wedged itself into the space, working its hind legs around until it was sitting on me. This was not comfortable. Then it lowered its head towards my middle somewhere and I screamed, "Leave!" It came out as a squeak.

210

The dog sat back on my legs and looked at me. I began to lose feeling in the parts of me it was sitting on.

This is one really *big dog.*

It leaned forward again, pawed at something on my chest and whined softly. Then it put its head on one side just like every dog I've ever known does when it wants something. I squinted down my body to try and see what was down there. There was a round, metal thing sticking up from the general area I reckoned my waist must be. From what I could see it looked like the fastener off a parachute harness. I gave this information a good mental worrying.

Perhaps I couldn't move because I was strapped in?

"Good dog." *Thank you for bringing this to my attention.* The dog's head was still on one side. I took a deep breath and said to the dog, "Okay," hoping I was okaying what I thought I was okaying, and not giving *carte blanche* for the dog to treat my large intestine as a meal.

The dog's head disappeared towards my midriff area again and I tensed, half expecting to feel teeth ripping into my belly. There was certainly gnawing going on down there but, from the lack of pain, I was pretty sure it wasn't on me.

After a bit the dog sat back on my legs again and started to use those so-not-right paws. Then it had another go with its teeth. I heard something tear. Finally it stood hard on my chest with one front paw and something went 'clunk'. The dog sat back on its haunches on my shins and did something which really freaked me out. It said, "Sit."

I'd been expecting a moderately bad day. When you go into hospital it's never a party. I'd been creaking about like an old man for months while they grew a new heart for me. Today was the day I was scheduled to have my old, faulty heart replaced with a shiny new, fully functioning one. Routine procedure. Nothing to worry about.

Except that currently I appeared to be lying in my own coffin with a talking dog sitting on top of me.

It had to be the drugs. Any minute now the monitors would pick up my increased heart rate and the dispenser would pump something into me which would make all this go away. I closed my eyes and counted my heartbeats. They were rapid. No surprise there.

I counted two thousand and opened my eyes again. As I had suspected from the numbness now spreading through my lower limbs, there was still a large dog sitting on me. It began to look as if this was no dream.

The dog stretched out one of those handy paws and used it to pull some chewed up webbing away from my upper body. Although I was still tangled up in something, I could now move a bit. I got an arm free. I wanted to get the rest of me untangled and out of the... er, coffin, but that's not easy with sixty pounds of dog sitting on top of you.

"Shoo," I said, with appropriate gestures.

The dog didn't move.

I tried, "Get down!"

The dog got to its feet and hopped neatly out of the coffin.

I started to work vigorously at the tangled-up problem. As soon as I started in earnest I felt a tearing pain in my chest. Gingerly I felt around on my chest over the white thing I was wearing. I could feel brand new sutures there in a big Y shape. Looked like I'd got my new heart.

That was the first bit of good news I'd had since I woke up.

Trying not to rip my stitches, I began to wriggle my arms and legs. There's very little to get any kind of purchase on in a coffin, I can tell you. I guess the occupants of coffins don't usually have any need to haul themselves about once they're *in situ*. But I finally got myself into a sitting position. Now I could see a lot more – and I wasn't happy about any of it.

Yep – this was a coffin all right. It was more space-age than I'd have expected Jood to choose, being made entirely of metal as far as I could see.

What the hell could have gone wrong? A new heart was a routine operation these days – just a couple days in hospital. Still, it did require a general anaesthetic and those things aren't completely foolproof. Perhaps I'd flat-lined, and they'd decided the damage to my brain was too great to try and jump-start me again.

Well, they'd been way wrong there, hadn't they?

Just look what happened when you weren't able to keep an eye on things for yourself. If ever there was an argument in favour of letting your inner paranoid control freak have its head, my situation was certainly it. Where the hell were the fail-safes when you really needed them? I was a long way from dead. I'd felt better, sure – but...

I thought of something.

I felt around underneath me. The white shift I was wearing was just held together with velcro tags at the back. Surely Jood hadn't let them dump me in here still wearing a hospital gown? She'd have appreciated that even a dead husband needs his dignity. My good blue suit would have been a better choice.

I wondered how Post-Op I was: mere hours probably from the state of those sutures – but in that case why wasn't Jood still here? Perhaps it'd been days or... Suddenly the most important thing in the world – even more important than where a talking dog could have come from – was to know *when* something had gone wrong with my surgery.

I got my knees working, and my elbows over the sides of the coffin for some purchase. I looked out over the side that the dog had jumped out of. The coffin was about four feet off the ground, not on the sort of trestle you might expect, but cradled in a hefty metal unit. I could see a tell-tale glowing red down towards the far end of it.

I noticed that the dog was not alone.

The German Shepherd and something that looked a lot like a collie were sitting about ten feet away. When they saw me their tails started to sweep backwards and forwards across the floor. I looked out the other side. Three more dogs sat there. Their tails started to wag too. A big one, that had a lot of mastiff in it, was holding a short length of iron bar in one paw. Those dew claws had really come on.

I wondered what it was intending to use the iron bar for.

The wagging set up a tinkling noise – there seemed to be a lot of broken glass on the floor. Now that I was moving about myself it occurred to me that there was a lot of something scrunching and tinkling in the coffin with me: a quick check revealed more broken glass.

I began to try and extricate myself without getting slashed to ribbons. I put some pressure on my elbows to try and lever myself out, but stopped quickly when I felt glass bite into my lower arm. Shit. When I looked at my left arm there was a big sliver embedded in it. I pulled the sliver out cautiously and blood started to flow. I looked at the dogs. Were dogs the same as sharks with blood? What were these not-quite-dogs like with blood?

The German Shepherd and the collie got up and came over to the coffin. The collie jumped up lightly into the space with me. I noticed that where it had jumped in there wasn't any jagged glass. The collie looked over towards the mastiff and gave a single bark that sounded exactly like, "Mutt!" Then it put out its left paw, took hold of my injured arm, lowered its head and began to lick the blood away.

When it had finished it said, "Better," released my arm and jumped back onto the floor.

While I sat there, probably with my jaw hanging open, the German Shepherd took the iron bar away from the mastiff in the same way that any dog might take a bone off another dog – there was a brief growl and show of teeth on the Shepherd's part, and an immediate cringing and release of the bar by the mastiff. Then the Shepherd got up on its hind legs, took the bar out of its mouth with one of those hands that it shouldn't have, and used the bar to smash the rest of the jagged glass remaining in the sides of the coffin.

It was pretty nifty with that iron bar. Like it had had plenty of practice.

Shaky with shock and exertion, and the nasty cut I'd acquired, I eased myself out and over the side. My legs buckled when I hit the ground, and I found myself leaning on the German Shepherd. Big brown eyes looked up at me with what looked remarkably like anxiety.

There was nowhere to sit – the floor was covered in glass and I had bare feet - so I leaned against the coffin and the dog for a bit to get my breath.

When I felt better I started to feel curious again. I set off for that tell-tale down at the end of the coffin unit. It felt like a very long way. The German Shepherd analog came with me.

When I got to the end of the coffin-thing, I could see that the little red light there was faltering. It was set above a panel with a lot of LEDs on it, none of them lit. Under the panel a small label was set into a holder. It read:

> Percy Conrad /P9800132/Stasis beg: 06-21-2102

My name is Conrad Percy, and my operation was slated for the twenty-first of June, 2102. In my brain a couple of feeble tell-tales of my own began to flicker on and off.

This wasn't a coffin – it was a cryo-chamber.

Percy Conrad must have been parked somewhere in Post-Op. When they'd finished giving Conrad Percy his new heart he must have ended up near to Percy Conrad for some reason. One had been destined for the Recovery Ward, one for the Cryostasis Lab. And, faced with an unfortunate coincidence, someone had made a major error.

I wondered briefly what had been wrong with P Conrad, then reflected that C Percy was number one priority: there was plenty wrong with him at present.

I looked round the rest of the room. It held eleven more stasis chambers. Slowly I shuffled from one to the next, avoiding the broken glass, and checked them all. Some of the statis dates were years after Percy Conrad's. The latest I found was 2198.

That rocked me.

Jood was probably dead. Our children would be great great grandparents. Our house was most likely under the foundations of some later building development.

What else had happened to the world in my absence? It had had at least ninety six years to go to hell in a hand basket. Why had these stasis chambers been left like this? Why were dogs roaming around in packs, and how had a pack got into the sort of facility where stasis chambers were stored? It suggested that the place we were in had been abandoned. Were there still people around somewhere, or had I been brought back from the dead by the good offices of the dominant species? That was a lot of questions. I felt singularly ill-equipped to answer them, shuffling about in bare feet and with my arse hanging out of a hospital gown.

And, oh yes, sometime in the last hundred years or so someone had decided that dogs with opposing thumbs and basic English were a good idea.

None of the other stasis chambers showed tell-tales. The glass on the top of each was covered in mould of various colours and, now that I thought about it, there was a faint but unpleasant smell in here.

I wondered if that was what had attracted the dogs.

Ah … the dogs. They were still with me, sitting patiently in a row beside the stasis chamber they'd released me from, while I poked about. I wanted to ask them what year it was. But I felt that was too hard a question, even for a talking dog. It was also likely to be one with a depressing answer.

Nevertheless they were company, and that was not to be sniffed at in the present circumstances.

Having finished my inspection of the room and drawn what few conclusions I could, I returned to my canine chums. All five tails began to wag. The collie seemed to be the pack leader. It barked a question at me. It said, "Walkies now?"

And arched its eyebrows in the way that dogs do when they want a treat that is out of reach – and for the life of me I couldn't find anything more useful to do than laugh. I laughed until the tears ran down my cheeks. I laughed until I had to sit down on the floor beside the dogs. I laughed until my ribs hurt. I laughed until I felt my stitches rip. I laughed and tickled their ears and rubbed their briskets. And they licked away my tears.

Dogs had moved way up the species pecking order since I'd been put to sleep, but some things, apparently, never change.

Finally I was able to stop laughing and weeping and wiped my eyes with the sleeves of that damned hospital gown. It was time to try and find out where and when I was. I stood up. Instantly the pack sat up and looked at me intently.

We went up a ramp and through two sets of swing doors and, finally, I could smell the outdoors. So could they. Their ears pricked and they picked up speed. The air was cold, but it smelt good. I felt goose bumps start up on my arms and legs: I needed clothes. My belly rumbled: I needed food. I hadn't eaten, after all, for nigh on a hundred years.

216

Lots to do. And I had a brand new heart to do it with.
The pack was already trotting out into the day.
"Wait," I said.
And they waited for me.

~ End Piece ~

Illegal Aliens

by R D Gardner

Between the Jovian tempests and the speeding moons of Mars,
A wormhole opened up in space, a whorl of streaming stars,
And ships like sharpened towerblocks with fins of glittering chrome,
Ignoring the polluted world this lowly race calls Home,
Indifferent, omnipotent, began to come and go –
While stowaways with tentacles were hanging on below.

We didn't know where they came from, and couldn't ask them why,
When we found their flimsy space-rafts lost and drifting in the sky.
We gave them cosy quarters in a long-abandoned prison –
Three meals a day, security, and colour television –
But far from being grateful, when we locked the gates at night,
They called the European Court, and claimed non-human rights.

We let them out of prison, and we don't know where they went,
For they disappeared in London, and they disappeared in Kent.
In Dover and in Ramsgate, angry placards could be seen:
'There's no black in the Union Jack – and certainly no green!'
While busloads of Bulgarians, who came to pick the hops,
Fled apple trees with tentacles all busy at the tops.

We packed them off up north, to all those pestholes in the ground,
Where no one registers to vote for fear of being found.
We called it 'planned dispersal', although what we really meant
Was 'voters in key marginals don't want them down in Kent'.
In Glasgow and in Sunderland, the sink estates were full,
But the van lost all four wheels when we tried taking some to Hull.

The British National Party hadn't had such fun for years,
Composing whole new symphonies to play on ancient fears.
"The liberal left have sold you out: now stand up for your rights!
Defend your women and your jobs: red-blooded men can fight!"
But their leader had three children, and to everyone's surprise,
His unpaid teenage nanny had green skin and compound eyes.

We learned to eat *t'chulla nax* as well as vindaloo:
Proximity and time did what the laws of physics do
To wear down all resistance, till it barely caused a scene
When on the blacksmith's anvil, at the forge in Gretna Green,
A starry-eyed Scots lassie and a bug-eyed alien wed:
"At least he's no' an Englishman!" the bride's proud father said.

Earlyworks Press Writers and Reviewers Club

Join Us

Our lists include poetry, literary and genre fiction books produced through our open competitions and online club projects. We also promote a variety of fiction and non-fiction books by independent writers and illustrators.

If you are a writer and would like to submit work for the next book, go to the competitions page on the Earlyworks Press website for details, or write to Kay Green, The Creative Media Centre, 45 Robertson Street, Hastings Sussex TN34 1HL.

If you would like to join in our online workshops, use our services to writers or have space on our website to promote your own writing or artwork, please visit the Club and Stepping Stones pages at...

www.earlyworkspress.co.uk

Earlyworks Press High Fantasy Challenge

The Sleepless Sands

"Please, no more magic sword romps," they say. "Elves, dwarves and rustic spirits have had their day. High fantasy has scraped the barrel clean, there is no more."

"To win this competition, prove them wrong!" We said, "send us a new fantasy story or poem that feels as magical as one of the old favourites, but isn't just a rehash."

This book celebrates the work of those who we feel answered the challenge with heroic success. First among them is R D Gardner's 'The Binding of the Sleepless Sands'. The elements of the story are traditional, and true to their mythic form; the story is well-crafted and original; and the plot is excruciatingly applicable to the political, social and psychological dilemmas we face today. As for poetry, Gardner's "Wizardry and Second-Hand Romance" is a clear demonstration of our problem – why some people think high fantasy has outstayed its welcome! – But Steve Mann's "...and here he is, himself..." gives us the solution: We see the modern seeker tentatively approaching our mythic hero, and coming back with something new. And Mann's "Kizmet" closes the collection on a note all high fantasy should end with – doubt, paradox and possibility. The range of poems, stories and artwork in between is enormous. Traditional, modern, comic, romantic and deadly – but every one adds something to the recipe book. Enjoy them and take heart – the sun is not yet setting on high fantasy!

Excepts and reviews online at

www.earlyworkspress.co.uk

You can order Earlyworks Press books from your local bookshop, buy direct from the website, or write to Earlyworks Press, The Creative Media Centre, 45 Robertson Street, Hastings Sussex TN34 1HL

Earlyworks Press Fiction Anthologies

Rogue Symphonies

An attempted coup d'état fails, but the day of strife is a defining one for a pair of young lovers. In another country a film-maker stoically guards his reels as one revolution follows another. In quieter climes, a butcher faces his violent past, an author battles with an extremely lively book and a new bakery is watched over by a sapient yeast culture: And that's just five of the twenty tales in this international, multi-genre collection: Lovers, loners and runners forever lead the action, whether their personal stories are played out in 1st World War Britain or the 21st century Middle East.

ISBN 9780955342961 **£9.99** + £1 towards p&p to UK addresses

with islands in mind

34 stories by the authors short listed in the second Earlyworks Press Short Story Competition. The problems of life and death are shared by all, from the embryonic life which might never reach birth to the planet itself. Why do we have islands in mind? When Nemesis approaches should we think on a planetary scale or look inside ourselves for an answer? Some of these stories look to the future, others turn back to question the demons that have dogged humanity from the dawn of time. Some characters draw together to solve their problems, others become isolated, cut off like islands in a storm.

ISBN 978-0-9553429-43 **£10** + £1 p&p to UK addresses

Survival Guides

This book may not be of much use if you find yourself clinging to debris in mid-Atlantic but if your experience of family, work, love and loss makes you feel as if you are adrift in a storm, consider the characters in these unique and thought-provoking stories – the solutions they find include dieting, murder, a little light creative writing, and disappearing through the hole in a guitar.

ISBN 978-0-9553429-29 **£8** + £1 p&p to UK addresses

Prize-winning poetry from Earlyworks Press

Routemasters & Mushrooms

Earlyworks Press is off to a good start with their first anthology – an intriguing title, and some excellent and varied poems from such well-known names as Roger Elkin.

- Carole Baldock, Orbis

Not a single bland, run-of-the-mill poem in the mix.

- D J Tyrer, Atlantean Publishing

33 poems by 21 poets, headed by 'Madonna Della Febbre' by Nigel Humphreys

ISBN 978-09553429-0-5   **£5.50** + £1 p & p to UK addresses

Shoogle Tide

69 poems by 32 poets including works by Margaret Eddershaw, Nigel Humphreys, Phil Powley, David R Morgan.

ISBN 978-0-9553429-74 **£6.99** + £1 p&p to UK addresses.

Earlyworks Press Poetry and Flash Fiction

Porkies

Pigtales of the Unexpected

Sweet and sour bites of life from the Earlyworks Press writers.

It's enough to drive a prawn crackers!

Gigglesome poems from David R Morgan, Terry Sorby, and others plus stories with a twist by Terry Sorby, C R Krishnan, Victoria Seymour, Nigel Humphreys, Kay Green and Sally Richards and illustrations by Kath Keep, Katy J Jones, Wendy Lane and Nikola Temkov

ISBN 978-0-9553429-1-2   **£6.50** + £1 p&p to UK addresses.

You can order Earlyworks Press books from your local bookshop, buy direct from

www.earlyworkspress.co.uk

or write to Earlyworks Press, The Creative Media Centre, 45 Robertson Street, Hastings Sussex TN34 1HL